SNOWED IN WITH MY BEST FRIEND'S DAD

AN AGE GAP, SECRET PREGNANCY, CHRISTMAS ROMANCE

AJME WILLIAMS

DESCRIPTION

3 things I want to do to my best friend's dad:
Slap him for being a cold, domineering and rude prick
Kiss him for being the hottest older man I've ever met
Climb into his bed when we're snowed in for Christmas...

I never meant to hookup with my best friend's dad... But when we're forced together during the merriest time of the year, I end up falling into his bed... and into his heart.

He may be a jerk, but Brett McKinnon is also totally irresistible. And off-limits... forever.

My friend would never forgive me for sleeping with her father...

Much less if she found out our heated encounter left me pregnant with Brett's baby. A man who is old enough to be my father.

I grew up with nothing and worked hard for everything in my life. This surprise pregnancy feels like a curse destined to ruin my life along with Brett's.

That's why I'm never, ever telling him.

PROLOGUE

Miranda

It was three days until Christmas, and like a dummy, I was out shopping for my roommate, Lindsey. God. How she and I were such good friends was a mystery to me. We were like oil and water. She came from a rich family with a father who spoiled her. My father might have spoiled me if he had the money, but alas, he didn't. Like me, Lindsay was raised mostly by a single dad after her parents divorced. I, too, had a single dad after my mother died. But whereas Lindsay's dad stayed single, mine decided to remarry, and what a disaster that was. Stepmom Loretta left him after spending all the life insurance money my father received following my mother's death.

But I suppose the biggest difference between Lindsay and me was that she went through life like it was paved with rainbows. Me? If I were going to have rainbows in my life, it was up to me to create them.

It could be hard to be with someone to whom life came so easily, and yet, I thought the world of Lindsay. She was fortunate in life, but she was sweet and kind, and I suppose her sunny exuberance in life was a nice offset to my constant feeling like I was under a cloud.

She was kind enough to invite me to her cabin in Westbrook for a few days during the Christmas break from university classes. I loved my father despite his terrible taste in second wives, but the holidays with him weren't anything special. Not since my mom died and wife number two took his money and ran. His holiday plans mostly involved drinking with his buddies.

Not that I wanted a fancy Christmas. Like my dad, I hadn't looked forward to the holiday since my mother died. But I definitely needed time away from Boston. The feeling was especially strong as I made my way through the bitter cold and the throngs of last-minute Christmas shoppers.

I made it to the little paper shop I knew Lindsey liked. She always had colored and patterned papers, pens, stickers, and envelopes around. Inside, I gathered a variety of paper products I thought she might enjoy, such as the paper with the hearts all over it. Yes, I did an eye roll at how girlie that was, but since Lindsey loved hearts, I added it to my bundle and made my way to the cashier.

Once paid, I put the paper products in my large purse to protect them from the cold and wind. Snow was expected tonight, although it had been clear when I'd left to go shopping.

As I opened the door to exit, a large man barged into me, knocking me backward. I stumbled, but it was no use and I landed on my butt.

"You should watch where you're going." He had a deep, dark voice that matched his size and attitude. Even so, he held out his hand.

I batted it away.

"I'm trying to help you up."

"Why? So, you can knock me down again?" I managed to get myself off the floor and got a better look at this jerk. Money. That was my first impression of him. He wore a suit that probably cost three months of my dad's mortgage payment. The man had silvery blond hair that couldn't have possibly been real. His gray eyes watched me, and I wondered whether he worried he'd gotten germs from having touched a lowly peon like me.

"Are you okay?"

"Do you really care?" I asked, righting my purse strap over my shoulder.

His eyes flashed with annoyance. "Are you always this rude to people who try to help you?"

I gaped. "You knocked me down!"

For a moment, he stared at me. It occurred to me that I should be leaving, so why was I still there gawking at him?

Finally, he sighed. "Let me buy you a drink."

"What? Why?" Was he trying to be nice? Or was it something more? It couldn't be more. He had to be nearly twice my age. Plus, with his suave demeanor and money, he likely had his pick of fancy women.

"To make it up to you."

"You could just say sorry."

His lips twitched upward slightly, and it annoyed me more that he was amused by me. "I'm sorry. Can I buy you a drink?"

"That's not necessary." My phone buzzed with a notification in my purse. I pulled it out to find a message from Lindsay.

Going over to visit Liam. Probably won't be home tonight. Stay safe.

Another evening alone. That was okay. I could get ahead on reading assignments due next semester. Or I could begin thinking about looking for a job once I graduated in June.

"Bad news?" the aggressive stranger asked.

"No. Just an update from my roommate."

"About the drink?"

I looked at him. "You're sure thirsty."

Finally, he let out a frustrated sigh and held his hands out to the side. "I'm chastised for trying to help and for not trying to help."

So now I was the bad guy? "I, ah—"

"Brett, darling, fancy seeing you here." A woman who looked like she'd walked out of a *Vogue* magazine stepped up to him.

"Just doing some last-minute shopping."

"Oh, how wonderful." The woman looked at me, her well-plucked brow arching in what I took to be distaste before turning back to the man. "We should get something to eat and catch up."

"Sorry. I'm having a drink with . . . ?" He looked at me expectantly.

"Miranda." What? Why was I giving my name?

"Miranda," he repeated to the woman.

"Really?" The woman looked between us, clearly not buying it.

His arm went around my shoulder. "Really. Shall we?" he asked me.

I must have been lost in la-la land, because I nodded and let him steer me out the door.

"Would you like something hot or cold?" he asked once out on the sidewalk.

I stared up at him, wondering what he was talking about.

"The drink?" He arched a brow. "Are you sure you're okay? You didn't hit your head, did you?"

"Why didn't you want to go eat with Ms. Plastic?"

His lips twitched up again. "Because she's Ms. Plastic."

"You don't like plastic?"

"Plastic can be okay sometimes. How about across the street?"

I glanced across the street to where there was one of the million Irish bars in Boston.

"Come on. Don't make me a liar to Candi."

I snorted. "Really? That's her name?"

"Really."

Ten minutes later, I marveled that instead of being at home microwaving mac and cheese, I was sitting across from the man who'd knocked me on my butt, sipping red wine. He had scotch and soda.

"So, tell me about yourself, Miranda."

"I don't think so, Brett." I remembered the woman calling him that. He didn't strike me as a Brett. He seemed more like a William or Edward. Old money names.

"Okay. No sharing of personal information. I like that. Strangers in the night sort of thing."

I shrugged and sipped the most excellent glass of wine. Normally, I ordered the cheapest on the menu, but Brett insisted on ordering something else for me. It had to be at least thirty dollars a glass.

"Are you regretting not going with Ms. Plastic?"

"Not at all. Believe it or not, I'm enjoying your company."

I shook my head. "You're right, I don't believe it."

"The fact that you're still here suggests maybe you don't mind me as much as you're trying to convey."

I shrugged. "The wine is fabulous."

He smiled then, a full one, and it was breathtaking. This man could have any woman, plastic or not, so why was he here with me? Pity, I supposed.

"I thought you'd like that."

I had to admit he was right. Not just about liking the wine, but also about not being so averse to his company. We didn't talk about personal things, but we still found topics to chat about that made for lively, engaging conversation.

Three glasses of fabulous wine later, we left the bar to find snow falling. This wasn't a Hallmark movie, glittery snow. This was the heavy, wet stuff coming down in glops.

"Ugh. My jalopy won't make it home in this."

He looked up toward the dark sky until wet snow plopped on his face. "I can drive you."

"Nah. It'll be okay."

He stepped in front of me. "That's not good enough." His hand pushed my hair from my face, his fingers brushing over my skin, sending an unwanted thrill through me.

Our gazes caught, and he let out a nervous laugh. "I find myself not wanting the evening to end."

"Funny. Me neither." Did I say that out loud?

His gray eyes darkened as his gaze drifted to my lips.

"Why are you looking at my mouth?"

"I've been looking at your mouth all night. I've wondered what it would be like to taste your lips."

"Really?" I squeaked. That couldn't be true.

"Really. I suppose I'm an old ogre to you."

I swallowed as intense waves of energy radiated between us. I wasn't unaware of lust, but I'd never felt it with a perfect stranger. And he was perfect. And a stranger.

"No. Not an ogre."

He laughed. "But old?" He pressed his finger over my mouth. "Don't answer that." He leaned toward me. "I'm going to taste you, Miranda."

"Okay." I'd lost my mind.

His lips settled on mine, and wild heat blasted through me. My body felt like I was standing in the middle of the desert, not in Boston on a snowy night. I moaned as his lips swept over mine. They were soft, but his kiss was firm, growing insistent as his arm banded around me. He pulled me into his body, and I gasped at the feel of his erection. It had to be significant to feel it through all the layers of clothes and coats.

"I'd like to get you on your ass again, only this time without clothes," he murmured against my lips.

My pussy clenched hard in what had to be *yes, please*. I gripped his coat, feeling like my world was spinning away. I mean, I couldn't go with this man and let him have his wicked way with me, could I?

"Too crazy?" he asked, his lips trailing along my jaw, making it impossible to think.

"Well . . . uh . . ."

"We could get a room in the hotel over there. Wait out the snow. We could have room service dinner and that's it, or we could engage in more carnal activities."

"I am hungry." Warning bells were clanging in my head, but I couldn't seem to heed them.

"Then let's get you some food." He led me down the street to the hotel. It wasn't a ritzy type, but neither was it a no-tell-motel.

He booked the room, and we were both silent as we rode the elevator up to our floor. Brett opened the door and let me in.

He headed toward the table by the window. "Here's the menu. Would you like to eat now?"

I don't know what came over me. He stood in his fancy suit, his silvery-blond hair glistening from melting snow crystals, and his mouth smiling at me . . . a mouth I could still taste on my lips . . . and I knew food wasn't what I wanted.

He tilted his head to the side. "Want to work up an appetite?"

I nodded.

He strode over to me, his eyes turning predatory. He maneuvered me back toward the bed. "I'm going to knock you on your ass again and not be sorry about it."

"Ah, okay."

He pushed me back. I bounced on the bed in a way that couldn't have been sexy. I had a moment of nerves. Well, I was all nerves because I'd never done this before. But I had a new set of them wondering if he'd still be attracted to me once he got all the layers of clothes off me. I wasn't like plastic lady who probably wore a size two except around her fake boobs. I was what my grandmother had called full-figured. Nor did I wear fancy underwear or wax my private parts, all of which I'm sure Ms. Plastic did.

He undressed me, but as my shirt came off, I crossed my arms over my plain white bra. He arched a brow. "Problem?"

"I'm not plastic."

"Thank God." He let me lie there, covering my lady bits like a silly girl. "I'm dying to see your tits, Miranda."

Arousal shot through me from his words. I pulled my hands away, and his hands immediately divested me of my bra. Moments later, I was completely naked and feeling vulnerable as he sat back on his knees and his eyes inventoried my body.

I shifted. "If you don't like what you see—"

"You're joking, right?" His fingers brushed over my nipple, making it ache with need. He leaned over, sucking it into his mouth.

"Oh!" I gasped as another shockwave tore through me.

"Fucking hell. This is going to be spectacular." He stood, taking his shirt and belt off but leaving his pants on.

"What about—"

"First, I'm going to taste every inch of your delectable body and make you come in a screaming orgasm. Then I'm going to fuck you. Are you okay with that?"

"Ah . . . yeah . . . okay."

He cocked his head to the side, his gray eyes studying me. "Are you new to hookups or sex?"

"What?" My brain was on the fritz, and I couldn't keep up the conversation.

"Are you nervous because you've never hooked up like this or because you're a virgin?"

My breath hitched. I'd let a total stranger lead me to a hotel room because my body was burning up from lust when I'd never, ever been with a man before.

"Hookup." He didn't need to know I was a virgin.

"Okay. Good."

"What if I were a virgin? Would you have stopped?"

"Only if you told me to. I'd just be more careful." He arched a brow. "Do you want to amend your answer?"

I shook my head. I didn't know why I lied to him. Maybe I was embarrassed that at twenty-two, I was still a virgin.

"Okay, then. It's time for me to feast." The minute his lips were on my skin, all my concerns and nerves ended. There was only sensation. Each touch of his lips or hands sent sparks of electricity coursing through me. I felt like a spring being coiled tighter and tighter.

I might have been a virgin, but I'd had an orgasm before, so I knew what the pressure meant. But touching myself was nothing compared to being touched by Brett.

He pushed my legs apart, settling his large body between my thighs. Nerves broke through. What if I was gross down there?

"Relax, Miranda. And hold on, because I'm going to make you scream."

I had just a moment to catch my breath before his mouth was on my pussy, doing the most wicked, glorious things to me. I gripped his head with one hand to make sure he never stopped. My other hand gripped the sheets as reality spiraled away. There was only pressure, building, building until it exploded. I screamed, and my body flooded with pleasure. It vibrated with it. Shuddered. It was the most amazing feeling in my life. I finally understood what the big deal sex was to my friends.

He trailed his lips up my body as I lay there completely boneless. "You taste fucking fantastic."

"Really?"

"Really. Now I'm going to undress and fuck that sweet pussy until you scream."

1

Brett – The Next Day

Christmas was two days away, and I was busting my hump finishing up my holiday shopping and making sure the cabin was ready. I was rich enough that I could hire people to take care of most of my tasks, but I wasn't going to pawn off chores involving my daughter, Lindsay, to someone else. I knew a businessman who did that shit, and he was always surprised by the gifts "he'd bought" for his wife and kids. Gifts were personal. If a man couldn't buy his family gifts, he was a shitty husband and father.

Still, I'd planned to have this done yesterday, but I got sidetracked. Who'd have thought the voluptuous woman I'd knocked over would have distracted me from my goal? I'd been in a pisser of a mood, just like now, for having to shop so late. Somehow, the holidays got away from me, so I was at the stationery store for last-minute stocking stuffers. Yes, I still filled a stocking for Lindsay even though she was twenty-one. We were going to the cabin to enjoy family time, and I was hellbent on making it special, as I'd always done since I won custody of her as a toddler.

I'd barged into the store, knocking down a woman. It was my

fault, but I was already pissed, and I started to take it out on her. When she batted my hand away and took me to task, I was strangely amused when it should have just pissed me off more. She wasn't wrong that my normal MO when it came to women was plastic. Plastic women were predictable. Shallow. Easy to enjoy a fuck with and then part ways.

Miranda wasn't plastic. She was messy and complicated, so it made no sense that the more I talked to her, the more intrigued I was. Not that I still wasn't after a good fuck and then parting ways. To be honest, I was surprised that she had a drink with me and then let me take her to the hotel. As I sank into her delicious pussy, I was even more shocked to learn that she was a virgin. She was tighter than fuck, and she had me coming after a few hard strokes. It was over too fast, so I convinced her to stay for a meal and then I had her again.

Just like outside the bar, I was reluctant to end the night once all the orgasms were done. It was strange and a little bit unnerving, especially when I considered asking for her last name so I could call her again. Had she asked me to stay, I might have, and that was one rule I never broke.

Thankfully, she said she had to get home. I offered to drive her, but she insisted she was okay since the snow had stopped, and while her car was old, it had all-wheel drive.

The next morning, I woke with a hard-on and happily conjured up the night before as I stroked my dick. It was hard to decide what to focus on. I'd never had a woman as curvy as her, and it was a shock to find out much of a turn-on it was. Her tits were large, which wasn't unusual for the women I was with. What was unusual was that they were real. I focused on them, imagining my dick sliding through those glorious mounds, her tongue snaking out to lick the tip with each thrust. In my mind, I sprayed my cum over her chest, getting some in her mouth and her licking it, enjoying it. God, I wished I'd thought of it last night.

I showered and dressed, made breakfast, and tried to contact Lindsay. I loved my daughter more than life itself, but holy hell, she could be so difficult to connect with. Oh, well. I'd see her at the cabin. That was when I remembered I still had shopping to do. And that I'd planned to go to the cabin today to decorate for the holidays.

I managed to make it through the holiday shopping without knocking anyone down or hitting anyone. But I was keyed up from the experience, so I headed to the gym. The place was surprisingly packed for two days before Christmas. It was mostly women who seemed to have the strange idea that extra days of exercise before gorging on a holiday meal would make any significant difference in managing their weight.

"Brett." Duncan, my business partner in the gym franchise and my best buddy, approached me.

"Dunc. I didn't know you were coming in."

He shrugged. "I thought you were out of town with the rug rat." The name was cute when Lindsay was two, but not when she was twenty-one. But Dunc was her godfather and closer to her than anyone besides me, so he got away with it.

"I'm heading out later. I wanted to get in a workout."

"Gloria is here."

Ah, hell. Gloria was fit, firm, and built like Barbie. If I met her in a bar, I'd have definitely accepted her advances. But I never fucked clients and she couldn't seem to get that into her head.

"Maybe I'll work instead." I headed to the office.

Dunc followed me. "I tried to call you last night."

"I was out. Turned my phone off."

Dunc laughed. "Only you would hook up with a woman while Christmas shopping."

I shrugged. "I'm lucky that way." I thought back to Miranda. Yeah. I was lucky to have run into her.

"What's that look?" Dunc took a seat on the couch in our office as I sat behind my desk. We'd tried separate offices, but we held different hours so it didn't make sense to have two offices. We turned the other one into a spa room.

"What look?"

"Like you were thinking about a woman sucking you off."

I snorted. "She didn't suck me off." But hell, another thing I wished I'd thought of.

"But?"

"I don't know what you're thinking. It was nice. Different?"

He arched a brow. It might have reached his hairline if he had one, but Dunc was bald. It added to his terrifying appearance. A former bouncer, he was built like a linebacker. What people didn't know was that deep down, Dunc was as softhearted as one could get. "You got kinks I don't know about?"

"You're a pervert."

"First, kink isn't perverted. Second, you're the one hooking up while you're supposed to be Christmas shopping. Third, my sex life is like . . ." He made a wanking motion. "I gotta live vicariously through you. So, how different?"

"She was the opposite of my usual."

"Short, fat, and ugly?"

I threw a pen at him. "No. She wasn't blonde with fake tits. She was curvy. It was sexy."

He nodded. "Nothing like round hips to hold on to while fucking."

"She was young. And while she denied it, she may have been a virgin."

"Jesus fuck, Brett. A teenager?"

"No! God, no." How old was she? I never asked. But she definitely wasn't a teenager. "Twenties."

"Like Lindsay?"

I winced. "Don't put it like that."

Dunc shrugged. "Like what?"

"Equating my fucking a young woman to my daughter. That is perverted."

He laughed. "You're the one going there, not me." He rose. "You need to work out all that tension. I'll go check to see if Gloria is gone."

When he left, I weeded through the work on the desk. Dunc and I ran a tight ship. We did our jobs well and hired the best managers, trainers, instructors, and other staff. It made working easy.

With the all-clear, I changed into my workout clothes and hit the treadmill. After running ten miles, I hit the weights. By the time I was done, the tension of the day was gone. I headed home, packed my bag, loaded up my SUV with presents and holiday decorations, and started on the two-hour drive west to the cabin.

When I arrived, I stepped out, inhaling the fresh air. I'd grown up in the area, and at eighteen, I was eager to leave. I still prefer the city to the country, but I couldn't deny that sometimes, getting away from the hustle, bustle, and pollution was a salve for the soul.

I had a little time before the sun set, so I hurried to put up lights on the outside of the house. When I finished that, I headed inside and grabbed a beer from the fridge that I had stocked by a local guy whom I paid to watch the place. With beer in hand, I set about setting up the fake tree and other decorations.

I texted Lindsay again. This time, I got a response that she was fine. That was it. Nothing about where she was or when she'd be here. But she was alive.

I made myself something to eat, and after dinner, I went out onto the back deck. My guy had cleared it of snow and prepped the hot tub, and I intended to use it. Since we didn't have neighbors, I stripped despite the fact that it had to be less than thirty degrees out, and I sank into the tub with a sigh. This was living.

I didn't grow up with money. Not that my family had been poor, but we had struggled sometimes. I worked hard, and today, I had more money than I could spend. Between the nationwide gym franchise I owned with Dunc, the Internet supplement and fitness nutrition company I started in college, and learning to invest, I'd never have to worry. Lindsay wouldn't either. And if she had kids, they wouldn't have financial strife either.

Yep, life was good. Maybe not perfect, but what was perfect? A wife and family? I tried that, and it didn't work out. I got Lindsay out of it, so it was worth it, but the minute her mother left, life improved. Of course, I had to fight for Lindsay and fork out a shit-ton of money, but today my ex was off with husband number three, and I couldn't be happier about it. Since then, I decided wives were overrated. At least for me. Lindsay was fine being raised by me, with some help from Dunc. I knew how to cook and clean. As sex went, I could get that without marriage. Besides, it was like having an itch. A biological function that needed to be scratched now and then. And in my case, after how quickly I came inside Miranda, perhaps I needed to scratch a bit more than I had been. Maybe I should have gotten her number. I very rarely fucked a woman more than one night, but I could make an exception for her.

2

Miranda

I woke up the next morning feeling sore in my nether parts. I brought my hands to cover my face, partly in shock and partly in giddy laughter at what I had done last night. I'd lost my virginity to a perfect stranger.

I knew society still suggests that people should wait until marriage before they have sex, but let's face it, that practice ended long ago for most people. At the very least, it was suggested that love and affection be involved when having sex, but I determined that I lost my virginity in the best way possible. I handed in my V-card anonymously, getting the deed out of the way without having to be self-conscious about my inexperience, causing a potential suitor to change their mind about me. Also, I'd done it with a man who clearly had a great deal of experience and, therefore, made it all that more enjoyable. Even the soreness I felt today was tempered by the memory of the pleasure I'd had last night.

I looked over at my phone alongside my bed, noting it was eight o'clock in the morning. Lindsay and I had made plans to leave for the cabin around noon. That gave me time to get cleaned up and packed for the trip, plus fit in a quick visit with my father before we left. I'd just finished putting the clothes in my bag when I got a text from Lindsay.

Sorry, Mira. I'm stuck at Liam's. Do you mind if we head up to the cabin separately? I'll meet you there at the regular time.

I grumbled as I sat on the edge of my bed. It would be weird to show up at the cabin on my own. Already, I felt like I was intruding on her family holiday, no matter how much Lindsay told me she wanted me there.

"I need a buffer between me and my dad. He's the greatest guy in the world, but I don't want to spend my vacation hearing how disappointed he is that my grade point average has fallen."

Normally, I didn't like to be late, but in this case, I thought I would delay my departure time so that she would already be at the cabin when I arrived because it would be even weirder if I got there before her. I'd never met her father before, but I couldn't imagine any parent wouldn't think it was weird to bring a roommate home for the holiday.

I texted her back that I would meet her there and then bundled up and grabbed my purse to head to my father's house. I drove through the working-class neighborhood I grew up in. Most of the families who lived here didn't quite reach the middle class but managed okay. Most lived paycheck to paycheck, which meant there wasn't a lot left over for things like landscaping and home upkeep. As a result, the neighborhood looked a bit rundown and tired. My father's house was no different, with peeling paint along the trim and part of the gutter hanging detached from the roof.

My father hadn't plowed the driveway or the walkway of snow, so I parked on the street in front of the house and trudged through the few inches of snow to the door. I stomped my feet on the front mat to shake off the snow as I opened the front door.

"Dad?"

"Miranda?" I stepped into the tiny entryway, making a right-hand turn into the living room.

My father was kicked back in his recliner, a beer in his hand even though it was barely eleven in the morning. The TV emanated sounds of sportscasters talking about football.

My father straightened, putting the chair back in place, and stood. "I didn't think I was seeing you for Christmas." He came over to me, giving me a hug.

My father wasn't very old age-wise. He was only fifty-six. But he looked more like he was closing in on seventy. His starting to look old for his age happened after my mother died. When he first started seeing Loretta, he had made an effort with his appearance, but when she left, he went back to not caring.

I had been supportive of his dating, knowing that he was lonely and, left to his own devices, didn't take good care of himself. Unfortunately for my dad, Loretta turned out to be the worst possible choice of companion.

I gave him a hug, noting how I could feel the bones in the upper part of his back. "Have you been eating?"

"When I'm hungry. I thought you were going away for Christmas. If you're planning to stay, I need to call the guys."

I shook my head. "No, I'm heading up to the cabin with Lindsay as planned. But I wanted to stop in and wish you Merry Christmas and see how you're doing."

"You don't have to worry about me, Miranda." His eyes sparkled with amusement.

I took off my coat and headed to the kitchen to make him something to eat. "I can't just turn off worrying about you, Dad."

He followed me into the kitchen and laughed. "I think that is supposed to be my line, kiddo. But I'm doing just fine. The last thing I want is you hovering around me when you have your own life to live." He grinned like the proud papa he was. "My baby girl is getting a college degree. The first one in the family. You're moving on to bigger and better things, and I don't want to hold you back from that."

I rolled my eyes as I spread mayonnaise on two pieces of bread. "Being with family doesn't hold one back." I finished putting together the cold cut sandwich, and then I poured him a glass of milk and handed both to him. "Now eat something. You can't live on beer alone, no matter how hard you try."

He took the plate and glass, setting them on the counter. "I got you a little something for Christmas."

"I thought we agreed we weren't exchanging Christmas presents."

"It's not big, but I still hope you like it." He hurried out of the kitchen. I picked up a sandwich and his milk, bringing them out to the table next to his reclining chair.

He returned a moment later with a brown sack with handles on it. He gave me a sheepish smile. "You know I'm shit for wrapping. I hope this is good enough."

I laughed. "It doesn't need to be wrapped." I took the bag, reached in, and pulled out a rectangular box. I sat on the couch, putting the box on the coffee table and lifting the lid. Inside was a picture frame.

"People who get college degrees frame them and hang them on the wall. That's for you when you get your degree."

Emotion welled in my chest, and my eyes filled with tears. No matter what else I got this Christmas, this would be the best gift of them all. The gift was the epitome of my father's love and pride in me.

I stood and walked over to where he'd sat in his chair, giving him a hug. "Thank you, Dad. I love it. I can't wait to put my degree in it. Maybe I'll hang it here."

He patted my arm. "Well, I wouldn't mind bragging about you to my friends by showing them your degree hanging on the wall, but that's supposed to go in your office when you get a job. It tells everybody how important you are."

"Well, if I'm so important, you need to eat."

"Yes, ma'am." He grinned as he picked up his sandwich.

I stayed with my father a little bit, watching *March of the Wooden Soldiers*, the Laurel and Hardy version. It was my father's favorite holiday movie. The bogeyman scared me when I was little, but now I enjoyed it as much as he did. It had been a Christmas tradition until my mother died. I wondered if the fact that we were watching it now meant we needed to make Christmas a bigger deal again. Maybe I shouldn't go to the cabin with Lindsay for the holiday.

My dad's phone rang. "It's Jerry." He poked the button. I couldn't hear Jerry, but my father said, "Yes, we're still on tonight."

I guess if we were going to re-establish our Christmas traditions, it would be next year.

Around one, I decided it was time for me to get on the road. "I've got to go. I'm sorry I'll miss the peewee scene." I stood and put my coat and hat and gloves back on.

"You be safe," my father said as he came over to give me a hug goodbye. "Don't let the bogeyman get you."

"I've packed my peewee darts."

He laughed as he walked me to the door. With a last hug, I trudged back out to my car.

Once I got out of the city of Boston, I relaxed and took in the scenery. For anyone who wanted to experience distinct climates, Massachusetts was the place to come. In the summer, the surrounding area was lush and green. And then in the fall, it was a burst of orange and yellows and reds as the leaves changed. Now, in the winter, the trees were bare, and the snow gave the landscape a picturesque beauty.

Nearly two hours later, I drove into a town that looked like it should be on a postcard. It made me think of *The Gilmore Girls* and I wondered if anyone actually lived a picture-perfect life.

As I exited the town to make my way to the cabin, I reached over to my dashboard, poking the start button for the GPS on my phone to get me the last part of the way there. Once again, I meandered through the countryside, taking in the beauty. It had snowed more here than it had in Boston, and the trees sparkled in the last rays of the setting sun. It was only after three, but winter days were short in Massachusetts. The sun would mostly be down by a little after four.

Realizing I didn't want to be out here when it was dark, I checked my phone since it hadn't given me any directions in some time. My screen indicated the phone was offline. That wasn't good. I poked at the screen, careful to keep my eyes on the road, but apparently, there was no service in this spot.

I continued up the road, looking for a place where I could pull off and text Lindsay. Even when my phone had no call service, I could usually get through with text. Up on the right was a driveway with a wide entrance. I pulled off the road into it. Taking my phone out of the holder, I texted her.

No GPS. Can you text me directions from town?

I waited a moment and received a notification that the text didn't go through. Dammit. I scrolled her past texts, looking to see if she had given me specific directions, but all she'd given me was the address. Surely, she had to know there was no service here. Why would she give me an address and expect me to use GPS when there was no service?

I sat back in my seat, knowing exactly why she did that. Lindsey was sweet, happy-go-lucky, and even intelligent, but not necessarily full of sense. When life came easily, one didn't have to anticipate problems.

I blew out a breath and looked up the road. Perhaps just this section was a dead zone for GPS. I pulled out on the road and continued on my way, hoping that I would hit a section where my phone would work again.

Luck was with me because as I came up over a hill, my phone told me that I would be making a left-hand turn in 500 feet. A text also came through.

I made the turn and then poked the text button to have the phone read to me what it said.

I'm so sorry Mira, I'm still stuck at Liam's. I'm not going to be able to make it. You go and enjoy yourself. Drink lots of wine and get in the hot tub. My dad will keep out of your way, so use the time as a respite.

. . .

SHE HAD to be kidding me. I wasn't going to spend Christmas with her father. What were the chances he'd stay at the cabin if she wasn't there?

I poked the call button to give her a piece of my mind. But of course, I entered another dead zone. This was a sign for me to turn around and go home. The road was narrow, so narrow that there was no center dividing line. While it had been plowed, mounds of snow piled up on the shoulder, making it impossible to turn around without risking somebody coming over the rise or around the corner and hitting me.

My hands gripping the wheel, I stared up the road ahead, looking for a place to turn around. Eventually, I saw what appeared to be a smaller road or an opening to a driveway. In my eagerness to execute my updated plan, I pressed on the gas slightly. As I approached the driveway, my wheels slipped and then slid.

Black ice.

If my father was correct, the solution to hitting black ice was to hold the steering wheel firm and take your foot off the accelerator, but don't put on the brakes. Unfortunately, my instinct took over and while I gripped the steering wheel for dear life, I also slammed on the brakes.

Immediately, my car began to spin, doing a complete one-eighty as if I were making a U-turn. But then it kept sliding until my wheels went off the road and I slid down into a ditch.

When my car came to a stop, I let out a breath. I was fine. Then my annoyance hit. Did I do something to deserve this?

While my car was tilted sideways, it wasn't so much so that I couldn't drive out of the ditch. I slowly stepped on the gas, but my wheels spun in the snow.

Okay, so this wasn't good. I tried to exit through the driver's side door, but the tilt of the car was so much that the door was too heavy for me to hold it open while I got out. So, I climbed across the passenger seat and got out on that side. I had all-wheel drive, but it wouldn't do any good if the wheels couldn't find purchase on the ground.

I looked around my surroundings, hoping maybe there was a pile of sand or mulch or dirt or rocks or boards or anything that I could put under the tires to help me get out. But the snowfall had covered everything. As I stood on the side of the road wondering what to do next, new snow began to fall and the sun began its final descent.

Don't panic.

I scanned the area again, looking for a house. I crossed the street to the driveway where I had planned to make my U-turn, but as I looked up the long road, I didn't see any dwellings. I shivered with cold and fear as I went back to my car, grabbing my coat, gloves, and hat and slipping them on. Should I walk to the place where I had phone service and call for help? I couldn't very well sit here and hope someone would drive by. It was almost Christmas. Traffic would likely be low.

I tried to think about how far it was from when that text came in from Lindsay to where I was now. Was it a half-mile? Was it five miles? I had no idea. But I had no other alternative.

Deciding I should put on more layers before braving the elements, I pulled my bag from the back seat and dug through the warmest clothes I could find. In the distance coming from the direction that I'd been driving before my accident, I heard a vehicle. This was good news, right? Except I had watched enough true crime television to know that a young woman being stranded in the middle of nowhere was a prime opportunity if the wrong person happened by.

I put my bag back into the car, shutting the door and walking back to stand behind my car at the trunk. I looked up toward the road as the vehicle approached. Pretty soon, a large black SUV came into range. As it approached, it seemed to slow down, suggesting whoever it was had seen me on the side of the road.

I tried to think quickly about how I could protect myself from this person while at the same time getting help. Maybe they would let me use their cell phone. No, that wouldn't work because there's no cell service. Maybe they could drive home and call for help for me while I sat in my car. Of course, that put me at risk for any other person who came by. But what were the chances someone else was going to come by? And if no one else was driving on this road, would I be an idiot to not let this person help me if they offered me a ride?

The vehicle passed me, and for a moment I was ready to call them an asshole for not stopping, but then they pulled into the driveway, pressing on their hazard lights. The person got out of the car, and by their size, I determined it was a man.

He turned to me, and I saw that he had silvery blond hair and gray eyes.

My perfect stranger.

No, it wasn't possible. Was he stalking me? I inched back toward the ditch with each step he took toward me. Then, for the second time in twenty-four hours, my mystery man had me falling on my ass as I tumbled into the ditch.

3

Brett

Holy shit. It couldn't be.

I was unsettled at seeing Miranda on the side of the road, two hours from Boston, here near my cabin. There was a part of me that was also excited. Admittedly, that part hung between my legs. Mostly, I was unsettled. I was a good judge of character, and Miranda hadn't given me obsessive or stalker vibes, and yet here she was.

I thought she had registered who I was, but as I moved closer, she stepped back, almost as if she were afraid of me. After the night we spent together, I would have thought she'd be grateful that I was the one who stopped to help her. In general, this was a safe area, but nowhere was immune from predators. Miranda was a sitting duck out here.

I started to say something when all of a sudden, she tumbled back into the ditch.

I moved quickly, careful of the slippery edge of the road. It wouldn't help if I slid down on top of her.

Tentatively, I made my way down into the ditch, holding out my hand to her to help her up. "Are you okay?"

Just like last night, she batted my hand away. "Are you stalking me?"

Did she just ask me if I was stalking her? What the fuck? "I have a home out here. I've had it for over twenty years, and not once have I ever seen you out here. So, let me ask you. Are you stalking me?" I dismissed the idea earlier, but maybe she figured out who I was or at least that I had money and decided to take advantage. If I wasn't worried that she would either freeze to death or would be picked up by a serial killer, I'd leave her in the ditch and head home.

She got herself upright and stood glaring at me the way she had the night before at the stationary store.

Feeling insulted and surly, I asked, "So? Are you stalking me?"

"Why would I do that?" she snapped as she dusted snow from her clothes.

"A woman doesn't make noises like you did, come as hard as you did, and not want more."

She gaped at me in shock, and I had to admit my words surprised even myself.

Finally, she lifted her chin. "I regret last night. If I could scrub the memory from my brain, I would."

I stepped closer to her, noting the way her eyes flared with heat as I did so. "Liar."

She stared up at me, and I could see her attempts to be strong, but her lips trembled, and it made me feel like the biggest fucking asshole in the world.

I stepped back. "Why are you here on the side of the road?"

She started up the embankment. "None of your business."

I followed her up to the road. "All right, then. I'm just going to head home, then." I started for my SUV. It was cold, and I figured I'd wait there to make sure that she got in her car and headed wherever she was planning to go. I might be an asshole, but I wasn't the type of man to leave a woman stranded on the side of the road, no matter how irritating she was.

I'd made it about halfway across the street when she called, "Wait. I'm stuck. I hit black ice and slid into the ditch and I can't get out. Maybe when you get home you could call me a tow truck?"

I turned around, setting my hands on my hips, studying her. "How about I give you a ride to my place and you can call a tow truck from there?"

She shifted, looking down at the ground. Was she nervous about being alone with me? Or maybe she didn't like needing help. Twice now, she'd refused my assistance when she had fallen.

"I'm supposed to be out here visiting a friend of mine. Maybe you can take me to their house."

That sounded even better to me. The last thing I needed was the woman I had fucked last night, and was still thinking about fucking again, in my house.

"All right. Where do they live?"

She pulled out her phone and rattled off the address. My gut clenched as I recognized it. And with it came a new revelation that made me sick. This couldn't possibly be the young woman Lindsay had planned to bring to stay with us over the holidays. Lindsay's friend was named Mira. Fucking hell. Was Mira a nickname for Miranda? I had received a message a few hours ago from Lindsay saying that they would be traveling here separately. But no. This woman couldn't possibly be my daughter's roommate. Could she?

All of a sudden, I couldn't breathe. Two very hard truths hit me all at once. I'd fucked my daughter's roommate, which made me a pervert. But because she was my daughter's roommate, I was even more obligated to help her.

"Yeah, I can take you there. Do you have a bag or something?"

She went to the driver's side of her car, opening the back door, which took effort since the car was tilted. I strode over to help her, holding the door and taking the bag from her. I carried it to my SUV, putting it in the back. All the while, my brain was scrambling to figure a way out of this. There was no way I could bring her to my home and not have her learn about who I was, was there? I could just drop her off, but it would be rude to leave her at an empty house.

Besides, I'd locked the door, so I'd have to unlock it, which would give away that it was my place.

Irritation grew. Why the hell was she here by herself? Where was Lindsay? I'd expected her by now but hadn't worried because she was frequently late. And why hadn't they come together as planned? Not that having Miranda walk into my home with Lindsay wouldn't still be a shock.

I cleared my throat. "Where's your friend now?" I held my breath, hoping against hope that this was a big misunderstanding and she wasn't Lindsay's friend. Maybe she got the address wrong. I was grasping at anything that would make it so that I hadn't hooked up with my daughter's roommate.

She sat in the passenger seat with her backpack. "We were supposed to come together, but she was detained."

Lindsey had texted me that she was coming on her own but hadn't given me details. I could only imagine what had detained Lindsay. A "fabulous purse" in a shop window. A stray puppy. TikTok.

We continued the drive in silence as my gut knotted even tighter. How was Miranda going to respond when she realized she'd fucked her friend's father? How did it happen in the first place? I thought back to conversations I'd had with Lindsay about her roommate. Lindsay described Mira as studious, hard-working, and determined. There never had been any mention of an active social life.

Dammit, I remembered having the feeling last night that hookups weren't something Miranda normally did. And fucking hell, I still felt pretty sure she'd been a virgin. My stomach rolled as nausea nearly had me pulling over to vomit. Did I take the virginity of my daughter's roommate? I tried to turn my mind off because the more I thought, the worse it got.

I reached our road, making the right hand turn up the long drive toward the cabin. Why did I let Lindsay talk me into this trip? We could have just as easily had Christmas in Boston and I wouldn't be in this situation.

"It turns out she's not coming."

At first, I didn't understand what she said. But then it sank in. Lindsay wasn't coming? She hadn't told me. "What?"

"Just before I spun out on the ice, I got a text from her saying that she couldn't make it."

So why was Miranda still coming to my place? Maybe she wasn't a stalker, but if she knew who I was . . . Maybe she saw an opportunity to get something out of our hookup, after all. Did she plan to blackmail me, threaten to tell Lindsay unless I gave her money?

"I was looking for a place to turn around. Hitting the ice worked, and I spun out, except I ended up getting stuck in the snow. Do you think it's going to be a problem getting a tow truck?"

She didn't talk like someone who was conniving, but that didn't mean she still wasn't up to something.

"I'll make a few calls and see if I can get somebody out here."

"That's okay. My friend's dad will be there, and hopefully, he'll help me."

I glanced over at her. Fuck. Fuck. Fuck.

I pulled up in front of my cabin, parking near the front steps. I got out of the SUV and rounded the back to get her bag. By the time I made it to the steps, she was already at the front door, knocking.

Taking a breath, I shoved my key into the lock and opened the door.

"You have a key to the McKinnons'?"

I gestured for her to enter and shut the door behind us, wondering how long it was going to take before she realized what was going on. I knew the moment the lightbulb went off because her eyebrows rose practically to her hairline.

"Oh, my God. You're Mr. McKinnon. You're Lindsay's father."

4

Miranda

Oh, my God. This couldn't be happening.

I stumbled back, feeling like I'd been punched in the chest. Brett reached out a hand, probably to steady me, but I pushed it away.

"Are you alright?" he asked.

"No, I'm not alright. I slept with my roommate's father."

His jaw tightened. "It's not as unsettling as having slept with my daughter's roommate. I guess even more so now, you wish you could scrub the memory from your brain." He stalked off, leaving me in the enormous open living area.

"Where are you going?"

"I need a drink. And then I'm going to call a tow truck and see about getting you home."

It was strange how hurt I was by the way he wanted to get rid of me. Like he was disgusted by what we had done. But why wouldn't the whole situation be as disturbing to him as it was to me?

I followed him into a large kitchen that had to be half the size of my father's house.

"Did you know who I was?" I don't know why I asked that. I guess it just seemed hard to believe that in a city as large as Boston, I would have hooked up with the one man I shouldn't have hooked up with.

He glared at me. "Maybe you should stop talking to me because all you do is piss me off."

“Oh, really?” I fumed.

“First, you accuse me of stalking you. Now, you think I knew who you were, suggesting I would fuck my daughter's roommate on purpose?” His hands jerked as he poured several fingers of amber liquor. “I picked you up by the side of the road. I brought you to my house, and I am going to get you help. So maybe you can stop treating me like I'm a psychopathic pervert." He downed his drink.

I swallowed and blinked at his tirade. Of course, he was right. "I'm sorry. I'm just having a hard time figuring out how this happened."

He poured more liquor. "You know what would be much more likely? That you set your sights on me."

I tensed, taking umbrage at his comment. "Why is that?"

"Lindsay told me about you, although she calls you Mira. She mentioned how you have to scrape for every penny. You saw an opportunity not to have to live that way anymore. And now, here you are again, in my house. Apparently, Lindsay isn't coming. How convenient."

My jaw dropped, shocked at what he was insinuating.

He pulled out his phone. "Where the fuck are you, Lindsay?" He started tapping on it. Finally, he pulled the phone up to his ear and listened. After a few moments, he put the phone down. His hard gray eyes stared at me. "This message came in a little while ago from Lindsay. And yet, here you are."

I felt sick to my stomach. "I am not a gold-digging whore. And I didn't get Lindsay's message until I was already mostly here. I told you, I was trying to turn around to return home when I ended up in that ditch."

"Right,” he said. His tone told me he didn't believe me. "And I am not the type of man to fuck his daughter's roommate." He shook his head. "My mistake was going off script with you. You're not even my usual type."

His words were a slap to my face. Hurt and anger boiled up. My fists clenched at my sides. "I wasn't enough plastic for you, eh?"

He downed his drink. "No. You're too immature."

I flinched.

"A grown woman would own up to the fact that she was as much of a participant in our fuck-fest as I was and stop blaming me."

I hated that he was right. It wasn't like he dragged me kicking and screaming into that hotel room. I'd gone willingly. He said *he* had changed his MO. *I* definitely had.

"If you need food or want something to drink, help yourself. I'm going to make some phone calls and see if we can get you out of here." He poured himself another drink, picked up his glass, and strode past me out of the kitchen.

I made a beeline to his liquor bar, grabbing the same bottle he poured from, not caring what it was. I found a glass, pouring a bit into it and downing it, willing the burn to undo this crazy situation. But of course, it didn't.

Knowing we both needed a little space, I decided to stay in the kitchen. I walked over to a set of French doors looking out on a vast deck. A hot tub sat on it. I remembered Lindsay telling me to use it so I could relax and treat this trip as a respite. At this point, I was experiencing the opposite of a respite.

"Fucking hell!" Brett bellowed from the other room.

That couldn't be good. As I continued to look outside, I noticed that the snow was coming down harder. It was sticking and accumulating. I had a sinking feeling his outburst meant that I wasn't getting home tonight. Unless Brett was willing to drive me in that fancy souped-up SUV. Sure, I had all-wheel drive in my car, but it was currently stuck in a ditch, and even if I got it out, everything about my car was old enough, including my tires, that it would make the trip difficult.

I thought back to the town, wondering if there was a hotel, not remembering seeing one. I imagined there had to be a bed-and-breakfast or lodgings, but they were likely well out of my price range.

"Bad news. There was some sort of multi-car accident up on the highway, so all tow trucks and wreckers are spoken for. And with the snow coming down the way it is now, they don't believe that they will be able to get to your car anytime tonight, especially since it's in a ditch and not blocking traffic."

I sighed and nodded.

"The fact that you don't want to be here, and I don't particularly want you here, would be motivation enough for me to drive you back to Boston, except, of course, there's a multi-car accident blocking one of the roads we need to take to get there. That means you're staying the night. I've put your bags in the guestroom, and you're welcome to make use of anything in the house. The Wi-Fi, food and drink, hot tub, whatever you want."

"But?" I turned to look at him. "It sounds like there's a 'but' in that statement."

"No but. I also just talked to Lindsay, who said that she felt you needed rest and relaxation. So, you have full run of the house and I'll do my damnedest to stay out of your way."

How was it that hearing the words I wanted to hear actually hurt a little bit? He was treating me like I was a leper.

"And in case you're concerned, you don't have to worry about my trying to come on to you." He held his hands up in surrender. "Enjoy your stay." And with that, he exited the kitchen again.

Both he and Lindsay had told me to make full use of the house, but I didn't feel comfortable doing so. I hurried out of the kitchen to catch up with him. "Can you tell me which room is mine?"

You gave me a curt nod. "It's up the stairs, first door on the left."

I made my way up the stairs and into the large, rustic room. My bag and backpack were sitting on the bed. The light was off, so the room was dark, but there was enough shadow that I could make out the window. I went over to it, looking out. The snow seemed to be coming down even faster and thicker. What if we got snowed in? What if tomorrow I couldn't get out?

I remembered Brett saying that he had talked to Lindsay, so I pulled my phone from my pocket, dialing her number.

"Oh, my God, Mira. Are you okay?" she said when she answered.

I sat in the window seat, letting out a long breath. "Yes. I'm safe and warm."

"I'm so glad that my dad found you. You could have been stuck out there all night. You could have died."

I rubbed my temple. "Yes, I was very fortunate."

"My dad promised me that he will give you space so that you can rest and relax. He can sometimes be a little gruff, but he's really a good guy."

My mind flashed back to the hotel room and all the good things that Brett had done to me. I gave my head a quick shake. I couldn't think of that stuff.

"I'm so sorry I'm not there with you. We'd have so much fun."

"What happened, anyway?" I asked her.

"My car went on the fritz, and I can't get anyone to fix it because it's too close to Christmas. Liam is letting me stay until I can find someone."

I'd never known Lindsay to be a liar, but there was a part of me that wondered if that was an excuse because she didn't want to leave Liam. They had only just started going out, and there was no doubt that she was infatuated with him.

"I'd much rather be there with you. Christmas is so much fun up there. Did my dad decorate? He can be such a Scrooge, but deep down, he's a softy."

I realized that I hadn't paid much attention to the home. I was so focused on the fact that I'd had sex with my roommate's father and that I was stranded there alone with him.

"Oh, I've got to go. Have fun, Mira. Relax, okay?" The call had ended before I could respond. I continued to sit in the window seat, looking out at the falling snow, thinking I'd stay there until I could actually leave. Sure, I was hungry, but I could fast until tomorrow when I was able to get out of this place.

I had no clue how long I'd been sitting there when I heard a movement in the hallway. I turned and saw Brett leaning against the bedroom's door frame, his arms crossed over his broad chest.

"I'm going to make some dinner. Shall I make enough for two?"

My instinct was to say no and stick with my plan to hide out here. But my stomach growled. It had other ideas.

Brett arched a brow. "I'll take that as a yes."

God, he heard my stomach from across the room? That was embarrassing.

"It's spaghetti. One of Lindsay's favorites."

I gave a wan smile as I noted that Lindsay was right. He came off surly and yet there was a sweetness about him. He had planned to make one of Lindsay's favorite dinners.

"I like spaghetti. In fact, I think I've had your spaghetti. Lindsay brought some home after a visit with you and shared it. You're quite the chef."

The tension in him lessened a little bit. "It will be ready in twenty minutes."

I nodded. "Thank you."

He stayed where he was, staring at me, and I wondered what he was seeing or what he was thinking about what he was seeing. It was clear that he regretted what happened last night, just like I did. The night before, he'd seen me as a sexual woman. Tonight, he was likely looking at me as his daughter's friend. Not a child, but still off-limits.

He finally left the doorway, and I turned my attention back out the window. I'd been rude and obnoxious to him, and he was right that I hadn't been owning up to my part in what happened. If I was completely honest with myself, if Brett wasn't Lindsay's father and I ended up stranded here with him, I'd be hoping to have a repeat of last night.

5

Brett

I was a fucking pervert. It was one thing to be attracted to a woman I didn't know, but it was entirely different to want a woman after learning she was my daughter's friend.

I watched Miranda sitting in the loveseat of the window, the snow falling outside and her silhouetted like she was an ethereal being, and my dick twitched. Fortunately, the fact that she was Lindsay's friend would be a deterrent from trying to seduce her again. Even so, the desire to touch her again was irritating. It wasn't often that I wanted a woman a second time, so the fact that I'd have Miranda in my bed right now if not for the fact that she was Lindsay's friend was odd. But since that wasn't an option, and my dick didn't seem to get the message, avoiding her would have been the best option. But I promised Lindsay I'd look after her friend. It would be rude to make dinner and not offer some to Miranda.

Down in the kitchen, I busied myself making tomato sauce and sautéing Italian sausage with vegetables as I waited for the pot of water to boil for the pasta. I was no gourmet chef, but I found cooking relaxing, and so I settled in, preparing the meal, letting it calm my nerves.

Fifteen minutes later, Miranda appeared in the kitchen. "Is there something I can help with?"

Seeing her again jolted me out of my relaxation. She was wearing a pair of faded jeans that hugged her curves and a red sweater over a white T-shirt that molded around her perfect tits. Her dark, wavy hair was piled up on top of her head in a messy bun.

She's Lindsay's friend. She's Lindsay's friend. I chanted in my head like a mantra to keep myself from putting her on the table and fucking her right then and there.

"You can set the table. Plates and silverware are in the cupboard over there." I nodded to the area of the kitchen that held our eating utensils.

She walked over to the area, and I had to stifle a groan as she turned her back to me, showing off that stellar heart shaped ass of hers. I was going to hell for sure.

I had her bring the large pasta bowls to me, and I served us both spaghetti and sauce. I handed a bowl to her and brought mine to the table. I grabbed a bottle of red wine, two wine glasses, and a corkscrew and brought them to the table. For a moment, I had to consider that serving alcohol might be unwise, but it was red wine, and she was just as disturbed by the fact that we were both connected to Lindsay, so I figured we were safe.

"I didn't make a salad or anything. But the sauce has zucchinis, peppers, and other vegetables. When Lindsay was little, she wouldn't eat them, so I always had to hide them in sauces."

She gave me a sweet smile. "She still doesn't eat vegetables."

I popped the cork and poured us both wine, and then I sat at the table. She put her fork in her spaghetti, twisting it and then taking a large bite, grabbing her napkin to keep from splattering everywhere.

"Do you cook?" I asked as I sipped the wine. I wondered if she'd recognize it as the wine she'd had the other night.

She swallowed her bite. "I do a little bit. When my mom died, I ended up doing most of the cooking. My dad took her death pretty hard."

Something shifted deep in my gut. Last night, I had seen her as a sexual being, and then this afternoon as my daughter's friend. Learning that her mother had died and that she had taken over the motherly duties began to turn her into a person. Not that she wasn't a person before, but I'd compartmentalized her. Now those compartments were beginning to emerge.

"I used to make spaghetti quite a bit, but at the risk of offending your senses, I used sauce from a jar."

I pressed my hand over my chest and feigned a heart attack. "Say it isn't so."

Her lips twitched upward as she picked up her wine. "I was only ten at the time. By the time I was fifteen, I did start adding vegetables, but not zucchini."

Jesus fuck, mother died when she was ten? No wonder she was such a scrapper. She was just a kid having to take on adult duties.

Lindsay hadn't been very old when her mother and I split, but Lindsay never had to take on adult roles in the family. Some would say she was spoiled, and I couldn't dispute that, but she was the center of my world. And so, I tried to be both her mother and her father, particularly when her mother stopped visiting her regularly after I won custody. While both girls were without a mother, I imagined Miranda's situation to be significantly more difficult because her mother was deceased, and she had to take on an adult role in the family.

"I'll give you the recipe if you like."

"I'd be afraid I couldn't do it justice." She took a sip and her brows lifted in surprise. "Is this the same wine from last night?"

I nodded, pleased that she remembered, but that was quickly followed by a worry that she might think it meant something. Like I was hoping to relive last night. And of course, I was, but no way would I act on it. "You noticed."

"It was hard not to." She set the wine on the table, her head tilting down, looking at her plate. "I'm sorry about the things I said earlier. I was just shocked to see you and then shocked to find out . . . well, you know."

"I apologize as well. I guess we were both a little shocked and took it out on each other."

I found myself wanting to ask her all sorts of questions, like had last night really been a first-time hookup for her? And I really wanted to know the truth about her virginity, hoping that she hadn't been a virgin because for some reason, taking my daughter's friend's virginity seemed even worse than what the situation already was.

But I determined it was best to not discuss what happened. "I think that starting now, we should act like who we are. Lindsay's father and her friend. We can leave the rest of it behind us."

She nodded. "We won't be telling Lindsay, right?"

"I hope not."

She seemed relieved as she twirled her fork in her spaghetti again. And her relief made me feel better as well. If I could just continue to see her as Lindsay's friend and not the curvaceous, passionate woman I met last night, everything would be all right.

To keep my mind out of the gutter, I steered the conversation to topics that would be normal for me to ask Lindsay's friends. "Are you finishing college this year like Lindsay is?"

"Yes."

"What are you studying?"

“I majored in history and am working on getting a teaching degree."

I sipped my wine, studying her over the rim of my glass. I hadn't pegged her as a history teacher, but my history teacher was a cranky old man.

"I'm trying to decide whether I'll go to graduate school first and get a master's degree. Maybe even a PhD."

"You want to teach at the college level?"

She shrugged. "That would be my preference, but graduate studies are expensive, and I might just get my bachelor's and get a job in a high school. I could pursue a graduate degree on the side."

I shook my head with a small laugh. "I wish Lindsay had your drive. It's bad enough she's getting a degree in art, which I'm having a hard time determining how it will translate into a job, but her grades leave something to be desired."

Miranda gave a little shrug. "Lindsay likes to live in the moment."

I laughed as I jammed my fork into my spaghetti. "I wish that moment was in her schoolbooks a little bit more." I didn't want to deny Lindsay the full college experience, which included activities outside the classroom, but I didn't want to waste my money on a useless degree and poor grades, either.

"It's a testament to the security that you give her that she can live life the way she does."

I looked up at Miranda, wondering what she meant by that. "A testament?"

"She knows that you will be there for her emotionally and financially. She has no worries hanging down on her. It gives her the luxury to embrace life."

My brow furrowed, intrigued by the way Miranda was explaining Lindsay's attitude toward life. "Is that a polite way of saying I spoiled her?"

Miranda's lips twitched upward slightly as she turned her focus back to her food. "Not exactly."

Feeling a little irked, I grumbled. "Then exactly what do you mean?"

She finished chewing her bite, but I had a feeling she was also using the time to choose her words.

Finally, she said, "Do I think Lindsay is spoiled? Yes, a little bit, but not in a way that makes her unlikable. Lindsay is the epitome of what life could be like if you didn't have to worry about anything. You can pursue any and every interest that you have. You can savor every moment. I sometimes envy that sort of freedom, but I also know that when the time comes for her to be encumbered by responsibility, it will be a challenge to her. It might even be sad to watch because she has such an exuberance."

I loved my daughter more than anything else in life, but I had seen the way she flitted through life while being irresponsible. But to see Lindsay through Miranda's eyes, I realized she was right. My goal in raising Lindsay was to give her the world. And so, who was I to be upset with her when she reached out to grab it, expected to receive it? She did it in a way that she wasn't acting entitled but instead wanted to fulfill every moment with happiness or fun. But had I set her up to not be ready when real life came her way?

"Maybe you should be studying psychology?"

"I'd rather teach." She studied me for a moment. "How did you decide what you were going to do when you were our age?"

"I didn't grow up with a whole lot. My family wasn't as poor as some, but we were poorer than most. I grew up in a rural area not far from here, actually." It was one of the reasons I didn't care much about coming to the cabin as much as Lindsay did. I much preferred the vibe, the energy of the city than memories of a more difficult life in the country. "I knew that if I wanted to do more, I needed an education and opportunity. I got a degree in business and parlayed my interest in sports and fitness into a line of supplements and sports drinks and other nutritional items. And then with my buddy Duncan, we opened a gym which is now several gyms across the country."

"So, in the end, you still pursued something that was close to your heart. Art is what fulfills Lindsay's heart."

“That may be, but what is she going to do with it?”

“She could become a fashion designer.”

“Yes, but who's going to build her business when she has no business or marketing background?”

She smiled. “Remember, Lindsay goes through life with the expectation that good things will come her way.”

“I suppose that's where I failed her.” Did I need to spend this last semester tightening the purse strings to help Lindsay learn to plan and be more responsible?

Miranda's eyes turned sympathetic. “The reality of life is going to come to Lindsay later than most of us. But it will come, and I know that you will be there for her when it does.”

She wasn't wrong. Despite the fact that I wanted Lindsay to be more committed to her studies and plot a path in life, no matter what happened, I would be there for her, which would perpetuate the problem. But it was what it was. Lindsay was my life. There wasn't anything I wouldn't do to make sure that she was happy.

Miranda finished her meal and rose from her chair. "I'll do the dishes since you cooked."

I was disappointed for the conversation to end, and because I was, I knew that it was time for me to disengage. It was one thing to want her sexually, but to connect to her at a different level that could enhance feelings of desire would be even more problematic. The idea that I would even be thinking this was a shock. I hadn't met a woman whom I wanted to get to know at a deeper level in a long, long time. Just my luck, the woman who interested me was one I couldn't have. So, for that reason, I needed to extricate myself from this situation.

I stood, carrying my plate into the kitchen. "Thank you. I was going to put a fire in the fireplace and finish decorating, but since Lindsay isn't coming and you'll be leaving as soon as the snow stops and the roads are clear, I don't see much use in it."

She turned on the water, her attention in the sink when she said, "I could help you if you wanted. I know I'm not Lindsay, but it's been a long time since I was in a home that was decorated for Christmas."

That stopped me short. She didn't celebrate Christmas? Then again, the fact that she was planning to spend it with Lindsay should've clued me in. "You don't have Christmas at your house?" I wondered if there was a religious or cultural reason for it.

She shrugged as she started to rinse the dishes. "Not really. Not since my mom died. My dad remarried for a short time, and we had Christmas then, but that was mostly because Loretta wanted fancy gifts. When she took off, Christmas sort of ended."

Holy hell. What sort of father did she have that he didn't try to lavish his daughter? I understood that money was tight, but I grew up in a family in which presents for birthdays and holidays were scarce, but there was always a celebration.

All of a sudden, the need to give Miranda a Christmas holiday became a singular focus. "I'll tell you what. I'll make some hot chocolate, and because you're old enough, I'll add a little peppermint liqueur to it. Then you can help me decorate the living area."

She didn't look at me, but a wide smile spread on her face. "I'd like that."

In my brain, warning bills were clinging. Spending more time with her would be problematic. Sure, my mind understood she was off limits as Lindsay's friend, but Lindsay wasn't here and my dick remembered all too well what it had been like to slide inside her.

But I was a strong man, right?

So, I ignored the warning and went out to make a fire in the fireplace.

6

Miranda

When Lindsay's dad left the kitchen, I blew out a breath and sagged against the counter. This emotional confusion was wreaking havoc inside my body.

My initial impression of him last night when we bumped into each other was that he was a curt, brooding, domineering man. Even after going to the hotel with him, that impression stayed with me. It was solidified tonight when we met alongside the road and returned to the cabin with the shock that he was Lindsay's father. So, seeing this kindness from him was a little bit unsettling. Unsettling because it made me feel all sorts of things I shouldn't be feeling.

Why was he going to continue to decorate and have his holiday traditions with me? I'd be a liar if I didn't admit that a part of me wanted to think it could be a prelude to seduction, but that was a stupid thought. The truth was more likely that he was just being nice to his daughter's friend. Hadn't he said at dinner that we were to act like nothing ever happened? Last night was in the past. Going forward, Lindsay was my friend and roommate, and he was Lindsay's father. That's how he was treating me. Like the friend of his daughter.

He probably took pity on me since I told him we didn't have much of a Christmas at my house. In some ways, that made my desire for him all the more unsettling since that meant he was treating me like a daughter. I shook the image of that out of my head.

I loaded up the dishwasher, finding detergent and starting its run. I washed the pots by hand and put them away if I could find their home. I left a few on the counter.

I'd just finished when Brett returned. "The fire is roaring if you'd like to go warm up. I'll make hot chocolate now."

I thought about telling him that he didn't need to go through all this trouble, but I couldn't find the words. The truth was, I wanted this evening. I wanted to see what it was like to celebrate the holidays with cheer and decorations. So I exited the kitchen, going into the large, open living area. The fireplace was huge, and the fire nearly consumed the entire space. It was the type of fire on Christmas cards or in holiday children's books.

I peeked into the box to see individually wrapped ornaments. It surprised me because it seemed like a very feminine thing to do. My dad just tossed all our stuff into a single box.

I wasn't comfortable starting the decorating process, so I took a seat on the large, comfortable couch and stared into the embers of the fire. A strange feeling came into my chest and slowly radiated out.

It took me a moment to realize what it was. It was a sense of comfort and safety.

The stress of my life involving finances and grades and caring for my father, and even worrying about having slept with my friend's father, melted away in the cozy warmth. I settled into it, remembering Lindsay's words about having a respite. I couldn't imagine that it was possible, and yet here I was, feeling like I was a world away from my world, where I didn't have to be responsible for anything. I determined that I would relish this feeling, this moment. Who knew when I'd ever have a chance to experience it again?

Brett returned from the kitchen carrying a tray that had two giant red mugs with white trim on them. Each had a candy cane sticking out of it. He set the tray on the table. "Hot chocolate with marshmallows, a little peppermint liqueur, and a candy cane to stir it with."

I couldn't help the happy little laugh that escaped. I suppose it was technically a giggle, but I never giggled. Giggling was what silly girls did.

"This is wonderful." I took the mug he offered me and settled back into the couch, taking a sip. Chocolate and peppermint burst in my mouth, and I closed my eyes to savor it as I knew Lindsay would. That was what this moment offered, I realized. I could be like Lindsay and be open to savoring everything. Well, maybe not everything. Brett took a seat at the other end of the couch, and while it was wrong, there was no stopping my appreciating that he was sexy as hell.

"Where would you like to start? We can do the tree first. Or we could decorate the rest of the room. I've got stockings somewhere around here that we can hang on the mantel."

"Let's start with the tree." But first, I took another sip of the hot cocoa, letting it warm me up from the inside out as the fire and the atmosphere warmed me from the outside in. I set my mug on the tray and went with Brett to the box to decorate the tree.

Many of the ornaments had clearly been made by Lindsay when she was a child, and they brought back bittersweet memories of similar ornaments I had made in school or crafting with my mother. Those ornaments were long gone. Once Loretta married my father, Christmas trees looked like they came out of a magazine with color themes and no room for sentimental child-made ornaments. It was sweet that Brett still had Lindsay's creations and put them on the tree.

A part of me wanted to ask what it was like being a single father and raising Lindsay, but I didn't. As much as I wanted to know about this man, bringing up Lindsay was only a reminder of what we did and what we couldn't do again. I didn't want that reminder now, not in this moment outside of my real life.

I was grateful that he didn't ask me anything more about my own Christmases or my friendship with Lindsay. I wondered if that was on purpose? Could he possibly be feeling similar to the way I was? I shook my head because it was unlikely he was feeling the attraction. More likely, he was avoiding those topics because he didn't want to be reminded about last night. He wanted to see me as Lindsay's friend.

Now and then, I would stop and take a sip of my hot cocoa and then continue decorating. When we finished the tree, we moved on to the rest of the room. There was a little manger scene that he let me set up on a table near the window.

I finished the last of my hot cocoa just as we set up the last decoration. I studied our accomplishment, noting how lovely and warm the room felt. It was quickly followed by sadness that it likely meant the end of the night.

Brett drank his hot cocoa, pulling his cup away and looking down into it. Then he looked up at me. "I'm out. How about you? Do you want another one?"

"Yes, please." I said it a little too eagerly. Like a kid on Christmas Eve. So much for appearing mature.

He took the cups and headed back into the kitchen. I took another look around the room, studying our handiwork. My eyes settled on a book facing outward on the bookshelf. I picked it up, realizing it was a photo album. I knew I should put it back, but instead, I opened it up and saw that it was a scrapbook of Christmases. I wondered if Brett had made it. Or maybe Lindsay had. I decided it was probably Lindsay because she was always doing artistic things with photos that she would hang in her room or put in little frames. Even on Instagram, her photos had added little flourishes beyond the filters.

I took the book and sat on the couch as I went through it, seeing pictures of Lindsay as a baby and then a toddler. By the time Brett returned, the pictures showed Lindsay in elementary school. Each year was filled with love and joy and celebration that made my heart squeeze tight with envy.

"Where'd you find that old thing?" he asked as he handed me a mug of hot cocoa.

"I hope you don't mind. It was on the shelf over there."

"Not at all." He sat next to me, so close our shoulders were touching as he looked into the book. "That was the year I taught Lindsay how to ski."

It took a minute for my hormones to stop frizzing out my brain to study the picture. Sure enough, there was Lindsay bundled up in outdoor gear with two little skis and a huge toothless grin.

"How old was she here?"

"Five or six, I think." His finger brushed over the picture with reverence. "That was when I decided that I was going to fight her mother for custody."

Lindsay didn't talk much about her mom. Only that she didn't see her very much anymore. After moving in full-time with her father, visits with her mother were regular for a short time, then they grew more and more sporadic. But I wasn't clear on why.

"I had to put up a hell of a fight. But when it came to Lindsay, there wasn't anything I wouldn't do."

I had no doubt that my father loved me, and he would say similar things, but I wasn't sure that he had the energy in him. The thought made me sad.

"What's wrong?"

My brow furrowed as I looked at him because I wasn't sure what he was talking about.

This thumb gently brushed across my cheek, sending waves of warmth through me. "Are you crying?"

I hadn't realized I was. Embarrassed, I wiped my cheeks. Then I closed the photo book, putting it on the coffee table. "I'm sorry."

He shook his head, turning his body toward me on the couch. "No, what's wrong?"

I sipped my hot chocolate, wanting to hide from my feelings, wanting to hide from him and the intensity of his stare.

"It's just bittersweet." I started to get up, but his free hand wrapped around my wrist, keeping me on the couch.

"Why? Is it something I said or did?"

The truth was that it partly was what he said and did, but not in the way he thought. This was the sort of Christmas I had until my mother died.

"It's just making me remember Christmas when I was a little girl. It was always special. Craft ornaments and hot chocolate, although mine didn't have liquor in it." I gave him a wan smile, but his stare was still intense.

"So I've brought back bad memories?"

I shook my head, pressing my palm to his cheek feeling, its warmth and only afterward realizing that I probably shouldn't be touching him. I started to pull my hand away, but again, his hand took mine.

"Not bad memories. They're sweet memories. Happy memories. But it's sad that it's all they are. I told you that my father didn't do well after my mom died, so Christmas and a lot of celebrations in life just fell by the wayside. He remarried, and for a short time we had Christmas, but it wasn't like this. It was all the commercial type of stuff. It was all about the gifts." I looked down, feeling self-conscious. To hide it, I took another sip of my hot chocolate.

"I'm sorry that happened to you."

I forced a perky smile as I looked at him. "It's not your fault. And in the scheme of life, there are worse things than not having a fancy-schmancy Christmas."

"But it's not fancy-schmancy, is it? It's the family."

I nodded, and then worried that he might think badly of my father, I quickly said, "My father loves me. He's really proud of me. I'm going to be the first one in the family to graduate with a college degree. But inside, he's a little bit broken."

Brett's head tilted to the side. "And you've taken it upon yourself to fix him?"

"I suppose maybe there was a time I thought I could. I know now that I can't. But I won't deny that I try to keep the pieces that are there together."

"No wonder Lindsay was so adamant that you have total and complete rest. A respite, she said."

I nodded.

His fingers brushed back loose hair that had fallen from the messy bun I'd hastily tied up.

"I can't give you family, Miranda, but I can give you respite." His gaze drifted to my lips and then back up to my eyes. "Do you really wish you could scrub your memory of last night from your brain?"

I swallowed as the air around me changed. It was the same energy I felt on the sidewalk last night as Brett invited me to a hotel room. I should disengage. He was Lindsay's father.

"No."

"So, you enjoyed it?" His thumb brushed across my lower lip.

I closed my eyes as an ache rushed between my legs. "Yes." This shouldn't be happening. Couldn't happen. I opened my eyes to say as much, but his intense gray stare made the words disintegrate. Instead, I asked, "Did you?"

He smiled. "Immensely. So much so, I'd like to do it again. What do you think about that, Miranda?"

I agreed, but . . . "What about Lind—"

His finger pressed over my lips. "How about a new rule for tonight? Instead of acting like last night never happened and treating each other by our relation to Lindsay, we act like the relationship isn't there and treat each other like we did last night?"

Sign me up was my first thought. The second was *Caution*. Surely, I was betraying Lindsay.

As if he understood my hesitation, he said, "Just one more night. Once we leave here, we play our roles in relation to Lindsay."

My gaze drifted to his lips, really wanting to taste them again, to feel them on my body. "A moment away from real life. We can live like Lindsay does. In the moment, without a care."

His head cocked to the side. "Yes, I suppose that's a way to look at it. Just here and now. Like a bubble."

The words sent a feeling of freedom through me. Like I could let go of everything about my life and who I was, and instead, indulge in make-believe. In fantasy.

"Can I do what I want to you?"

Wild heat flashed in his eyes. "What do you want to do to me?"

Nervousness slid down my spine. He was a man with experience. All I had was what I'd learned last night. But I wanted to learn more. Learn it all. Learn it with him.

"Suck you."

He let out a low groan. "You can suck me all you want. Anything else?"

I couldn't really think of anything else. I was aware there were different positions and ways of achieving sexual gratification, but I couldn't think beyond wanting to touch him, to watch him come from my ministrations.

"Just that."

His gaze stayed on me as he stood. He shucked off his shirt as he toed off his shoes. I watched with rapt excitement as he unbuttoned his jeans and pushed them down his strong legs. His dick was straining behind his boxer briefs.

I licked my lips, and he groaned again. "You look hungry."

I looked up at him, feeling a little self-conscious. I'd never done this before. What if I sucked? In a bad way?

He pushed his boxer briefs down, his dick springing out, long, hard, thick. I started to reach for him, but he sat down next to me.

"Get on your knees in front of me," he commanded.

I did as he asked, kneeling between his knees. For a moment, I just sat there, not sure what to do. Did I just grab his dick? Should I engage in foreplay, and if so, what?

"Take your shirt off, Miranda. When I come, I want to do it all over those gorgeous tits of yours."

The naughtiness along with his praise of my breasts sent another rush of arousal to my center. I pulled off my sweater and then my shirt. A mixture of self-consciousness and excitement filled me.

"While you're at it, take everything off. That way, I can eat that cream pie of yours when you finish me off."

I stood, turning away as I undid my jeans.

"What are you doing?" he asked.

"Getting undressed." Again, nerves made me second-guess myself. I was no supermodel. No plastic beauty.

"Why are you hiding? I want to see that sweet body of yours."

Sweet body? Really?

I turned, and unable to look him in the eyes, I finished undressing.

"You have a body made for fucking, did you know that?"

I shook my head.

"I'll prove it, but first, come suck my dick with that hot mouth of yours."

I resumed my position on the floor between his knees. He positioned himself at the edge of the couch and leaned back, his gray eyes watching me.

I swallowed, rethinking this whole thing. "What . . . What do you like?"

"You haven't done this before?"

It was that obvious, eh?

He took my hand and pressed it around his dick. "Feel that?"

"The skin is soft." I don't know what I expected, but that hadn't been it.

"But underneath, I'm hard as a rock." He guided my hand, stroking him from tip to base, slowly. "Up here." His thumb slid along the rim of his dick. "This is the sweet spot. Especially on the bottom."

I rubbed my thumb over the spot he'd indicated.

He hissed. "Yes. Right there."

I leaned in, licking the spot. His hips jerked up.

"That's right. More of that."

Enthralled and wanting to explore, I pushed his hand away. I focused a bit more on the rim but then moved on, wanting to touch every inch of his dick. I massaged the sacks below, marveling at how soft and fragile they seemed.

"Use your mouth, Miranda. Suck my cock."

It looked huge, but I was eager for the challenge, hoping I didn't disappoint him. I pressed my lips around the tip, lapping my tongue over it to feel it, taste it.

"Yes. Fuck." He groaned, and I looked up at him. His head fell back and his eyes closed.

I took him in deeper, pressing my lips tightly around him.

"Mmm, more. More." His hand pulled out my hair tie, and then he pushed my hair to one side. It cascaded over his hip. I glanced up, and this time his gaze was on me, his eyes fixed on my mouth.

I sucked him as deep as I could without gagging, then reversed, sliding back up. I repeated, taking him in, sliding him out, up and down, listening to his breathing quicken, his words turn dirtier.

"Fuck my cock. Yes. Take it all."

I wrapped my hand around his shaft and focused my mouth on the tip, moving it in and out of my mouth faster, my tongue lapping at the spot underneath.

"Fuck. Yes. Right there. Fuck, don't stop." His hips rocked and his breathing turned to panting. "Oh, fuck." He pushed me back and sat up. "Hold up your tits, baby. I'm gonna come."

A little surprised by the quick change, I sat back on my heels and held my breasts up.

"Oh, yeah." He stroked his dick, the tip touching my nipples. "Tell me to come on you."

I enjoyed his dirty talk, but I wasn't sure I could pull it off.

"Tell me to cream your sexy tits."

"Come on me."

He groaned, his hand stroking faster and faster. Fascinated, I watched the way he touched himself. It was mostly short, fast strokes along the tip.

"Fuck. I'm there." White, creamy cum shot out, hitting me on the chest. He kept stroking, and each time, more cum sprayed until my breasts were dripping with it. "Lick the rest." He pushed his dick toward my mouth. Not sure whether I'd like it, I was too caught up to refuse. At first, I tentatively wrapped my lips around his tip.

"Yes. God."

Emboldened, I sucked his dick into my mouth. It was smaller, softer, and tasted salty.

"Jesus fuck." He sank back onto the couch.

I released him and waited.

Finally, his eyes popped open. "You're a fucking natural." He took my arm, hauling me up onto the couch and kissing me hard. "Now it's my turn to feast, and you're going to ride my face."

7

Brett

Turns out I wasn't that strong. At least not stronger than my dick when it came to Miranda. If there'd been a moment when I could have let smarter minds prevail, it vanished the minute she said she wanted to suck my dick. And while having a woman who knew what she was doing around a dick was generally ideal, the idea that my dick was the first one in her mouth was a turn-on I'd never experienced.

Fucking Miranda was wrong, but at this moment and time, I didn't give a fuck. Instead, I justified it by telling myself that Lindsay would never know. Like Miranda said, "a moment away from real life." So as long as what happened at the cabin stayed at the cabin, everything would be alright. No harm, no foul.

Right now, I wanted to drink in that sweet pussy of hers and I wanted to do it with her riding my face. Her expression was a mixture of excitement and nerves. That told me she hadn't ever ridden a man's face before but she was willing to try.

If I had doubts about her being a virgin before, I was pretty sure that question was answered now. Guilt tried to nag at me. I had nothing to offer Miranda except a few mind-blowing orgasms while we were here. A woman who waited until her twenties to sleep with a man was usually saving herself for love, if not marriage.

But Miranda was game for our sexual encounter last night and tonight. She never said she was a virgin when I asked. So I pushed away any guilt about taking her virginity and focused on how fucking hot it was to think about all the things I could teach her.

First, I grabbed a napkin from the tray to wipe her off. She shivered.

"Are you cold?" Before she could answer, I tugged her to the plush rug in front of the fire. I lay spooned behind her, my dick nestled against her ass cheeks.

She came willingly. There was something sweet about her innocence and apparent trust. My guilt tried to rear its ugly head again, but I pushed it away.

"Are you aching?" I asked as I slid my fingers between her pussy lips, finding her dripping wet. She moaned and arched in response.

I lay on my back. "Straddle me." I used the commanding voice I'd used when I had her suck my cock.

Her expression was tentative, but she complied.

"I want you to scoot up until your pussy is over my face."

"Are you sure?"

I pressed my hands on her ass to urge her on. "You'll love it, I promise."

As she moved over me, the scent of her sex filled my nostrils and my dick thickened. Before she left tomorrow, I'd be inside that pussy again, I vowed.

I looked up at her, wanting to reassure her. Taking her hips in my hands, I pulled her down as I lifted my head and slid my tongue through her pussy.

"Oh, God." She gasped, her hips jerking. Her hands covered mine on her hips. "Brett!"

Hell yeah. Nothing better than hearing my name on a woman's lips when she's experiencing pleasure.

I focused on the job at hand, giving her pussy the feasting of a lifetime. I sucked and licked. I thrust my tongue inside her as my nose flicked over her clit. It didn't take long for her to come. She cried out again and her juices flowed. I drank it all like a man dying of thirst.

As her body went lax, I maneuvered her until she was lying on the plush rug, her breathing still labored.

For a moment, I watched her, and a strange sense of calm settled inside me. Perhaps it was because I knew our secret would be safe. Or maybe it was because she was so open to exploring the physical attraction between us. Or maybe it was something else . . . but I didn't want to look at it too closely.

"Are you okay?"

"Mmm." A sweet, sated smile came to her lips, and that feeling of calm morphed into something that filled my chest. It unnerved me.

I started to pull away, ready to end the night even though I hadn't fucked her fully yet.

"I don't know that I've ever been this relaxed," she murmured, as if she was on the verge of drifting to sleep. "Thank you."

Jesus fuck, did she just thank me for giving her an orgasm?

Her head tilted toward me, and her sated smile still teased her lips. "I hope it was okay for you."

I rubbed my hand over my chest, hating the feeling there but powerless to make it stop. "It was more than okay."

"Really? Because . . ." She turned her head away, looking toward the fire. "The truth is, I am . . . or was . . . a virgin."

"I figured that out." Unable to help myself, I tucked in close to her, spooning around her. "I hope I didn't hurt you."

She let out a light laugh. "I felt many things, but hurt wasn't one of them."

I smiled, even though I was feeling off-kilter. "I'm glad." I kissed her temple. "What made you decide to give it to me?"

She was quiet for a moment. "I don't know for sure except in the moment, I wanted what you were offering."

"I made you horny?"

She laughed, finally looking at me again. "I guess that's it."

"What about a boyfriend?" I didn't know why I asked that because I didn't want to know about boyfriends, past, present, or future. Not here in our bubble. Here, she was mine.

She shrugged. "I had a boyfriend in high school and dated a little bit in college. There's one guy who showed an interest in me in my Ancient Law and Society course. Mostly, I'm focused on work and school." She sighed. "And looking out for my dad."

I had this strange urge to want to finance her life. Not in a kept woman sort of way. I wanted to make life easier for her. Help her get ahead in life.

I recalled that she was here for a respite, and thinking about her dad, work, school, and whoever the fuck the guy in her Ancient Law and Society course was defeated the purpose.

Before I could change the subject, she asked, "Why did you invite me to the hotel? I know I'm not your usual. Linds—I've heard you like plastic women."

She stopped herself from saying my daughter's name fully, but not soon enough to avoid bringing the situation between us again. It told me that Lindsay talked to Miranda about our lives, and likely how I dated a lot but never settled down again after my divorce.

"I like a good fuck every now and then," I admitted. Why color-coat the truth? I didn't want Miranda to think badly of me, but neither did I need to impress her. Like my past women, this moment would be a one-and-done situation. We'd have our fill and then go on.

"But why me?"

I wasn't quite sure. "You made me horny."

She laughed then. Not a giggle or a light laugh. She burst out laughing. I found myself mesmerized by how free and full it sounded.

"Is that funny?"

"I've never heard those words before. Not directed toward me, anyway."

Feeling light and free myself, I rolled on top of her, pressing my hard dick against her pussy. "You make me horny now."

She gasped and looked up at me as her legs opened to invite me in.

I sat back on my heels. Gripping her hips, I tugged them toward me, repositioning my dick at her entrance. "I want to fuck you now, Miranda. I want to fuck you hard and fast until you're screaming my name. What do you say to that?"

Her fingers gripped the rug underneath her. "I say fuck me hard and fast, Brett."

The wild, hot storm of desire consumed me. I drove into her and let go. I gave full rein to the powers of sex and physical need. I lost myself in the sensation of my cock sliding in and out of her tight pussy, the friction building, building, until I was mad with the need to come.

"Brett!" she screamed, her pussy clamped around my cock like it would never let go.

Stars burst behind my eyes as my orgasm slammed into me, charging through my body like a fucking freight train. "Fuck!" I continued to drive into her, thrusting, grinding, coming until my body gave out, and even then, my dick continued to pulse inside her.

I collapsed over her, feeling sated, yes, but unsettled as well. I withdrew, moving us so that we were on our sides, and I spooned around her again. This way, I wouldn't have to look at her while my mind was a torrent of confusing thoughts.

What was it about this woman? Why was it that fucking her felt like more than scratching a physical itch? And why was it that just after coming so hard, I shouldn't be able to get it up again for a week, my dick twitched as she settled her ass against my groin? And why did I feel like even after tonight, I'd still want more?

I DIDN'T MEAN to fall asleep on the floor, but apparently, I had as I woke up with Miranda still tucked into my body. The sun wasn't up, but the sky was starting to light up, telling me it had to be close to six thirty. For a moment, I lay with Miranda's body warm and soft against me. Her breathing told me she was still sleeping.

I was well and truly fucked. I didn't spend the night with women. I didn't wake up next to them. This time, I overrode my dick, which was at full mast, ready to sink into Miranda's sweet body again. Now, it was time to go back to reality.

I carefully rolled away and stood. I grabbed a blanket from the couch and covered Miranda. She smiled but didn't wake up. A pull in my chest had me wanting to lie down next to her again, but I ignored it. I was doing a lot of that lately, ignoring my instincts.

I grabbed my clothes and headed upstairs, where I took a quick shower and then set out to see how much snow we had and how soon I could get Miranda on her way home.

I figured it would be some time before our road was cleared, but I crossed my fingers it would be by noon or so. Then hopefully, we could dig out her car and get a tow truck to pull it from the ditch.

I didn't get an answer from the towing company when I called, so I made coffee and set out clearing the snow from my front steps. I'd moved my SUV into the covered area next to the cabin so I didn't need to dig it out. I needed to deal with the driveway, but not yet. Instead, I went to the back to clear off my deck and around the hot tub. Maybe I'd take a soak in it later once Miranda headed home. I had an image of Miranda in with me, riding me.

Fucking hell.

When I finished, I returned inside ready to make breakfast. I checked in the living room but Miranda wasn't there. The blanket was folded on the couch and her clothes were gone. For a moment, I was disappointed, but I ignored it, of course.

I pulled out bacon and eggs and bread for toast. A few minutes later, Miranda entered the kitchen. Her long hair was wet, suggesting she took a shower. She wore jeans and a green sweatshirt with a reindeer that had Christmas lights in its antlers. It was a reminder to me that she was young and not someone I should be fucking. The thought irritated me.

"You slept through all the chores, I see."

She flinched, her eyes rounding, making me feel like a dick for speaking so curtly.

"I'm sorry. I didn't realize—"

"Doesn't matter. Are you hungry?"

She studied me for a moment, probably wondering what the fuck was wrong with me. "I was going to call about my car."

"Sure thing." I cracked three eggs into my pan as I pushed the lever on my toaster down.

Miranda took her phone from her back pocket and started to leave the kitchen.

Let her go, let her go. "You really should eat something."

She stopped. "I should call."

"The roads won't be clear for a bit." I slid the cooked eggs onto a plate, pulled bacon from the oven where it had been warming after cooking, and took the plate to the table. "I've got toast too."

She bit her lip like she wasn't sure what to do.

"Sit. Eat." The toaster popped up. "Do you like butter on your toast? What about jam?"

She watched me like I was a predator, ready to pounce on her at any time, but she sat at the table. "Butter is fine."

I prepared the toast and made my plate, then sat at the table. I took a breath to get my shit together. "Sorry I snapped. Hangry, I guess."

"I'm happy to help with chores. I'll do the dishes—"

"Eat first."

She began to eat but remained quiet. The severing of whatever the fuck had connected last night was complete. Soon, she'd be on her way. She'd be back to her life, and I'd be back to mine.

So why did I feel like shit?

8

Miranda

I woke up this morning disoriented. Why was I sleeping on the floor?

When my eyes popped open and I saw the fireplace, the night before came flooding back. Christmas decorating, hot chocolate with peppermint liqueur, and incredible sex. Just as before, I was shocked at my behavior. But unlike last time, I also felt guilty for knowingly sleeping with my roommate's father. But if I was going to be completely honest with myself, I had no regrets. Brett had been sweet, sexy, naughty, and I loved every moment of it.

My only real concern was whether being with him now would ruin me for relationships in the future. I couldn't imagine any other man making me feel the way Brett made me feel.

I had turned over, wondering if perhaps the morning could start the way the night before had ended, but Brett hadn't been there. It was a reminder that it was time for me to leave this fantasy world and reenter the reality of my life. I rose from my spot, getting dressed and folding up the blanket that he had put over me. I heard him out in the back doing what sounded like shoveling. I headed upstairs, showered, and got dressed, packing my bag. I was disappointed that I would be leaving, but I was used to disappointment.

When I headed downstairs, I followed the scent of bacon, my stomach grumbling. What I hadn't expected was for Brett to snap at me for being lazy. It told me that he had regretted last night and he was eager to get me out of his house. The sooner I could call to get help with my car and on the road back to Boston, the better.

I imagined it was guilt over his curt demeanor that had him serving me breakfast. I'd accepted it, not so much because I was hungry but because I wanted to placate him. I even offered to help with chores, including doing the dishes.

If I was leaving, I wondered if he would be too. I hadn’t heard from Lindsay since yesterday, but it sounded like she hadn’t planned to come up at all.

"Will Lindsay be coming up later?" I asked.

He cocked his head to the side, his eyes narrowing as they studied me. "Not that she told me."

"I guess that means you won't be spending Christmas here. I can help you take the decorations down again."

His jaw tightened, although I couldn't imagine why he seemed irritated by that. "That won't be necessary. Just focus on getting your car out of that embankment so that you can get home."

I suppose his irritation was that my helping him would mean that I’d be here longer. He wanted me gone. I hadn't finished my breakfast, but I wasn't hungry anymore either. I picked up my phone to search for a tow truck service that could come pull me out of the ditch. I imagined it would have to dig me out too after last night's snow.

"I'll call. You can finish packing."

The urgency with which he wanted to get rid of me hurt, and I felt like such an idiot for the flights of fancy I’d entertained about him. I knew that there was nothing beyond this cabin for me and Brett, and yet, I had felt something last night. Something beyond physical pleasure.

I nodded and headed up to my room, not bothering to tell him I was already packed. At this point, I figured it would be best to stay out of his way until I could leave.

Back in the guest room, I sat in the window seat, staring at the blanket of white covering the landscape. Being in a funk, I couldn't fully appreciate the beauty of it.

I wasn't sure how long I sat there when Brett made an appearance in the doorway to the room. His expression was grim. I decided that meant only one thing—I was stuck here a little bit longer.

"Last night, the snow was pretty wet, which means trees are down all over the area. Apparently, there are several on the road, so they can't even plow yet."

"How long do you think it will take for them to clear out the trees and plow?"

"There are other roads that have higher priority than Bucknell Road at the moment, but maybe by later this afternoon or this evening. Of course, clearing the road and plowing isn't the only issue we have. We need to pull you out of that ditch too, but until the road is clear and plowed, there's no sense in calling someone."

I nodded and turned to look back out the window, unsure of what to say.

He let out a sigh. "Don't feel like you have to hide in here until we can get your car back to you. Same as yesterday, you have access to the house and all the amenities with it. I promise to stay out of your way."

"Thank you." Of course, I had no desire to make use of the amenities of the house. While his words told me I was welcome, his behavior earlier made it such that I wanted to avoid him at all costs. I didn't feel welcome, so I would stay out of his way the best I could.

After he left, I sat in the window seat a little longer, staring out the window, but that was quickly getting boring. I wished I'd brought schoolbooks so I could at least study for the upcoming semester. I did the next best thing and found my earbuds, putting them on and listening to an audiobook.

I was able to hide away in the guest room until midafternoon. But finally, hunger got the best of me. I made my way down the hall and stairs into the kitchen without making any noise. All the while, I looked around corners, wondering where Brett was.

I entered the kitchen and, looking through the French doors to the deck outside, I saw Brett's head poking out from the hot tub. His back was to me, so I was able to study him. Study the strong upper back and shapely, sculpted shoulders. He had his arms spread eagle along the rim of the hot tub, one hand holding a glass of something that I suspected was liquor.

I was about to go to the kitchen and make lunch when my conscience told me I should offer to make him something too. The guy had already made me breakfast and dinner and served me hot cocoa. I needed to pull my own weight. Reluctantly, I opened the French door and stepped out into the frigid air.

He turned his head and then maneuvered his body to the side of the tub so that he could see me better. "The water is perfect if you'd like to come in."

What was it with him? He was like Dr. Jekyll and Mr. Hyde. Sweet and attentive one minute and then rude the next.

I schooled my face to hide my annoyance. "Thank you, but my swimsuit is packed and who knows when we'll be able to get a tow truck so I can head on home."

He brought his drink to his lips, taking a sip before resting it again on the side of the tub. "I know it won't be tonight."

What? No. I can't continue to stay here.

"They anticipate getting Bucknell Road plowed later this evening, but another storm is coming through. They'll be plowing and treating the road at the same time. So" —he motioned his free hand over the tub— "you might as well make yourself at home."

"Thank you, but I don't think so."

"I'm sorry I was such an asshole earlier." He cocked his head to the side. "Surely, you understand why?"

I couldn't guess the specifics, but I suspected it had something to do with my being Lindsay's friend. Why that would make him act the way he did, though, I wasn't sure.

"Have you ever wanted something that you shouldn't have?"

I nodded. "Sure." He came to mind. So did binging on chocolate cake.

“Have you ever allowed yourself to indulge in it, just a little bit? Thinking it would sate the craving, only to find out it fueled it?"

We could have been talking about chocolate cake, but I realized he was talking about me. The tension and irritation I’d been holding onto around him began to wane.

"It's fucking frustrating, Miranda, to try to avoid something you want badly when it's hovering in your orbit." He took another sip of his drink, but his gray eyes stayed on me. "Do you know what I mean?"

"I know exactly what you mean." And I did. Brett was my chocolate cake. The thing I wanted but shouldn't have. The thing that taking a single bite of would only lead to my wanting more.

"You do?"

"Yes."

His gray eyes watched me. "You feel it now? Here with me?"

"Yes."

"How good are you at resisting your cravings?"

"It depends on how appealing the thing I want is."

He studied me for a long moment and then set his glass down at the edge of the hot tub. He stood, turning his body fully to me, holding his hands out to his sides. He was completely naked. It had to be over one hundred degrees in the tub, but it was only in the twenties outside, so he had to be freezing.

"Is this appealing?" he asked.

Yes, yes, it was. "You're going to catch a cold."

He shrugged as he sank back into the tub. "Clearly, not appealing enough."

"I didn't say that."

"Then why don't you come in here with me? Same rules as last night."

I wanted to. I really did. "And what happens tomorrow when you regret indulging your craving?"

"I won't take it out on you."

I stood looking at him, wanting to join him and at the same time knowing it was a bad idea. Partly because of Lindsay, but also partly because as much as I loved his attention when he showered it on me through his touch, I didn't like it so much when he was irritated.

His expression had been like a dare, but then it morphed into resignation. "I won't be in here much longer if you'd like to come in later."

Now that it felt like the choice had been taken away from me, I wanted to run and cannonball into the hot tub.

"It's just that my swimsuit is upstairs."

He arched a brow. "You don't need a swimsuit. And if you don't want me to touch you or see you, I can get out and you can use the tub alone."

A feeling of excitement shimmied up my spine at doing something so deliciously erotic as being naked outside. I stepped out the door, closing it behind me and making my way toward a bench next to the hot tub. I took off my clothes, shivering as the cold air bit into my exposed skin. I had to have looked like a lunatic as I charged up the steps to the side of the hot tub and then sank into it, the heat as searing as it was cold outside.

He smiled from the opposite side of the hot tub. "See? I told you it's perfect."

"It seems a little crazy to be naked outside when it's so cold."

"That's part of the fun of hot tubbing in winter. The contrast."

I closed my eyes, letting my head drop back on the edge as I took in the heat of the water, the scent of the chlorine, and the cold air on my face.

"Are you disappointed that you're stuck with me here on Christmas Eve? That you're going to wake up on Christmas morning with a grump like me?"

I opened my eyes to look at him, wondering if he was serious or joking. "Only when Scrooge is here."

He let out a laugh, and it occurred to me it was the first time I saw him laugh like that. Open and reaching to his eyes. He really was an amazingly handsome man.

"I'll try to keep my inner Scrooge contained."

"Then no, I'm not disappointed." The truth was, if he kept his word, I would have another night like I did last night. One without stress or worry. One where I could give in to sensations and pleasure.

Our gazes held for long moments, and the energy between us charged again.

"Just so you know, Miranda, I'm not going to try to seduce you."

In an instant, all the sexy feelings evaporated.

"So, if there's something that you want from me, you're going to have to initiate it."

I appreciated that he was leaving the decision to me but self-conscious about taking that step. "Is there something you want from me?"

"I think I've made that clear since the moment we met." His gaze drifted down, and I realized my breasts were bobbing in the water. My nipples tightened, and it had nothing to do with the cold air.

Remembering that I'd been open to him about my sexual inexperience, I decided he could teach me the art of seduction. "How do I go about seducing you?"

His lips twitched upward. "It is amazingly easy. You just need to straddle my legs and press those magnificent tits into my face."

"That sounds easy enough." I slowly crossed the hot tub, still feeling self-conscious but daring. I straddled his thighs, looping my arms around his neck. "How's this?"

"Fucking fantastic." His hands kneaded my breasts, lifting them from the water. Cold air assaulted my nipples. He groaned as he rubbed his thumbs over them, making me moan too. His lips wrapped around one, sucking, tugging. My hips rocked, seeking his dick. It was hard pressed between my pussy and his belly. I ground against him.

"Are you going to fuck me, Miranda?" His hands left my breasts. One reached behind me, grabbing my ass. The other slid between us, his thumb flicking over my clit.

"Yes," I said in a gasp, rising to take him in. I sank down, closing my eyes to savor the pressure, the pleasure as he filled me.

"Fuck, yeah," he groaned. "Love your tight pussy. Now ride me, Miranda."

I'd learned that sex involved a lot of instinct, at least when it came to intercourse. There had been many times when I'd been unsure, but once he was inside me, my body knew exactly what to do. I rocked my hips and then rose and sank down again. My hands gripped his shoulders as I moved. I was aware of the cold on my exposed body, but I didn't feel it. The only sensations were building tension and pleasure as I moved faster, faster, seeking, reaching for release.

His fingers dug into my hips as he helped me move over him. He dipped his head, his tongue snaking out and lapping at my nipple. I felt it straight to my pussy, launching me into the sweetest pleasure.

"Oh, God!" I cried out into the openness as wave after wave of sensation flooded my body.

"Yes. I'm coming," he growled out, his hips bucking up and warmth filling me.

When the pleasure subsided, I sank against him, boneless. Thoughts and feelings rushed into my mind, all having to do with Brett. The one that took hold was why did something that was wrong feel so right?

9

Brett

W*hy fight it?* That was the rationale I used when I invited Miranda into the hot tub and to fuck me. When I resisted her, all it did was irritate the shit out of me and make me act like an asshole. Since we were going to be stuck here together again, why make it hard? Why torture myself if I didn't have to? We could have another sex-filled night in this little world away from reality and nobody would be the wiser. Once we left, we'd go back to our regular lives. And because I wouldn't see her again, I wouldn't have to fight the near-constant state of arousal I felt when Miranda was near.

Seeing that she was wary of me, I put the decision of *to fuck or not to fuck* into her hands. If she wanted me to stay away from her, I would. Thank God that wasn't the choice she made.

As our orgasms subsided, she went boneless over me, and I banded my arm around her, holding her there. We had nowhere to go and nowhere to be, so we might as well just stay here with my dick deep inside her hot, wet pussy until I could get him up again. Fun fact —with her, it rarely took very long.

I brought my other hand up to her tit, lifting it out of the water, watching as the nipple tightened and puckered as the cold air hit it. She let out a soft moan as I flicked my thumb over it. I wrapped my lips around it, sucking. With each tug of her nipple, her pussy pulsed around my dick, coaxing him back to life.

She shivered.

"Are you cold?" If necessary, we'd take this party back inside.

"No." She lifted her head and rocked over me, making my dick twitch. She was a fast learner. I liked that about her.

I took both her tits in my hands again, playing with them, sucking on one nipple as I pinched the other.

"Oh." She gasped, her head falling back.

"I'd like to fuck these beauties." I could see it already, my dick sliding between them, coming all over her chest. Not now, though. Later. I sucked hard on a nipple, wrangling another gasp, and her pussy tightened around me.

"Time for something new." I maneuvered her off me, loving how she whimpered at the loss of contact. "Turn around and rest your hands on the edge."

She did as I asked. I stood behind her, the biting cold air adding pain to the pleasure. Pushing her ass down to the water, I dropped to my knees and then positioned my dick at her entrance. "Hold on, Miranda."

I thrust in, fast and hard.

"Oh, God. Mmm." She rested her forearms on the side of the tub, arching her back, giving me a lovely view of her ass.

"You like that, don't you? You like when I fuck you hard." I withdrew and plunged in again.

She moaned. "I like all the ways."

Fuck, I did too. It was going to be hard to follow up after this. I pushed that thought away. This was about enjoying the here and now. I moved in hard thrusts. The bubbling water around us splashed each time I drove in. Miranda let out tiny mewls that I found incredibly arousing.

"Are you close? Are you going to come on my cock, Miranda?" I'd learned over the last two nights that she liked it when I talked dirty to her.

She moaned in response. "Brett."

"Tell me, baby. Tell me you're going to come."

"Oh, God, I'm going to come." She'd been resting her forearms on the side of the tub, but now she rose, gripping the edge with her hands, her ass pushing back, telling me she was close.

"Talk to me, Miranda. Talk dirty." I wanted to be sure I'd come when she did.

"Brett."

"Do it. Tell me what you want." I gripped her hips, my thrusts coming faster, harder.

"Fuck me."

Hell yeah. "More."

"Fuck me hard."

The tension in my dick coiled tighter, pushing me closer to the edge. "More."

"Oh, God! Fuck me, Brett. Come inside me."

Jesus fuck. In an instant, my balls drew in and my orgasm shot through me.

"Yes, Brett." Her pussy grip my cock like a fucking vise.

"Fuck!" My voice echoed out through the backyard. Chances were good someone could hear us, but I didn't give a shit. Pleasure skyrocketed through me until every cell in my body was humming with it.

Miranda moaned and mewled. Her pussy pulsed, milking my dick until I couldn't see straight. I collapsed over her, pulling in deep breaths. I felt like I'd just sprinted a marathon.

Finally, I sat down, pulling her with me, taking us both deep into the water to warm up.

"Is it always like this?"

My heart stopped in my chest, worried about what that question meant. Was she attaching some sort of emotion to sex?

"What do you mean?"

"Is it always so . . . intense, explosive?"

I couldn't stop the satisfied smile on my face. A man always liked hearing when he'd rocked a woman's world.

"Not always. But when there's high levels of attraction and chemistry, like there seems to be between us, plus a sense of adventure, then yes, it can be intense and explosive."

"Is it the same for you?" Her courage to ask questions or reveal her inexperience was sweet.

"I wouldn't be fucking you if it wasn't."

The smile that spread on her face matched mine. She might not have experience, but there was no doubt about what she brought out of me.

"I'm going to get the towel and robe and we can go inside. I'll make us something to eat."

"That's why I came down here. I was going to offer to make lunch for us. I still can."

"We can make something together."

I exited the tub, hurrying as I grabbed the towel to wrap around me and the robe for her. I picked up her clothes for her, and we hurried out of the cold and into the house.

Once we were both dressed, we met back in the kitchen, making tomato soup and grilled cheese sandwiches. We worked together well, moving in the kitchen without getting in each other's way and yet efficiently getting the food prepared.

I made a fire in the fireplace again, and we ate our lunch out there, talking about anything and everything unless it involved Lindsay. I learned that Miranda had a very eclectic taste in music and movies and books.

"The creative arts always have a snapshot of society in them," she said. "I can read Dickens or Jane Austen to learn about life in their day. They weren't writing historical fiction. They were writing contemporary fiction for their time. Writing today is the same. So are music, art, and even movies."

"I hadn't thought about it like that." Her insight made me realize just how intelligent she was. In my mind, studying history was all about boring dates and people who'd been fortunate enough to make history. But to her, history was a way to understand the world. She viewed history not as dates and events but about people and society.

"You can see how social norms change through the arts," I commented.

"Yes. What used to be taboo a hundred years ago may not be today. With that said, there are still some taboos that will never change."

"Like having sex with your daughter's friend?" The words were out of my mouth before I could think better of it.

She blinked and looked down at her sandwich. "Maybe. Although two hundred years ago, a widower would very likely marry a woman even younger than me, who might have been his daughter's friend. But that would've been a matter of having an heir."

"So, not simply pleasure?"

She shrugged. "I imagine, for him, there might have been some pleasure. Maybe for her too. But security would've been a bigger desire for them."

Hating that I had taken the wind out of our lively conversation, I decided to change the subject. "Since you're so good at history, how good are you at trivia?"

She smiled, giving me the impression that she was glad I was moving on to a new topic. "I'm not bad."

"It's *Trivial Pursuit* or *Candyland*, and if I never play another game of *Candyland* again, that will be just fine."

She laughed. "What do you have against *Candyland*?"

"Until kids can count, there's not very many board games they can play. *Candyland* is one of them, and Lindsay couldn't get enough of that game. I must hold the world record in playing *Candyland*."

"That would mean Lindsay did too."

"Father-daughter world record team."

"Well, I do like *Candyland*, but I'm happy to play *Trivial Pursuit*."

As it turned out, Miranda was very good at Trivia and it all had to do with her interest in history. Not only did she see the arts as being something that informed history, but sports and entertainment as well. She knew a crap ton of useless facts.

We played several rounds with me losing most of them and then made dinner together. Afterward, we did the dishes, and I made more hot chocolate as we settled back into the living room where I added more wood to the fire.

As midnight marking Christmas approached, I patted my lap, telling her to sit and tell me what she wanted for Christmas. I don't know what she asked for because the minute that fine ass of hers was in my lap, I was rock hard.

“Santa has a present for you.” I pushed her back on the couch and made good on my desire to fuck her tits and then later, her pussy again.

When the final orgasms subsided, we were on the floor, both exhausted. I pulled the blanket from the couch and covered us both. Maybe I should have brought her up to my bed, but this place in front of the fire, with Christmas lights twinkling around us, was our place.

I woke up the next morning still spooned around her. I watched her sleep, amazed at how beautiful she was. *If only she weren't Lindsay's—*

No. I couldn't think like that. Not only because of the situation of her being Lindsay's friend, but also because I was a committed bachelor. There was no *if only* that suggested something more than a brief affair. Love and marriage hadn't worked out for me, and I had no interest in it. I had Lindsay as my family and that was all I needed.

As it turned out, it was lucky that Miranda was off-limits because it was clear she was the type of woman who could tempt me to break my vow of bachelorhood. Holy hell, did I just think that?

She let out an “mmm” sound. "I feel like you're staring at me. "

"I want to see what Santa brought me." I pulled the blanket down her body, letting my knuckles caress her smooth, silky skin. “I must have been a very good boy.”

10

Miranda

I didn't realize that sex came in so many variations. I didn't mean positions because, of course, I knew about that. But I hadn't been aware that it could have different pacing and moods. Fast and furious. Fun and flirtatious. And now, slow, steady, like a lazy Sunday morning. But even with the variety, there was still an intensity. Every time Brett touched me, kissed me, looked at me as he pistoned inside me, it stole my breath. The emotion of it settled deep in my soul, and while I was grateful for the experience, I was already starting to grieve that it would be over soon.

He lay over me, his hands clutching mine held over my head. His gray eyes watched me as he moved slowly, steadily, inside me. My heart ached, wishing this meant more.

"Wrap your legs around me."

I did as he asked, using my legs to pull him deeper each time he drove in. While the rise wasn't as crazed and desperate as before, when I reached the peak and my orgasm rolled through me, it was still as powerful. And then it was over.

I couldn't say that this was the best Christmas morning ever because I'd had some wonderful ones as a child, but it definitely was the best since losing my mother. I had some guilt for feeling that way. Like it was a betrayal to my father. Perhaps it was just that the entire experience was so new, so different. My life had been so much 'the same' for so long.

Since it was Christmas, we both agreed that it was unlikely my car would be towed out of the ditch even if the road crew was able to clear the trees in the roads. I suspected that was the only reason Brett didn't turn on his Mr. Hyde persona. Mentally, I had to prepare myself for the moment I could leave knowing that he would likely withdraw. Of course he would. We had both agreed that this was a moment out of time. Once we went back to the real world, everything that happened here would cease to exist.

I rubbed my hand over my chest as I pulled out my clothes for the day. Once we rose from our spot in front of the fire, I went up to my room to shower and dress. We didn't have plans, per se, but since I didn't have a Christmas gift for him, I thought I would make cookies. I had today, this last day, to fully embrace the joy and pleasure of the holiday.

When I made it to the kitchen, I studied Brett without his seeing me, checking to see if he was still going to be the fun and sweet man I had spent yesterday and this morning with. He was at the stove, cooking something with one hand and taking a sip of coffee with the other.

He looked up and smiled. "I hope you like French toast."

Feeling safe, I entered. "I love French toast. You may have noticed that there isn't much food that I don't like."

He frowned and then rolled his eyes. "You're not one of those women who are always comparing yourself to plastic magazine women, are you?"

I shook my head. "If I did, I would diet and exercise more."

He gave a curt nod. "Good."

"I'm surprised you say that considering you own gyms and have a nutrition line."

He shrugged. "Health comes in many sizes and shapes. Physical health is important, but so is mental health. Mental health can have an impact on physical health. You look happy and healthy and that's what matters, right?" He gave me a sly smile.

I was happy to hear him say it.

We enjoyed breakfast, and then I pulled out all the ingredients to make sugar cookies. I was pleased to discover that he also had powdered sugar, which meant I would be able to make frosting. He didn't have food coloring or sprinkles, but I found fruit and figured we could use that to decorate them.

After cookies, we ended up in the hot tub, naked, and of course, nature prevailed.

The evening proceeded just as it had the night before where we had dinner and afterward hot chocolate with peppermint liqueur, ending the evening on the floor in front of the fire enjoying each other's body until fully sated.

As we lay in front of the fire, Brett spooned around me, his slow, steady breaths telling me he was asleep. I thought about how quickly the day had passed. Too fast. I wasn't ready for our time together to end. I wasn't ready to let him go.

Although it was futile, I tried to figure out what to say so that we could continue to be together. I knew it could only happen if Lindsay never found out, which created guilt at betraying her. But the heart wanted what it wanted, right?

I thought I could tell Lindsay I was going off to study and then I could see Brett. Maybe sometimes, we could sneak back up here to be together. I fell asleep imagining a life that I knew I couldn't have.

I WOKE in the morning feeling chilled. My eyes opened to find the fire was out and Brett's body was no longer wrapped around me. I hoped that he was off making breakfast, but deep down, I knew the truth. Today, this magical Christmas holiday ended.

I got up, slipping my clothes on, folding the blanket, and putting it on the couch. I peeked into the kitchen but didn't see him. So, I went upstairs to my room to shower and pack. Deep down, I hoped that the roads were still impassable, or perhaps my car couldn't be pulled from the ditch, but I forced myself to look at reality. I had to be grateful for this experience even as it grieved me to let it go.

I carried my bag and my backpack down the stairs, setting them near the front door. I entered the kitchen, smelling the brew of coffee. Brett was looking out the French doors of the kitchen with coffee in his hand.

He turned as I entered. His cheeks were flushed, his blond silver hair looking windblown, telling me he'd been outside.

"There's coffee if you like."

I couldn't say that his voice was curt, but neither did it have the smooth welcoming it had yesterday.

"Thank you. I'm all packed." Perhaps if I signaled to him that I understood our time together was over, he might not be compelled to be rude.

"Good. The roads are passable, and I met the tow truck down by your car this morning. We dug it out and towed it back. It's out front."

I glanced at the clock on the wall, noting it was eight in the morning. He must've been up before dawn to do all that. It told me he was eager for me to be gone.

"Thank you for that. If you give me the bill—"

He shook his head. "It's all right. I handled it."

Our gazes held for a moment, but then he abruptly turned away, walking around the counter to the main part of the kitchen. "Are you hungry? I was thinking of eggs and hashbrowns this morning."

I really wanted to stay and have breakfast, to draw out our time together for as long as I could. But what was the point? I should treat this like a Band-Aid—just rip it off and leave.

"I should probably get on the road soon. There will probably be lots of after Christmas traffic as I get closer to Boston."

He nodded, and I swore I could see relief in his eyes. He came around the island, leaning against it and crossing his arms over his chest. "Before you go, I need to make sure that we are clear—"

"I know." I snapped more harshly than I should have. "Lindsay's not to know."

"I'm sorry if that hurts you, but I was clear from the start about how this would work."

"That you were."

His jaw ticked as if he didn't like my answer. Perhaps I had a bit of an attitude, but I didn't like being reminded that I didn't mean anything more than a few days of physical pleasure.

"Considering we never met through Lindsay before, I imagine we won't have to worry about seeing each other again." The words came out as if he was stating a fact, but behind the words, I heard a warning to avoid him.

Inside, my heart felt heavy, but on the outside, I did my best to stand strong and act like this whole thing was nothing to me either. "It's not going to be a problem avoiding you at all."

He studied me for a moment, and I began to think that he worried that I might have a crush on him, that I might seek more from him.

"You don't have to worry, Brett. I'm not going to go join a gym or lurk outside your house. I've got bigger goals and more important things in my life than pining for you. I've got a semester to finish and then graduation and then getting a job."

His eyes flashed with something that I couldn't decipher. It couldn't have been pain because I was telling him exactly what he wanted to hear.

I jerked my thumb over my shoulder. "I should get going."

"How about some coffee? I can put it in a to-go cup."

"That's all right. I can stop on the way. Besides, if I have your cup, then I'll have to return it to you, and we wouldn't want that, would we?" I turned and headed to the door.

He was behind me in a few strides. "Let me help you with your bags."

I wanted to tell him no. I wanted to end being near him at this very moment. But instead, I let him help me put my bags into my car. I got into the driver's seat and he stood by the open door.

"The roads are clear, but that doesn't mean they're not a little slick, so be careful."

"I will."

He continued to stand blocking my door, looking at me. I wondered if there was something he wanted to say. All sorts of words were flitting through my brain, but nothing I could say out loud.

A moment later, he gave another curt nod. "I wish you all the best in your life, Miranda."

"Thank you." I tugged on the door, and he stepped away from it so I could shut it. The finality of the goodbye in his words brought tears to my eyes, but I fought them. Instead, I started my car, carefully maneuvering down his driveway as I headed back out toward the main road.

I wanted to regret what happened between us because the feelings that it brought now were so heavy. At the same time, I was grateful for the last couple of days. I experienced things I didn't imagine I'd ever experience. Oh, sure, someday, I'd meet somebody else and probably get married and have kids, but it was hard to imagine there would be the intensity that had been between me and Brett. I suppose your first love never leaves you.

11

Brett

I fought myself the entire morning to keep from asking Miranda to stay. Even as her car drove away, a part of me wanted to run after her, bring her back, and spend yet another day buried in her delicious body. The woman had a crazy hold on me and it pissed me off. Because she was wreaking havoc on me, she had to go. Goodbye. Adios. It would be the only way to break whatever spell I'd been ensnared in.

Frustrated, I stomped back into the house, slamming the door behind me. I stood for a moment, unsure what to do next. It was still morning, but I strode into the kitchen, grabbing a bottle of scotch and pouring myself two fingers. After downing the glass of potent liquid, I decided I'd take a day to myself. Get my shit together. As I started toward the living room and as I passed by the French doors, I looked outside to the hot tub. A vision of Miranda riding me swept through my mind.

I growled at the annoying memory and headed to the living room, but she was there as well. Jesus fuck. I couldn't escape her. I pulled out my phone and called Lindsay.

"I'm sorry I didn't call you on Christmas, Dad," she said when she answered.

Holy shit. I hadn't thought to call her, either. It was another reminder of how deeply I'd fallen into Miranda. I scraped my hand over my face. "It's all right, sweetheart. I'm calling to find out if you have any plans to come up. Otherwise, I'm closing up the house."

"I'm sorry, Dad. I don't have much more time off. Maybe we can go up in a couple of weeks?"

Feeling like a shitty father for not being more attentive the last few days, I asked, "Is everything alright with you?"

"Yes, of course." There was nothing in her tone to suggest that she was lying. "I heard about the snow. Are you okay?"

"Everything is fine."

"How about Miranda? You didn't bug her, did you?"

"No," I said through gritted teeth. The last thing I wanted, though, was to talk about Miranda with Lindsay. What if I said something or had a tone that hinted at the dirty things I'd done with her? "She's on her way home. I'm going to pack up and head out as well."

"Okay. We can connect later."

"How about New Year's?" I suggested.

"Oh, I'd love to, but I have plans. Now that I'm twenty-one, I want to go to a big New Year's party."

I had no illusions about Lindsay never partying until now, but I didn't press her on it. "Another time, then."

"Drive carefully, Dad. I love you."

"I love you too, sweetheart."

Once I was off the phone, I grabbed the boxes and pulled down all the Christmas items, packing everything up for next year. Once everything was cleaned up, I texted the guy I'd hired to care for the cabin while I was gone to let him know I was leaving. I tossed my bag into my SUV and made my way out, heading back to Boston. I hoped to hell that somewhere between here and home, I would fully eradicate Miranda from my psyche.

Two hours later, I arrived home at my brownstone along the Charles River. I pulled into the basement garage and made my way upstairs. I tossed my bag into my room and then went to the kitchen to make something to eat. I took my sandwich and beer to the living room, eating as I caught up on sports on TV. When I finished, I decided to call Duncan.

"Are you snowed in?" Duncan asked when he picked up the line.

"Not anymore. I'm back in Boston." I leaned back in my recliner and sipped my beer.

"I thought you and Lindsay were going to spend the week there."

"Something came up and Lindsay couldn't make it, so I came home today." There was no reason to mention that Miranda was there. "Now that I'm home, I thought I'd check in with you to see if there was anything I needed to deal with."

"It's a good thing that I like you, Brett, otherwise I'd take offense at the idea that you don't think I can run the business for a few days."

I laughed. "It's the reverse, Duncan. I'm worried you can run it without me and you don't need me around."

"Well, that goes without saying, but since I like having you around, it all works out. But no, there's nothing going on."

"You want to come over for a beer? We can catch up on sports."

"Now you're speaking my love language. Give me about forty-five minutes."

When I hung up with Duncan, I wanted to make sure that I had enough beer in the fridge. Determining that I did, I made my way to my home office, deciding I would check in on my nutrition business. Duncan was, in fact, a good businessman and could absolutely run the gyms without me. This turned out well, allowing me the time I needed to run my other business. I checked my email and scanned a few reports and determined that everything was fine there too.

I returned to the kitchen, scrounged for some cheese and crackers and chips, and waited for Duncan to arrive. Once he showed up, we ate party food and drank beer as we watched television.

"Hey, I meant to mention that I have dates for us on New Year's. I was thinking we'd take them to The Bluebloods Club. We could get a private room."

"I don't need you getting me dates." I shifted in my seat as a total lack of desire to be with another woman besides Miranda settled through me. I didn't like that.

"Don't worry. She's recently divorced and only wants to have a good time. Plus, she's got tits the size of cantaloupes, just like you like."

The memory of my dick sliding through Miranda's tits flashed in my head. Mother fucker! "I don't—"

"You don't have to fuck her. It's just a night out. And it's a done deal, Brett. It will be fun."

"Yeah, whatever." I got up and went to the kitchen to get another beer. When I returned, there was no more talk about New Year's or tits, so I was able to relax and enjoy Duncan's company and TV.

By the time he left several hours later, I was feeling like my equilibrium had returned. I headed to bed thinking that the last few days with Miranda would finally fade and become nothing but a memory. Perhaps every now and then, I'd think of her when I needed to jerk off, but the tether that had latched on to Miranda was finally severed.

WELL, mostly because I woke the next morning with a hard-on that I took care of by thinking about Miranda on her knees, sucking my dick. Once I came, I pushed her memory away and dressed, had breakfast, and drove to the offices of my nutrition company.

I strode in an hour earlier than usual, not surprised to find my admin, Connie, already hard at work.

"Anything I need to know about, Con?"

"All the messages are on your desk," she said without looking up from the work she was doing. Connie was a no-nonsense battle-axe who made my life as a CEO amazingly easy. She could be grumpier and meaner than me, which served me well since she did a fantastic job at being my gatekeeper. Very few people got through her. The only ones who got automatic access were Lindsay and Duncan. She scared most people off so thoroughly that they didn't bother to try and come back.

"Thank you. Did you have a nice holiday?"

She shrugged. "I'm glad to be back at work and away from the chaos." She finally looked up from her computer. "And you?"

"Glad to be back at work myself." I headed into my office and got to work.

At lunchtime, Lindsay came strolling in. My daughter could exasperate me, but I loved her beyond belief, so seeing her put a smile on my face. I rose from my desk to give her a hug.

"I brought your present. I'm sorry I missed Christmas at the cabin."

"It's okay. I'm sorry, I left your present at home."

She plopped down on the couch in my office. "That's okay. It wasn't too weird with Mira, was it? She usually keeps to herself."

I swallowed, putting my focus on the package Lindsay gave me to avoid giving away my secret. "It was fine. What did you get me? Another tie? Cuff links?"

"Open it."

I tore the paper and opened the box. Inside I found shaving and grooming supplies and a massage gun.

"You've been so keyed up lately, I thought a little massage and spa would be good for you."

I laughed. "I didn't realize I was stressed."

She studied me, her eyes narrowing in scrutiny. "Maybe all you needed was some time at the cabin. You don't seem so stressed now."

Again, Miranda and her sweet body came to mind. Worse, I wondered what sorts of things I could do with her and this new massage gun. Fucking hell. Now Miranda was on my mind and I really wanted to ask Lindsay how she was doing.

"Thank you, sweetheart."

"Of course. Do you have time for lunch?"

"For you, always." I rose from the couch and got my coat. "I'm assuming Miranda arrived home okay?" I kept my body turned away from Lindsay.

"Yes. She, of course, went right to the books. The semester hasn't even started and she's already studying. And don't say you think I should take after her."

I shrugged. "A little studying on your part couldn't hurt."

She threaded her arm through mine. "Dad, I want to start a business and I figure the best place for me to learn about that is at Dad University."

Was I tickled that she wanted to become an entrepreneur like her dad and learn all I had to impart? Of course. But that didn't mean I wanted her to give up on her studies.

"How about lunch and you can share this business idea you have with me?"

Her smile was brilliant. "I've got it all figured out."

"You still need to study, Lindsay."

She rolled her eyes. "I know. Come on. I want Irish stew. It's so cold out today."

I took Lindsay to one of the many Irish pubs in the area for stew, enjoying how she chattered away about an idea that involved art and antique curation.

"So you want to open an antique store? An art gallery?"

She rolled her eyes in a way that suggested I was dense. "No, silly. Well, not really. I want to help people find great works of art."

"So an art broker?"

She shrugged. "I guess. I was thinking Mira and I could do it together."

My stomach clenched. "I thought she wanted to be a teacher."

"She does, but she won't ever rise out of her financial situation on a teacher's salary. She knows so much stuff about art and history."

I remembered how Miranda kicked my ass in *Trivial Pursuit*.

Lindsay pouted. "You're just not understanding."

"That's not my fault, Linds. If you want to start a business, you need to develop your ideas. Create a business plan. Study the market to know if there are buyers and if so, who and where are they? Perhaps you should take a business course next semester."

She let out a frustrated grunt.

"Enthusiasm and excitement are all well and good, but they don't build a business."

"All right. I'll think about it."

"Good." Deciding to change the subject, I asked, "So, what are your plans for New Year's?"

"Liam and I are going out. I'm trying to get Mira and Liam's brother, Oliver, to come too. They'd be perfect for each other, both total study nerds."

A ball of jealousy formed in the pit of my stomach at the idea of Miranda with another man. Goddamn it. Would I ever be rid of this woman?

12

Miranda

"I can't believe I let you talk me into this." I stared at myself in the full-length mirror, not recognizing myself. The red, satiny dress hugged my body so close, it looked like I had been dipped in the fabric. My long hair that I normally just washed and let dry had been styled by Lindsay, so it was fluffed into a wild main. I'd done my own makeup, except then Lindsay came in after me, darkening my eyes and putting on red lipstick over the more subtle shade I'd had on before.

"You look fabulous, Mira. Every guy at the club tonight is going to be drooling over you. I'd be shocked if Oliver didn't notice as well, and he's always got his head in a computer."

I didn't want every guy drooling over me. I wasn't the type of woman who liked to get attention, especially the sexual kind. Unless, of course, it was Brett. But I knew my time with him was over. I pushed thoughts of Brett aside as they were always accompanied by guilt when Lindsay was around.

Since the moment I arrived home the day after Christmas, Lindsay had been working on me to go out with her and Liam and

Liam's brother, Oliver, for New Year's Eve until I finally gave in. Sometimes, it was just easier to go along with her than to try and fight the constant barrage.

Lindsay stood next to me, her dress a shimmery silver, making her look like an old Hollywood starlet. The sides of her long blonde locks were pulled up with the rest hanging down in wavy streams, highlighted with pink strands. Maybe if I stayed next to her tonight, I wouldn't have to worry about male attention as it would all go to her.

"We look hot. Maybe I should cancel with Liam and Oliver and we could go out on our own."

"I doubt Liam would like it if you went out alone to attract men."

She shrugged. "Maybe he'd appreciate me more if he knew that other men would want me."

I looked at her and frowned. "Is there trouble in paradise?"

"I just feel like he sometimes takes me for granted. That's all."

"You talk like you two have been an item for a long time, but you haven't." I worried that maybe Lindsay was too attached to Liam, who sounded like he didn't feel the same about her.

She ignored me. "Come on, Mira, let's go give them hell."

Reluctantly, I put on my nicest wool coat and headed out into the cold night with Lindsay. She'd arranged for a ride for us, and it took us to the most exclusive club in Boston, The Blueblood Club. Where I had come from a blue-collared background, the Bluebloods were considered rich old money in Boston. Of course, new money could show up there as well. Money was the key factor in this place. It was unlikely I was going to see anybody from my old neighborhood here.

Lindsay leaned closer to me as we approached the bouncers. "I'm using my dad's name to get us in, okay?"

My stomach tightened. "Is he here?"

"Nah. I doubt it. He's too old for the club life."

We showed our IDs after Lindsay told them who her father was, and they let us pass. Lindsay and I had been out to clubs before, but this one reeked of money even as it was dark and music pounded like in the other ones. Maybe it was because everyone was dressed to the nines or that most of them looked like they had stepped out of a fashion magazine.

"Look, there's Liam and Oliver. Come on."

“How’d they get in?” I wondered out loud. I didn’t know much about Liam, but I was sure he didn’t come from the type of money Lindsay had.

“They used my dad’s name too.”

I followed Lindsay through the crowd toward the bar where Liam stood with another man. Lindsay introduced me, and I could see that Oliver resembled his brother, although a less coiffed version. I didn't get the impression that he tried as hard as Liam to look nice. His hair was a little bit longer, and until we showed up, he’d been looking and tapping into his phone, whereas Liam had been schmoozing with everyone around him.

"Mira, this is Oliver. He's a graduate student in cybersecurity. Oliver, this is my roommate and best friend, Mira. She's the smartest person I know."

I couldn't help the twitch of a smile at Lindsay's praise of me. She was always like that. Always positive. Oliver extended his hand. "It's nice to meet you, Miranda."

"You too, Oliver."

"Come on, let's get a table. Do you think you can name drop your dad and get us a private room? Or at least a nice table?" Liam asked Lindsay.

Oliver frowned at his brother. I wondered if he thought Liam was taking advantage of Lindsay, just like she was thinking.

Lindsay shrugged. "I can try."

"Hey, Lindsay?"

We all turned to look where a large bald man who looked like a bouncer except for the tuxedo approached us.

"Uncle Dunc." She let out a little squeal and launched herself into the man's arms, giving him a hug.

The man looked at all of us and then at Lindsay. "What are you doing here?"

"I guess the same as you. Celebrating the new year."

He crossed his arms and scowled, although he appeared to be feigning. "Since when are you old enough to come into a club?"

She smiled and nudged him with her elbow. "I'm twenty-one, Uncle Dunc. Meet my friends. This is my roommate and best friend, Miranda, and this is Liam and his brother, Oliver." It was interesting to me that she didn't qualify who they were to her uncle Dunc. I'd never met him, but I'd heard her talk about the man who was like a second father to her.

Dunc extended his hand and shook all of ours in greeting. "Your dad's in the back room. You should come say hello."

I froze. Brett was here?

Liam draped his arm around Lindsay. "Yeah, we should go say hi."

I definitely was getting the feeling that Liam wanted access to the money and power Lindsay got through her father. Oliver's disapproving glare told me he was likely thinking the same thing.

"We don't want to disturb their good time," I said. God, the last thing I needed was to see Brett right now.

"We'll just say hi. We won't party with them," Liam said, although I was sure he hoped to change that once we were in the private room.

"Yeah, sure, we can say hello," Lindsay said.

I tried to think of an excuse to avoid going with them but found myself swept up by the group as we headed back to another section of the club.

Dunk opened a door to a private room and stepped in, holding the door open. "Hey, look what I found."

Lindsay walked in, followed by Liam and Oliver. I did my best to stay outside the door, but Dunc looked at me, arching a brow. "Come on in. Despite his reputation, he doesn't bite."

Taking a breath, I stepped into the room.

My gaze immediately went to Brett. God, he looked beyond handsome in his tux. My breath caught with a mixture of awe and yearning. That is until I saw the woman on the plush couch with him. She was the epitome of plastic, practically in his lap, with her breasts nearly in his face. He was enjoying it if his hand on her ass was any indication. Envy bloomed hot even though it was stupid.

He frowned for a moment and began to disentangle himself from the woman. "Lindsay. What are you doing here?" His gaze ran down the line from Lindsay to Liam to Oliver and then to me. For a moment, I thought I saw a reaction, but then he turned his attention back to Lindsay.

"Doing the same thing you're doing, Daddio. Ringing in the new year. This is Liam, and Oliver, and you remember Mira, right?"

He gave a curt nod. "You didn't tell me you'd be here."

Lindsay cocked her head as if she was only just now noting that her father wasn't pleased to see her. She put her hand on her hip and glared at him. "And you didn't tell me you were going to be here. Don't be a grump, Dad. We're not going to party with you." She turned to Liam and Oliver and me. "Come on, guys, let's get some drinks and dance."

I was out the door as fast as my legs could move. We were nearly at the bar when somebody who worked there approached us. "Mr. McKinnon has arranged a special area for you all to enjoy the evening festivities."

"Hot damn," Liam said.

We followed the man to another section of the bar that appeared to be reserved for VIP guests. There were plush couches and chairs roped off from the rest of the crowd, but still in the mix of all the excitement. We took a seat, and the man who led us over waved down a server, who immediately took our drink orders.

"Come on, let's dance." Lindsay jumped up, grabbing Liam's hand to pull them out to the dance floor. "You too, Mira, Oliver. Come on."

I looked at Oliver, who shrugged. "If you're anything like I am, you're going to indulge them by going out on the dance floor."

I let out a laugh. "You're right. How is it that they have such an influence over us?"

He stood and reached out his hand toward me. I took it, and he helped me off the couch. "I suppose it's because they are endearing. Liam can be a bit self-centered, but he's a good kid. I just wish he'd grow up a little bit more."

I nodded, often feeling the same about Lindsay.

We headed out to the dance floor, and despite being self-conscious in my painted-on dress, I let the music move me. I enjoyed dancing, but a glance at Oliver told me he didn't. Still, he made an effort as he bounced and stepped side to side. I was going to ask him something but noticed he had his attention on Liam. Was he worried about him? Then again, Oliver could be watching Lindsay. In fact, the way his eyes drifted down and then up as if he was taking her in suggested he was. Huh? Was he into her too?

The floor was crowded, making it impossible not to get jostled. Another dancer bumped Oliver, pushing him toward me.

His hands reached out, landing on my hips as he tried to avoid running into me. "I'm sorry. I probably should've warned you that I'm a klutz on the dance floor."

"That's okay. It's crowded."

I looked over to where Lindsay and Liam were dancing, curious again about their relationship and Oliver's reaction. Motion behind them caught my eye. Looking beyond them, I saw Brett watching us, watching me. He had that same broody Mr. Hyde look on his face I'd come to know at the cabin. I could only imagine that he was pissed off at seeing me since we were never supposed to see each other again.

A dancer bumped me from behind, this time propelling me into Oliver.

"I'm sorry."

He laughed. "It's okay."

I stepped back, feeling a bit panicked. "Excuse me, I need to go to the restroom."

"Yeah, sure. I'll meet you back at the table."

I gave a quick nod and hurried off toward the ladies' room. The problem was, I'd never been in this club and I didn't know where it was. I headed down the hallway, but clearly, it was the wrong place. There were several doors, but none said *Women* on them.

I turned around, walking into a solid wall of man. His hand wrapped around my upper arm and he tugged me into a room, shutting the door. "What the hell are you doing here?"

"I didn't know you were going to be here. I didn't even want to come. Lindsay talked me into it." Why was I babbling? I had every right to be here.

"Is that Oliver kid the guy from your class?"

I looked up at him, surprised by his question. "No."

"Are you going to let him fuck you?"

What? I shook my head, wondering if he'd been drinking. Well, of course he had. We were in a club, but had he drunk too much? "No. I've only just met him."

Brett stepped closer to me. I stepped back, hitting the closed door behind me. "You'd only just met me when I fucked you."

I pressed my hands against his chest, intending to push him away, and yet I didn't. The scent of him, the heat of him, brought back all the sensuous memories of our time at the cabin.

"Now that you know how to fuck, I bet you can show him a really good time."

When his words finally reached my brain, I gaped and pushed him hard. I wanted to slap him. "All of a sudden, I'm now wishing I could scrub you from my brain again." I turned to open the door, but his hand pressed on it, pushing it shut again.

"Are you lying to me again?"

I turned around, feeling exasperated. "What is wrong with you? I'm not here to see you. I'm not following you. I'm definitely not going to tell you who I'm going to fuck or not. And I don't know why you care when clearly, you've got a woman who's ready to fuck you in the other room."

He leaned closer to me, his gaze drifting down to my lips. "Yeah, but her tits are plastic." His gaze drifted back up to my eyes. "I much prefer your tits."

"Well, that's unfortunate for you." I was proud of my indignation because on the inside, I was burning up and not from anger.

"Are you saying that you wouldn't much prefer my dick?"

"I'm telling you that I find your behavior offensive. You're pissed off that I'm here and yet now, you're talking about your dick."

He let out a breath and dropped his forehead against mine in a surprising gesture that seemed to show vulnerability. "It's that craving again, Miranda. That wanting something that I know I shouldn't have."

I closed my eyes and willed myself not to fall for his words, to not let his nearness affect me.

"Well, I guess it's a good thing that we're not at the cabin anymore. We're in the real world. Lindsay's in the other room."

He shifted, and I heard the snap of what sounded like a lock on the door. "In here, it's just you and me."

He pressed his body against mine, his erection hard on my belly making me gasp. "Tell me that you don't want this."

"It's not that I don't want it—"

"One last time, Miranda. Let's end the year with one final bang."

Oh, God, I wanted to. My brain screamed for me to leave. He had a woman in the other room. His daughter was here. We were in a public space. But when he was so close to me like this, the world shrank until it was just me and him.

"What about—"

He pressed his fingers over my lips. "It's just you and me right now. Have you overcome your craving for me?"

I nearly groaned. "No."

"I jerked off thinking of you the other day."

My gaze jerked to his. "You did?"

His intense stare ensnared me. "I did." He fingered a strand of my hair. "Do you touch yourself, Miranda?"

I swallowed, self-conscious about answering such a personal question.

"Do you think of me and touch yourself?"

God, only nearly every night. "Yes."

"Do you make those mewling sounds when you come?"

"I . . . ah . . . I don't know."

"I want to hear them." His hand slid up my thigh, lifting my dress. "Are you wet?"

Dripping.

His finger slid under my panties and through my folds. He moaned, bringing his fingers to his lips and sucking.

"Brett," I said with a mixture of a sigh and a moan.

"Are you going to tell me to stop?"

How could I? I looked up into his gray eyes, not wanting to be reactive in this moment. I wanted the confidence and courage he had.

I cupped him, loving how he hissed in response. "No, I'm not going to tell you to stop."

13

Brett

What the fuck was I doing? The last thing I should be doing is fucking Miranda. We were in a public place. I had a date in the other private room. Lindsay was here, for fuck's sake. But when I saw Miranda in the red dress that left nothing to the imagination, something inside me snapped. I couldn't deal with the idea that every man in this club would see her and know every curve of her.

So I excused myself from my group and hunted her down. I knew where she'd be because I'd arranged a secluded seating section for them. But she wasn't there. She was on the dance floor with that Oliver kid. His hands were on her. In a flash of rational thinking, I considered that she'd moved on. I even told myself that it was a good thing. Our secret was safe.

But that thought was immediately overridden by jealousy, which pissed me off. As per my MO, I had to take it out on the source of my anger and frustration, namely, Miranda. It didn't help that she stood up to me, calling me out. Her defiance didn't make me want to punish her more for making me feel the way I did. It made me want her more. And so here I was, in a private room of a club, pushing Miranda up on the table as I freed her tits and lifted her dress so I could fuck her. I needed to pound away this clawing need that threatened to consume me whole.

If caught, we'd likely be arrested. There would be a scandal that could hurt both of my businesses. Then there was Lindsay finding out. I'd have thought that losing my daughter's respect and love would have been a strong enough motivation to stop, but it wasn't. At this moment, nothing was more important than getting inside Miranda's sweet pussy.

My lips latched around her nipple as I fumbled with my pants to free my dick.

"Open for me, Miranda. Jesus fuck." I felt like I was going to spontaneously combust. I yanked her panties down and then positioned myself at her entrance. Gripping her hips, I drove in until my hips slapped against her.

I let out a feral moan that filled the room. If they had cameras in here, I was truly fucked. And yet, I didn't stop. Instead, I withdrew and thrust in again. And again. And again. Each time, the tension cranked up. The beast clawing to be free became more incessant.

"Oh, God," Miranda cried out, her head falling back as her pussy convulsed around my dick.

Sparks flew, radiating out until every cell in my body was on fire. "Fuck yes." My orgasm rammed into me. Like a feral animal rooting, I fucked her hard and fast, working to hold onto the sweet release.

When I pumped in my last shot, the irritation returned. I hated how weak I was to resist Miranda. Hated the pull she had me.

I withdrew, yanking my pants up. The anger at how she stole my strength and made me a slave to my libido swirled deep in my gut.

Just like the need for sex, my anger got the best of me. "You got what you wanted, now leave me the fuck alone." I didn't need to see the shock and hurt in her eyes to know my words were offensive. I hated how cruel I could become and decided to blame her for that too.

She slipped off the table, putting her dress back in place. "Back at you, Brett." She gave a humorless laugh that put me even more on edge. Was she really laughing at me?

"And you called me immature." She walked toward the door, stopping just as she stepped next to me. She glared up at me. "You're like a teenage boy who can't manage his dick. Thanks for reminding me what an asshole you are." She strode to the door, and a mixture of regret and anger filled me. I wanted to stop her even as I was relieved to watch her go.

She stopped at the door, turning to look over her shoulder at me. "You are effectively scrubbed from my memory. I won't think of you ever again, and if I do, it will only be to remember what a jerk you are."

"Mir—"

She opened the door, disappearing into the hall.

I dragged my fingers through my hair, hating the man I'd become. I resented Miranda for turning me into such an asshole, even though I knew it was my flaw.

Fucking hell. I hurried from the room, hoping to catch her to apologize. I scanned the club but didn't see her. Maybe her anger at me was for the best. Clearly, I couldn't control my libido or my asshole behavior around her. This way, she'd make sure to avoid me if our paths ever crossed again.

I pulled out my phone and texted Dunc that I was leaving. I wasn't in the mood to party or throw off the advances of my date, Debbie or Donna. I couldn't remember. I'd already been trying to concoct excuses to not fuck her before Miranda showed up. My date would think I was rude, but I didn't give a shit.

What's wrong? Came Dunc's text.

Migraine, I lied.

I headed home, making a beeline for my liquor cabinet, grabbing the closest bottle, and sinking to my couch. I flipped on the TV just in time to see the ball drop in Times Square.

I held up my bottle, saluting my reflection on the TV. "Happy fucking New Year, asshole."

14

Miranda

The minute I left Brett, I wanted to sink against a wall and catch my breath. My legs wobbled and my heart felt like it had been crushed by an anvil. I was a smart, independent woman. How had I allowed myself to be seduced by a man I knew could be so cruel?

I didn't sink into the wall, though. I used the strength I'd found to tell him off to propel me back to the main part of the club and eventually, to the bathroom. Only locked in a stall did I give in to the humiliation and pain. I heaved into the toilet bowl.

"Mira?" Lindsay's voice echoed through the restroom.

"Yeah?" I did my best to hide my tears.

"Have you been here the whole time? I've been looking for you."

"Ah. Yeah." I hated to lie to her, but it wasn't like I could tell her the truth.

"Why didn't you answer when I was here before?" Her feet appeared under the stall door.

"Uh. I'm not feeling well. I was probably being sick." That wasn't a total lie.

"Oh, no. What can I do for you?"

"Nothing. I'm . . . I'm going to call for a ride home."

"We can drive you."

"No. I don't want to ruin your night." I couldn't allow Lindsay to care for me when my source of ailment was her father. All I wanted was to be alone.

"You're sick. Of course, I'll take you home."

"No, please. You stay." I opened the stall and headed to the sink to wash my face and rinse my mouth out. I couldn't look at Lindsay and not see her father's face and hear the vile things he said to me.

Lindsay studied me. "You look terrible."

"I'll be fine." And I would. No matter what, I wouldn't let Brett keep me down. "Stay and enjoy the night. Really."

She pursed her lips and then tapped something into her phone.

"What are you doing?"

"I'm arranging a ride for you."

Panic shot through me. "I don't need a ride from your dad."

Her brow furrowed at me. "Not my dad. I doubt I could pull him away from that T and A clawing him. Oliver will give you a ride."

"I don't want to ruin—"

"Don't argue. Come on."

When we exited the bathroom, Oliver was already there. He gave me a sympathetic smile. "Under the weather? Let me get you home." We walked up the hall to the main part of the club.

"You don't have to drive me home," I said to him.

"Please, let me drive you."

"See? It's all settled. Oliver will take you home, and I'll check on you later." There was no sense in arguing with Lindsay.

As Oliver led me outside, I said, "You really don't need to drive me."

"You're doing me a favor by letting me take you home."

I eyed him skeptically.

"No, really. I didn't even want to come tonight." He winced. "Not that I didn't want to meet you—"

I held up my hand. "I understand. I was talked into tonight as well."

He gave me a sheepish smile. "Are you really sick or did you find an excuse to leave? If so, it was brilliant. I wish I'd thought of it. "

"I'm not ill," I admitted.

"Your secret is safe with me."

Oliver was very sweet, and I was grateful that he took me home. He walked me to the door and assured me again that he wouldn't reveal my secret. I sure was gathering a lot of secrets these days.

Once inside, I went to my bathroom, stripping and getting in a hot shower to scrub Brett off my body. If only it was just as easy to scrub him from my mind. I hoped that with time, he'd become a distant regret. That the humiliation would subside. I could look back and chalk it up to the ignorance of youth.

I put on pajamas and climbed into bed. Only then did I cry. I grieved for giving myself to a man like Brett. For the hurt and humiliation that I felt. I'd give myself this night to wallow in self-pity. Tomorrow was a new day, a new year. Tomorrow, I'd leave Brett in the past and focus on my future.

My plan worked well. The next day, I cracked open my books to get a head start on the new semester. Two days later, school started, making it even easier to forget Brett. Well, not forget, but distract me from thoughts of him. I spent all my waking time in class or studying.

Lindsay thought I was nuts. “It's all downhill from here. You don't need to study so much.”

“I want to finish my college life strong.”

She shook her head. “You're going to burn out, girl.”

By the beginning of February, I was starting to think Lindsay might be right. I was hit with exhaustion that made going to class and studying difficult. I decided to take the weekend to rest my brain and body by sleeping in and napping as much as possible.

I was half dozing Saturday morning when I heard Lindsay in the bathroom.

“Oh, thank God!" she cried out.

When she exited the bathroom, I called out from my bed, "Is everything alright?"

She popped her head in my door. "Did I wake you?"

"Nah. What's up?"

"I'm not pregnant!" She did a little dance in my doorway.

I arched a brow. "Was that a possibility?"

"Liam and I had a little mishap a week or so ago. But my monthly friend showed up today." She let out a breath. "My dad would kill me if I got pregnant. He already thinks I'm irresponsible."

"Your dad is no saint." The words were out of my mouth before I could stop them. Another testament to the fatigue.

"What makes you say that?" Her question seemed more like curiosity than offense.

Thinking quickly, I said, "Look at the plastic bimbos he dates."

She rolled her eyes. "He is a player, isn't he?"

I nodded, feeling relieved that I didn't tip my hand.

"He lives his life and I live mine. And thankfully, mine won't involve a kid anytime soon. Right now, I never thought I'd be so glad to have my period."

"No doubt."

"Well, I'll let you rest. I'm going over to Liam's with the good news."

"Have fun. Use birth control."

She laughed.

I turned over to rest, but a thought intruded. *When was my last period?*

Immediately, I pushed away the concern. There was no way I could be pregnant. It was more likely the stress of lying to my friend. Stress of being swept up by a jerk like Brett. The stress of finishing school. Wasn't that why I was taking the weekend off? I snuggled back into bed.

But the niggle of doubt remained, making it hard to go back to sleep. There was only one way to settle my nerves. I had to take a pregnancy test.

I threw off my covers in exasperation and headed to the shower.

After I cleaned up and dressed, I put on my coat, hat, and gloves, and headed out into the cold February day. The heater in my car worked, but it took about ten minutes to warm the interior. I decided to go to a pharmacy in another part of town. I didn't need to see anyone I knew as I bought a pregnancy test.

Pulling my hat low, I entered the store and found the aisle with the tests. To be sure of the result, I bought two, looking around to make sure no one was watching, then picking up the tests and heading to the self-checkout.

On the way home, I stopped at a drive-thru coffee joint. For a moment, I worried about having caffeine if I was pregnant. But no, I couldn't be pregnant, so I ordered a large mocha with whipped cream.

When I got home, I made sure Lindsay hadn't returned, then went to the bathroom.

"This is ridiculous." I opened the boxes and followed the directions. I let them sit as I went back to my room and changed out of jeans and a sweater, back into sweatpants and a long-sleeved shirt. By the time I was ready to settle back into my lazy day, I'd talked myself into believing I was overreacting.

I returned to the bathroom to toss the tests. I picked up the tests and opened the door under the sink where the trash was kept. As my hand hovered over the waste bin, that niggle of doubt returned. With a huff of annoyance at my silliness, I looked at one of the tests.

Pregnant.

I froze. There had to be a mistake. I checked the other test.

Pregnant.

I sank down on the toilet seat in disbelief. This couldn't be happening.

Still in denial, I returned to my room, grabbing my phone and searching the Internet for the efficacy of pregnancy tests. I was dismayed to learn they were highly accurate. Then I researched birth control, wondering if my brand of pills had been recalled for being defective. No, they hadn't.

What I did learn was that the low dose pills I was on to regulate my period could be less effective if not taken regularly. I always took my pill, although not always at the same time each day. Like at the cabin, when, instead of getting up from Brett's arms in front of the fire, I took the pill the next morning.

Oh, God.

I sank back into bed. No matter what I did, from this moment on, my life would change.

I ran through all the possible choices and decisions in front of me. I couldn't imagine giving my baby up for adoption, but this wasn't just about me. I had a child to think about. I wasn't an incapable woman, but at this point in my life, could I give a child what they needed? There were couples out there wanting to be parents who couldn't. They'd give my baby a good home. The problem I discovered was that Brett would need to be involved in the adoption. So that option was out. Looked like I was going to be a parent.

The biggest barrier was financial, which I knew Brett could help with.

Leave me the fuck alone.

I let out a strangled laugh at the memory of Brett's words mixed with my current situation. I could only imagine the heinous words he'd come up with if I told him I was pregnant.

I didn't have to tell him, did I? I suppose I should, but he'd accuse me of trapping him or deny paternity. Chances were good he'd offer me money to go away. Maybe I could use the money to raise the baby.

By the end of the day, I'd ruminated over every possible scenario. It was interesting how the terror of an unplanned pregnancy could change into excitement. Well, maybe not excitement, but by the time I went to bed, I was resolved to keep my baby. I'd grown to love the tiny being forming inside me. I didn't know how I'd manage it, but I'd start figuring it out tomorrow.

The next day, I woke up afraid but determined to finish school, have my baby, and live a happy life. The first issue I needed to figure out was could I finish school while pregnant? I decided this was yes, since I'd only be five or six months pregnant at graduation. I knew women worked until their due dates, so I could finish school.

Getting a job after graduation might be harder, although if I could teach, maybe I could find a job starting in the fall after the baby came.

The next issue was Lindsay and Brett. At some point, I wouldn't be able to hide my pregnancy. What would I tell her? For a moment, I wondered if Oliver would pretend to be my baby's daddy, but that was nuts. The biggest worry was what if Lindsay told Brett that I was pregnant? Would he know he was the father? Could I persuade him that it was someone else's? I should've never admitted to being a virgin.

The solution would be to move back home and hide my pregnancy from Lindsay and Brett. My heart ached at letting go of Lindsay's friendship, but it had to be done.

I spent the next week executing my plan. I made arrangements to take online versions of my classes and do my teacher internship closer to my dad's house. I packed up my things, which wasn't much since Lindsay had furnished everything. I basically rented from her.

It was cowardly of me, but I waited to leave until she was off with Liam. I left her a note telling her I was sorry, but I had to leave.

In my old car, packed with everything I owned, I headed home. On the way, I stopped at the cell phone store to get a new number to cut all ties.

I arrived home, knowing my father would take me in and support my decision to keep the baby, but I was also sure he'd be disappointed at my irresponsibility. He'd tell me to make the baby's daddy pay his share, but I was ready to tell him I didn't know the father. That he was an anonymous hookup at a New Year's party. He'd be shocked and disappointed about that as well, but it had to be done.

I parked in the driveway and lugged my bag up to the house. I knocked and then opened the door. "Hey, Dad. I'm home."

15

Brett

January was always a hopping month in both of my businesses as people made New Year's resolutions for better health. By February, business was nearly back to normal as they abandoned their goals. Now mid-February, life was back to normal, or as much as it could be after my encounters with Miranda. The woman was proving hard to forget. The worst was the guilt over the way I treated her on New Year's Eve. The things I said . . . I would have liked to apologize, but seeing her wasn't a good idea. The fact that she took off without letting Lindsay know where she was going told me she didn't want to be found.

Aside from all that, life was back to homeostasis. Even Lindsay had found time to visit tonight. I was making her spaghetti, and of course, it brought back memories of Christmas at the cabin with Miranda.

The front door opened and then shut. "Dad?"

"In the kitchen, Linds."

She entered carrying a bottle of red wine and headed to the

drawer to get the corkscrew. Her movements were abrupt, as if she were pissed at my cabinetry.

“Is everything okay?" I asked as I stirred the sauce.

“I'm pissed at my roommate. Or should I say, my former roommate.” She continued to scrounge through the drawer.

I tensed, not wanting to ask about Miranda but knowing I needed to if I was going to be a good father. "What happened?"

"She just left. Poof. Gone." She let out an exasperated *ugh*. I wasn’t sure if it was because of Miranda or her inability to find the corkscrew.

I nudged her aside, finding the corkscrew and taking the bottle from her to open it. "What do you mean, she just left?"

“I mean, I came home one day, and she was gone. Her phone is disconnected. She’s gone.”

Worry grew. Had something happened to her? "Did you call the police? When did this happen?”

"About a week ago, and no, I didn't call the police. She wasn't kidnapped. She packed all her things, left a note that basically said she had to leave, and she moved out. No advance notice. No reason. No nothing." She took the wine I handed her.

"Did you have a fight?"

"No!" She looked at me in exasperation. Then she shook her head. "I don't know what to think. I mean, maybe she had a breakdown or something. If that’s the case, then I’ll feel like a shitty friend for not noticing that she was cracking up and being pissed.”

"A breakdown?" What the hell? Miranda struck me as a strong woman. Then again, she’d endured a lot in her life and I was truly despicable to her.

"She’s been acting differently ever since the new year started.”

My gut clenched as the guilt burned. This could be my fault.

"At first, I just thought she was gung-ho about the last semester of school. She's studious like that, and don't say anything about my not being studious."

I held my hands out in surrender and pursed my lips shut.

"Anyway, she was even more so this semester. All she did was go to class and study. I warned her that she couldn't live like that without burning out, and I thought she realized I was right when she said she was going to spend the weekend resting. But when I finally got home, she was gone. And I haven't been able to find her on campus."

If she was overdoing the studying, then it wasn't my fault she left, right? "How could she pack up her stuff so fast and leave before you got home? Where did you go?" Realizing my noodles were about to overcook, I pulled them from the stove and drained the water.

"I went to Liam's."

I ran cold water over the noodles to stop them from cooking. Lindsay became quiet, so I turned to her as the water ran.

Lindsay gave me a sheepish smile. "I got back Tuesday."

I frowned. "When did you leave?"

"Saturday."

I arched a brow. "Did you talk to her during that time?"

"No, but we talked before I left, and everything was fine. I know she wasn't sure about Liam, but she wouldn't just up and leave because I was spending so much time with him, would she?"

I didn't think so, but how well did I really know Miranda?

"I tried to text and call, but her phone was disconnected."

"Is she having financial problems? Maybe she had to move home," I offered, reaching back to turn off the water.

"Then why not tell me?"

"Maybe she's embarrassed or proud."

Lindsay shrugged. "It seems like she just wanted to get away from me."

Was that my fault? Was Lindsay a constant reminder of what a dick I'd been to her?

"Maybe I should have known something was wrong when I found her puking in the bathroom at the club on New Year's."

"Puking?" Jesus fuck, this was getting worse and worse.

"Something made her sick, so Oliver took her home, but maybe it was the start of whatever had her leaving." Lindsay's eyes filled with tears. "I should have gone home with her. Maybe I shouldn't have been gone so much." She'd gone from being angry to feeling guilty. She'd have to stand in line because I was reeling from the guilt.

I pulled Lindsay in for a hug to comfort her as I considered that Miranda became sick due to the way I treated her. Or hell . . . could she be pregnant? I dismissed that thought because it had only been a week, ten days at the most, since we'd first had sex. I knew from when Lindsay's mom got pregnant that it took several weeks before we knew if she was pregnant, and it had been a few weeks more before she felt symptoms.

Lindsay sniffed and pulled away. "It was shitty of her to leave like that." She was moving back to being pissed. It occurred to me that she learned that behavior—getting mad when you couldn't manage your own feelings and taking it out on others—from me.

"Have you gone to her home to ask her what happened?"

"No. She was loud and clear that she didn't want to be my friend anymore. Besides, I don't know where her dad lives."

"Really? You're good friends with her, but you don't know—"

"It's South Side somewhere. I bet she doesn't know where you live," she said defensively. Then she frowned. "Did she say something to you at Christmas? Was she pissed that I didn't make it?"

I swallowed as memory after memory of Miranda and me flashed in my brain. "She didn't give me that impression."

"Well, it doesn't matter. I've already given her room to Oliver. Since he and Liam were living together and needed to move, I said they could move into my place."

My gut tensed again, but this time it had to do with the idea of my daughter living with a boy. "By move into your place, do you mean Liam and Oliver will share Miranda's room?"

She gave me an eye roll. "No."

"What the fuck, Lindsay. You're moving in with a boy you just met?"

She shook her head and pursed her lips. "I didn't just meet him, Dad. It's been nearly six months."

I returned her eye roll. "That's not long enough to decide to live with anyone. Not at this stage in your life. You need to finish school, get a job . . . heaven forbid if you got pregnant."

"You don't look as old as you act."

"I'm an old man who is your father."

"Can we just eat?"

"Right." I turned back to preparing dinner as Lindsay set the table. We were silent, and I knew that our behavior when things got tense wasn't necessarily right.

But once I got the meal on the table, the evening went well as long as we stayed away from the topic of Liam. Even so, my mind was never far from wondering what happened to Miranda. Why the hell did she pack up and leave and not want to be contacted by Lindsay?

The question nagged at me for the next week. So much so that I hired a private investigator to find Miranda and to let me know what she was up to.

"Are you looking for anything specific? Cheating? Stealing?"

"No. I just want to know that she's okay. Is she still in school? Working? Where is she living?"

The PI seemed perplexed by my request but took the job. Two weeks later, he returned with a report and photos.

"She's living with her father." He handed over a photo while he rattled off an address. The house looked tired and in need of repairs. It made me think of the home I grew up in.

"What about school?" I had a gnawing worry that she quit to get away from Lindsay, not because of Lindsay but because of me.

"She's taking her courses virtually."

Thank fuck, and yet, it was still strange.

"She's student teaching at a nearby high school."

Relief flooded me. It was bad enough that I'd been so cruel to her. I didn't want it to have impacted her life.

"Is she working?"

"She has a part-time gig as a tutor. She does some in-person and some online."

Even better. She was finishing school and pursuing her dream.

"She mostly stays home except for her student teaching or tutoring, which she does at the local library." He handed me pictures of her at school and the library. I felt guilty looking at them. I was a voyeur into her life.

"The only other place she's gone in the last two weeks is a women's clinic. "

I looked up at him. "Is she sick?" The idea of it unsettled me, especially since Lindsay indicated that she'd been ill on New Year's and pushing herself too hard in school.

"That I don't know, and with privacy laws, it would be difficult to get that information."

"You got the school information." Surely, the school had privacy laws.

He smirked. "I said she was up for a job after graduation so they confirmed that she was still enrolled but was taking courses virtually. As far as the clinic, it's one used by people in the area who don't have good insurance or any insurance at all. It provides free screenings for women, so it was probably that. My wife goes to the doctor every year to get her 'girlie bits'—her words, not mine—checked out."

That made sense but didn't fully alleviate my concern. "Thank you." I slid the pictures back to him.

"They're yours. And here's my report." He put the pictures into an envelope and handed it to me. I felt dirty for having them. Like I'd violated Miranda all over again.

I stared at the envelope on my desk, determining I'd take it home and burn it.

After the PI left, I followed him out for a meeting with Dunc. As expected, the gyms were doing well. Dunc ran over ideas for the "getting ready for the beach" promotion.

"It's barely even March." The bitter cold told me summer was still several months out.

He smiled. "Some people need three months to lose the winter weight."

"I suppose you're right."

"I also want to look at adding kid classes this summer just in one gym. A pilot program that, if goes well, we can roll out next year to the rest of them, or at least the ones in the suburbs."

"Kids play. They don't need fitness classes."

"First of all, not all kids do physical activity when they play. Secondly, I was thinking about things like games and yoga."

"Games? Like tag?"

"Yes, or obstacle courses. Maybe even a dance class. I met a woman—"

I arched a brow. "You got this idea from a woman?"

He grinned. "She teaches a hip-hop dance class through the rec center. I figured she could teach for us too."

I know Dunc had thought this all through before sharing with me. I only had one real concern. "How would that impact insurance?"

"Not at all. Parents would need to sign consent and do all the same paperwork our adult clients do."

Truth be told, it sounded like a good idea. Just as his idea to offer childcare for our clients had been a good idea. "It's a go for me, then."

I returned to my office. Connie didn't look up from her work when she said, "Your daughter is in your office."

"Did it look like she broke up with her boyfriend or she needs money?"

She shrugged. "I don't speak teenager." I didn't bother to tell her that Lindsay was twenty-one, especially since Lindsay often acted like a teenager.

"Anything else?" I asked as I made my way to my office.

"Nothing that needs your attention."

I stopped by her desk. "What does that mean, exactly?"

She looked up at me with annoyance. I wasn't sure if it was because I was questioning her or interrupting her work. "I dealt with calls and a walk-in who didn't have an appointment."

"What did the walk-in want?"

She pursed her lips. "We didn't get that far. She didn't have an appointment, so I sent her on her way."

I frowned. "No message?"

She let out a sigh like my mother used to when I got on her last nerve. “No.”

I shrugged and walked into my office to find Lindsay sitting at my desk.

She looked up at me with a mixture of annoyance and shock. "What's this?" She held up the pictures the PI gave me.

My stomach dropped. "What are you doing going through my stuff?"

"I was bored waiting for you and it was here on your desk.”

"Jesus Christ, Lindsay. The world doesn't revolve around you."

"I know that," she said defensively.

"Do you?” I strode toward her, intending to take the incriminating evidence. "Just because you're bored doesn't mean you can invade people's privacy.” I motioned for her to get out of my chair.

“What reason do you have for invading Mira's privacy?” She rose from my chair, moving away from me.

Fuck, fuck, fuck. What could I tell her that would make sense? “What do you care? I thought you were past her."

She made a face. "Nice try, Dad. Seriously. Why are you spying on her? Did she steal something from the cabin?”

Yes. She stole my sanity. "No."

"I didn't think so. Tell me the truth.”

Think fast, Brett. I took a moment as I sat in my chair and cleared my throat. It was enough time to come up with a plausible reason to find Miranda. "I did it for you.”

Lindsay arched a brow. "For me?” She didn't sound convinced.

"You were so upset with how and why she left that I thought I’d find her for you.”

She pursed her lips. "So why are you mad that I opened the envelope?”

“You took the envelope without knowing it was for you. You don’t respect my things.”

She studied me. "Is this true?"

"Why else would I look for her?” I hoped to hell she couldn't see through my lie.

All of a sudden, her expression showed insight. It was like a light bulb lit up over her head. "Oh, I know what you're doing. You think Mira will come back and I'll kick Liam out."

"Ah. Busted." Thank you, Lindsay, for giving me a reason for my egregious behavior.

"Get over it, Dad. I'm an adult now."

"Yes, one who still relies on her father. You can't have it both ways, Lindsay. You can't expect me to pay your way through life and not have input on how you live it."

She made a face. "First, I'm making Liam and Oliver pay rent, so my cost is less. That's good money sense, right?"

"Who pays the mortgage on your place?"

"Why can't you give me credit for anything?" She shook her head, looking dejected. I wasn't wrong, yet I felt bad for making her feel like that.

"I came here to see if you wanted to go for coffee."

"Is everything alright?" I asked. She didn't usually stop by for coffee unless she had something she needed.

She looked at me with indignation. "I had news that I thought would make you happy. I have a job lined up after graduation, but now I know you won't think it pays enough or doesn't have good benefits. You'll be disappointed about something."

I hated making her feel I wasn't proud of her. Especially since I spent the first few minutes of her visit lying to her.

"Lindsay. Congrats. How about we get champagne, and you can tell me all about your job?"

For a moment, I thought she'd turn me down.

"Okay. But no talking about Liam, alright?"

"Deal."

I left the office with Lindsay feeling like I'd dodged a bullet . . . unless, of course, now armed with an address, Lindsay reached out to Miranda.

16

Miranda

I sat in my car, my fingers wrapped tightly around the steering wheel, feeling equal parts anger and humiliation. I should have known better than to come to Brett's corporate office in an attempt to talk to him. I'd resolved to raise this baby on my own, but after a visit with the doctor and a discussion of potential medical issues that could cost a fortune I didn't have, I had to consider letting Brett know about the baby. I had no doubt that he would be angry and say cruel things to me. And he would definitely want me to keep the secret of the baby's paternity from everyone, especially Lindsay. But maybe he would offer financial help in case I needed it.

I couldn't deny that deep down, a part of me hoped he would be different. That he would want to be a father to this baby. That he would want me. It was laughable how stupid that was, considering the last time I saw him. The man wanted me sexually, but it also made him angry to want me. Why I still pined for him made no sense. I guess I was longing for the sweet Brett, but that part of him wasn't who he really was. I knew that when I called in sick to my student teaching and drove to Brett's corporate office after looking it up on the Internet.

I was able to make my way to his office, but his secretary, a woman who could give the Wicked Witch of the West a run for her money, stopped me. I understood that it was her job to be his gatekeeper. And I didn't have an appointment. But her attitude toward me went way beyond simply telling me I couldn't see Brett. Her eyes scanned my body, her lips distorting into something that looked like disgust. Granted, I wasn't dressed my best, but I wasn't wearing dirty, smelly clothes either.

"Good for you for wanting to get control of your health, but Mr. McKinnon isn't a trainer. You should go to one of the gyms."

I frowned as I looked down at my body. Her words and her expression told me she thought I was fat. "I'm not here about a gym membership. I need to see—"

She rose, her eyes piercing to the point where I felt like I wanted to wither away. "No appointment, no visit."

I glanced at the door to his office wondering if I could make a run to it. She was tall and svelte, but her pencil skirt would limit how fast she could move to catch me.

"He isn't even here. If you don't leave now, I will be forced to call security."

Maybe this was a sign that I needed to do exactly as Brett had told me. Maybe I needed to stay the fuck away from him.

I held my chin up as I left the area, entering the elevator to return to the ground floor. By the time I reached my car, I couldn't decide whether I was more humiliated or angry and decided that I was both. She was a cool, condescending woman, so I suppose it made sense that she worked for Brett.

I started my car, pulling out and heading down the street. The route I took brought me in front of Brett's building again. As I slowed for the light, I saw Lindsay walk up to the building's door and enter, clearly going to visit her father. I saw an open parking spot and quickly pulled into it to watch and wait for her to come out. I didn't want to talk to her. I wanted to know whether the secretary had been lying to me or not. After fifteen minutes, when Lindsay didn't appear, I knew I'd been lied to. Brett was in his office.

I pulled into traffic and headed south to the library where I did tutoring after school. It was still early in the day, but I figured I would use the time to read up on pregnancy, potential complications, and what I could do to have the healthiest pregnancy and baby possible. One thing I knew I wouldn't do was ask Brett for help.

But even thinking that, I knew it wasn't true. This wasn't just about me. If it turned out my baby needed help, I would definitely ask Brett for help, and I wouldn't care if anyone found out about me and Brett. My child's health was the most important thing. But unless and until that happened, I was resolved to raise the child on my own. That was the way Brett would want it anyway. It would be the only way for me to do what he asked me to do, which was to stay away from him.

I spent the afternoon reading at the library and then meeting with the two students I was tutoring, one in World Civilization and the other in American History. Afterward, I headed home with a stop to pick up dinner from the hot bar at the grocery store. For me, it was a salad filled with vegetables, chicken, and hard-boiled eggs for protein. For my dad, I loaded up on a little bit of everything from chicken wings to barbecued ribs, potato salad, and green beans. There would likely be enough for him to take to work tomorrow.

As I pulled up to the house, I noticed a car parked out in front. As I passed it to pull in the driveway, I realized it was Lindsay's car. Panic shot through me. Why was she here? I supposed I wouldn't be hard to find, but why had she come now? I'd been gone for nearly a month.

For a moment, I sat in the car, contemplating not going in. But I wasn't a coward, so I grabbed the food and my book bag and headed up to the house. I opened the door, peeking in to see my dad sitting in his chair and Lindsay on the couch, both of them in the middle of a good laugh.

As I stepped in, my father's attention turned to me. "Well, speak of the devil."

I looked over at Lindsay, wondering what her reaction was going to be. She had to be angry at the way I left, and at the same time, Lindsay was one of those people who didn't hold onto grudges.

She stood and looked at me. "I want to be mad at you, Mira, for what you did, but I'm just too happy to see you." She came toward me, giving me an enthusiastic hug. "I'm sorry that I wasn't there for you. No wonder you left. I was such a terrible friend. Here you were, dealing with an unplanned pregnancy. I didn't even know you were seeing anyone. That's how terrible a friend I am."

I shot a look at my father. Why had he told her I was pregnant? He gave me a sheepish smile and a shrug.

Lindsay pulled back. "Will you ever forgive me?"

My emotions were reeling, and at the same time, I couldn't deny that it was good to see her, to be around her energy that was always positive, even in a negative situation.

I nodded. "There's nothing to forgive. I didn't leave because you weren't a good friend. I just needed to go." I didn't know what else to say.

She took my hand and dragged me to the couch. I set the food on the coffee table.

"Is the daddy Oliver?" she asked as she tugged me down next to her. She looked at me strangely. It was as if she didn't want it to be Oliver. Then she shook her head. "It couldn't be Oliver, though, could it? I mean on New Year's when I found you in the bathroom, was that morning sickness even though it was at night, right? I don't think you knew Oliver before that night."

In the past, I'd always been entertained by how Lindsay could have a whole conversation between us all on her own.

"It's not Oliver. It's not anyone you know."

"It's not anybody, anybody knows," my father said, earning him another glare from me.

"Well, I can help you find him if you want. Or maybe you don't want to find him. No matter what, though, I'm here for you. And if the baby daddy does show up and he hurts you, I will make his life a misery. I promise you that."

My father regarded Lindsay with approval. He turned his attention back to me. "Is that dinner? I'm starving."

"Yes."

He rose from his chair. "Will you be staying with us, Lindsay?"

I shook my head. "You're not going to want what I bought. It's just from the hot bar at the store."

Lindsay's eyes sparkled. "I love food from the hot bar." She rose and picked up the bag. I stood, and she looped her arm through mine as we walked to the dining room.

My father brought out plates and utensils, and all I could do was sit and watch as my father and Lindsay developed an unlikely friendship.

As I ate my salad, I realized that with Lindsay knowing about my pregnancy, she'd likely tell her father. Could I possibly ask her not to tell him? What reason could I give her to keep the secret? Especially to him.

"So, how far along are you, anyway?" Lindsay asked as she poked at the potato salad on her plate.

"Only about six weeks." I looked at my father, hoping he wouldn't correct my lie. He was gnawing on a rib and didn't seem to notice. I figured he probably hadn't paid attention when I had told him I was pregnant. I was actually closer to eight to ten weeks. But if Lindsay told her father that I was six weeks pregnant, that would put me after Christmas and New Year's as the time of conception.

"This is so exciting." She gave me a sheepish smile. "I mean, I know it's not planned, and it's probably scary. But you're growing a human life. A little person. And I know you well enough to know that you're going to make it work. I mean, you're still taking classes, and you're working. I have no doubt that you're going to get a really great teaching job which will be perfect for raising a baby, right? You'll get holidays and summers off."

"Well, I haven't been hired yet, and considering when I'm due, it will be difficult to start at the beginning of the school year. I have found some online teaching opportunities. Maybe I could do that while the baby is little."

"Isn't the Internet amazing?" She beamed. It was so strange how happy she was for me. I wanted to bask in it, but all I could think about was Brett and what he was going to do when he learned I was pregnant.

"What about you, Lindsay? What are you doing when you finish school?" my father asked as he wiped barbecue sauce from his chin.

"I'd like to start a business, but I have a job lined up because my father is worried about me."

"Why is he worried?" I felt defensive for Lindsay. Granted, I had sometimes felt that she was a little too cavalier and flaky in her life, but she was surely capable of starting and running a business.

"Oh, you know, the same old stuff. But I got a job as a collections assistant at the Gardner Museum."

"Wow, Lindsay. Good for you."

She arched a brow at me. "Why do you sound so surprised?"

I laughed. "I'm not surprised you got the job. I'm surprised you applied. That's great." And I meant it.

"I still want to start a business, but I figure getting experience would help. I was hoping that you and I could go into business together since you know so much history. But I understand that you need a job with health insurance and a steady paycheck. But I'm not giving up. Be prepared in a couple of years for me to try to steal you away."

I do admit that the idea of owning a business sounded exciting, but I needed to keep my career grounded. Just as she said, I needed a steady job with benefits.

For the rest of the meal, the discussion was mostly between Lindsay and my father, and I just watched as the two of them talked about football and assorted other sports. I hadn't realized how much she knew about sports and decided it was probably because of Liam.

When it was time for her to leave, she gave me another hug and I embraced her back. I was genuinely happy to have my friend in my life again. It definitely complicated things where her father was concerned, and I hated that I was lying to her, but it had to be done. Now, I just had to hope that Brett wouldn't suspect or care if or when she told him the news about me.

17

Brett

I was just about to walk into a charity fundraiser at the art gallery when my phone rang. I looked at the caller ID, seeing that it was Lindsay. The only thing I could think of was that she was calling me to tell me she'd seen Miranda. I wanted to ignore the call and at the same time I needed to know . . . was my secret out?

Thinking about it, I doubted it because Lindsay was the type of person who would confront me face-to-face about something like fucking her friend. Hell, maybe I was reading too much into her call. She probably just needed money.

Although technically, it was practically springtime, it was still cold outside, but I decided to brave it when taking her call to avoid eavesdroppers in the gallery.

"Lindsay. Is everything all right?"

"Oh, my God, Dad, everything's great. I saw Mira and you won't believe it."

Her enthusiasm was a relief. Whatever she was excited about, it wasn't that I had fucked her friend.

"What won't I believe?"

"Mira is pregnant."

My hand shot out against the wall of the building, bracing myself as a wave of nausea threatened to consume me. Jesus fuck.

"I don't completely understand why being pregnant made her feel she had to totally end our friendship, but it is why she moved home and is now taking online classes. I feel terrible, though, because I should've noticed that something was wrong."

I remembered Lindsay telling me that Miranda had been sick on New Year's Eve. Surely, that had been too early to know if she was pregnant. But what other explanation was there? And holy hell, I'd fucked her and then berated her that night.

"Dad? Are you there?"

"Yes, honey, I'm here." I scanned my brain for what the next logical question should be. What I wanted to ask was who was the father, but a decent person would ask how she was. "How is she doing?"

"She seems alright, although I guess it's still early because she's not showing. She says she's only about six weeks pregnant. But in true Mira fashion, she's gone into full planning mode and is finishing school and working in tutoring and doing her student teaching and —"

"She's keeping the child?"

"Yes. I don't really know what the deal with the baby's daddy is. Her dad seems to think that she isn't sure either, which is weird. Mira isn't really a hookup kind of girl. I totally thought she was a virgin."

The length of Miranda's pregnancy finally sank into my brain, and doing the mental math, I realized I couldn't be the father. Relief started to settle in until I realized that meant Miranda had slept with somebody else. The jealousy flared deep in my gut. It made no sense how angry that made me. This woman had an unhealthy hold over me in that I would be more upset to learn she'd slept with somebody else since me than worried about knocking her up.

"Anyway, I just wanted to tell you that all is well. And from now on, I'm going to try and be a better friend to her."

"That's good to know," I said absently.

"Are you alright? Where are you?"

"I'm at a charity event."

"At the gallery? I was thinking of going to that, but Liam and I are going to see a movie instead."

I frowned. Lindsay loved art, and the fact that she would give up something like this to go see a movie with her boyfriend bothered me. I didn't want her to give up her goals and dreams for a boy.

But she had to live her life. I suppose I needed to be grateful she wasn't pregnant. Jesus fuck. I was a nearly forty-two-year-old man who fucked a twenty-one-year-old girl and possibility got her pregnant. Was I really that guy? Well, no. I wasn't the father.

When I got off the phone with Lindsay, I considered going home, but then I caught sight of the open bar in the gallery. I went inside, making a beeline to it. "Double scotch. Neat."

A moment later, I downed the scotch, feeling it burn through my gut. Unfortunately, it did nothing to quell the insane jealousy brewing there.

"There you are." Dunk stepped up next to me. He glanced at my empty glass and at me. "Something wrong?"

I shook my head and rolled my shoulders, as if that would get rid of the torrent of emotions swirling through me. "Everything's fine." I spoke in a clipped voice as I scanned the room. My gaze stopped on Naomi. Naomi somebody. I couldn't remember her last name, but eight or ten months ago, she'd been a good fuck when I was at another charity event. I waited for the bartender to pour me another drink and then I picked it up and made a beeline to her.

When she saw me, she smiled knowingly. This was exactly the woman for me. Long, blonde hair that was probably extensions, but if I didn't tug too hard, they would pass for real. Large, round, firm, fuckable tits, also not real. An ass my hands could grip as I pumped deep inside her. And when it was done, I could leave and nothing about her would haunt my mind.

"Hey, Brett," she cooed, sidling up next to me.

"Naomi." I noticed she didn't have a drink. "Can I get you something?"

She gave me a smile that told me she knew exactly what I was after and was going to be more than willing to give it. She took my drink and with a sensuous smile brought it to her lips. "I'll just have a little of yours."

She coughed, and I probably should have warned her that there was no mixer in the drink. But she recovered. "You like them stiff, don't you?"

I slid my hand over her ass. "If I remember correctly, you do too." She turned her body into mine, pressing close, closer than was acceptable in public. It should have been exciting, erotic. I had a ready, willing, and able woman with a body made for fucking grinding against me. My dick wasn't interested. The little bastard didn't even twitch.

I took my drink back and downed it, thinking maybe I needed to calm down and then my dick could get into the mood. "I need to look at some art first."

She nodded. "Of course."

We moved together, looking at each exhibit from a mixed media artist. We stopped at a piece that had a combination of old toys, pages from what looked like a fairytale book, and paint.

"I just don't get how this is art. I mean, I could do something like this. My niece could do something like this. All they did was paste paper and toys and then slap on a little paint."

I closed my eyes for a moment as her comment grated on me. I opened my eyes and studied the artwork. If Miranda were here, she'd likely see that the pages on the art piece all depicted fairy tales in which women were destitute, pushed into servitude. The toys were symbols of what was traditionally girly—pink, feminine, and smacking of subservient domesticity. While the paint was somewhat abstract, it was clear to me that the artist was showing that women, in many ways, are still held back by these old beliefs.

"Women have come farther since then, but not as far as many would think. Women still earn about thirty percent less than men. They still do seventy percent more of the housework." I could hear Miranda's voice saying if she were here. "And while some companies fight to fund birth control on their insurance plans, they have no problem finding Viagra." She'd told me that little tidbit during our *Trivial Pursuit* game at the cabin. She'd shaken her head. "Women today still can't win. Men want to have innocent, virginal wives and yet want to have sex all the time with women who aren't their wives. They can't have it both ways." Her comment had made me laugh because I decided she wasn't wrong.

"And men act like women don't like sex. At least the ones that they'll bring home to meet the family." When she said that, I'd asked her if she liked sex as I pushed the game aside. I'd also pushed away the knowledge that I wouldn't be bringing her home to meet the family, either.

Jesus fuck. Why was I thinking about her?

"What do you think, Brett?" Naomi asked.

I considered telling her the whole thing about representing the plight of women but decided it wouldn't interest her. Wasn't that why I chose her? All style and no substance?

She arched a brow and her hand cupped my dick. "Maybe we've seen enough art?"

My dick actually shriveled into my body. I stepped away, my jaw tight. "I need another drink." I left her there, heading straight for the bar. When I got there, I glanced over my shoulder and she looked at me with that same arched brow. I gave a slight nod. When she sidled up to another man, I knew she'd gotten the message. I wouldn't be fucking her tonight. Probably not ever.

For the next hour and a half, I stood at the bar, consuming drinks. Next year, I probably wouldn't be invited, or they would have a cash bar to recoup all the booze expense I was drinking.

Dunk came over, standing next to me. "Now, I know something is wrong. Thank God this bar is here or you'd be flat on the floor. What the hell's going on?"

I shrugged off the hand he settled on my shoulder. "Nothing a little booze won't take care of."

"You're beyond the little booze, Brett. Come on, let me take you home and we can talk about it."

"I don't want to talk about it."

"Fine. Let me take you home, then." Dunk had the appearance of a bruiser, but deep down, the guy was soft. He liked to talk about feelings. I didn't want to do that, but neither did I still want to be here, so I nodded.

"Did Janine call you or something?" He asked about my ex-wife as he drove me home.

My head rested against the window as I willed the booze to stay down in my gut. "Why would you say that?"

"Because the last time you got this drunk was when you thought you might be losing custody of Lindsay."

"Lindsay's a grown woman now. I'm not going to lose custody of her."

We drove a while longer in silence, and I was hopeful that Dunk would give up trying to find out why I was so fucked up, not just drunk, but emotionally as well.

"Listen, there's something going on with you and I'm not trying to pry—"

"Yes, you are. It is none of your business."

"It is my business, Brett. First, we're partners, and if you're going to start going around getting drunk in public and having women grope you where everyone can see, I need to know that because I'm gonna need to hire a really good PR firm. Second, we're friends, man. Brothers. Maybe I can help."

"You can't." That was the most fucked up thing of all. There was no solution to this torment.

"Maybe I can't help, but it can't hurt to talk about it."

We arrived at my brownstone, and Dunk helped me inside, plopping me down on my couch as he got water and pain reliever for me.

Then he sat in a chair and studied me. "What's going on, Brett?"

For a long moment, I didn't respond. I wasn't planning on saying anything. I leaned my head back and closed my eyes, willing the booze to numb me. "I fucked someone I shouldn't have. I seem to have developed feelings for somebody I shouldn't have. She's pregnant with somebody else's kid." There. I said it.

When Dunk didn't say anything. I peeled open my eyes enough to see him staring at me. "I'm not sure which shocks me more. That you would have feelings for somebody or be upset that they were pregnant by somebody else."

I dug the heels of my hands into my eyeballs, willing all this to stop.

"Does she know how you feel?"

I made an attempt to roll my eyes except it made my stomach heave. "No. And it wouldn't matter if I did. She's totally, completely, one hundred percent off limits. And besides, she's clearly moved on. I initiated her into the pleasures of the flesh, and now she's off sharing herself with other men."

Dunk arched a brow. "You think she was a virgin?" Dawning came to his face. "It's that woman you met before Christmas, isn't it?"

I tapped the end of my nose to let him know he'd guessed right.

"After one night, you fell head over heels for her?" His voice was incredulous.

"It wasn't one night. More like three or four. And no, I'm not head over heels." I didn't know what the fuck I was feeling, but it couldn't be that.

Dunk was quiet for a moment, and I was hoping that now that he knew my secret, or at least some of it, he'd leave me to suffer alone.

"If she was a virgin, how can you be sure you're not the father of her baby?"

"The timing. She says she's only six weeks along. But I was with her just before Christmas and—" I bit down on my tongue as I realized I was about to tell him about New Year's Eve.

Dunk was smart, and he might put two and two together and suspect it was Miranda.

"Well, I don't know a lot about women's bodies or pregnancy, but I do know that women, like men, aren't beyond telling mistruths. Maybe she just said that so you wouldn't think it was your baby."

His words sent the most interesting terror and hope through me. Had Miranda lied to Lindsay, knowing that Lindsay would tell me she was pregnant? That would mean Miranda didn't want me to know about the baby. That pissed me off.

"I can see that you're thinking it's a possibility." Dunk was quiet again, and when I finally looked at him, he was studying his fidgeting hands, a sure sign that there was something he wanted to say or ask. He lifted his head. "Does this have anything to do with Lindsay's roommate, Miranda?"

"What the fuck, Dunk?"

He shrugged sheepishly. "As Lindsay's godfather, she and I are in contact a lot. So I know that she didn't make it to the cabin over Christmas, but her friend did. I also know how upset she was that her friend disappeared all of a sudden and that now, that friend is pregnant."

I could only stare at him. I probably looked like the proverbial deer in the headlights.

"Wow, Brett."

Rage erupted in me. "I don't want any lectures from you, Dunk. Just leave me the fuck alone." I winced as I realized those were the last words I'd said to Miranda.

Dunk rose from the couch, holding his hands out to his sides in surrender. "I'm not going to lecture you, Brett. You're both consenting adults. But—"

"I said no lectures."

"But if you're the father of that girl's baby, you have to do the right thing. At least you have to find out the truth. Get a paternity test. And also, if you don't think Lindsay can figure this out, then you're dumber than the women you normally fuck."

I shot up from the couch, but the room began to spin and I ended up popping back down on my ass.

"Do yourself a favor and just stay there for the rest of the night. Take the water and pills. And with that, I leave you."

After the door shut behind him, I wallowed in my anger. I took the pills and downed the water and immediately began to think about getting more booze. But the more I sat, the more I stewed, the more I needed to see Miranda and find out the truth once and for all.

Somehow, I managed to pull out my phone and order a rideshare. It pulled up in front of my place just as I managed to get out of my house. I gave him the address, and when we arrived at Miranda's father's house, I told the driver to wait, offering him an extra hundred dollars if he did.

I made my way up toward the tired-looking house, wondering if Miranda was playing a game with me. I could be her ticket out of living paycheck to paycheck. Somewhere in the back of my mind, I knew that didn't make sense because clearly, she was trying to hide her pregnancy. But booze and anger swirled and I decided to lead with the anger.

I pounded on the door. It was several minutes later before it opened. Miranda stood in front of me, wearing dark leggings and an oversized faded sweatshirt with her hair messily pulled back in a bun on her head. How was it that looking like this, she was more beautiful than Naomi?

"Brett?"

Remembering why I was there, I straightened, rising to my full height, wanting to look intimidating. "Are you a gold digger or just a fucking liar?"

18

Miranda

I was in my room studying when the knock came on the door. It had to be my dad being escorted home by his bar buddies and unable to find his key. But when I opened the door, Brett stood on my doorstep. At first sight, my heart squeezed hard in my chest. He looked like a fairy tale hero in a tuxedo. But when I studied his face, I saw rage in his glassy eyes. Had he been drinking?

"Are you a gold digger or just a fucking liar?"

His words struck me just as surely as if he'd used his fist. I tensed, stepping back, wanting to shut the door and lock him out. It was clear that Lindsay had told him I was pregnant, but I really thought he'd be relieved. He had to have done the math and determined the child wasn't his.

His eyes, as dazed as they appeared, took a long inventory of me, and when he was finally looking at my face again, he said, "You look like hell. Aren't pregnant women supposed to glow?"

"Mr. Hyde, I presume," I murmured. This had to be the real Brett. I feel like I saw more of this side of him than the sweet side I'd fallen for.

"Oh, no. You don't get to make me out to be the bad guy here. What game are you playing? Not just with me but with Lindsay as well?"

"No game."

"Did you take everything I taught you about fucking and now you're sharing with other men?"

I swallowed, knowing that if I were to keep my secret, I'd have to lie, but I found it difficult to do so to his face.

"Are you a gold digger? Did you see your friend's wealthy single father and think maybe you can get some of that?"

I tried to glare at him in indignation, but all the while, my emotions ran from hurt to fear. He was angry at me, and if he found out the truth about the baby, would he take it from me? Just like he'd taken Lindsay from her mother?

Somehow, I found my voice. "There's no winning with you. You're angry either way." I shook my head. "If you weren't so self-centered and you took the time to know me and assess the situation, you would know the truth. And who are you to be lecturing me on sleeping with someone else, anyway? How many plastics have you been with since New Year's?"

His face contorted. "None. And that's your fucking fault."

I wondered what that meant.

Several lights from homes on the street flipped on, a sure sign the neighbors were hearing Brett's diatribe. I didn't want my neighbors to know about my business, but neither did I want to invite Brett into the house. Thank God my father had gone to the bar with his friends. Who knew what he would've tried to do to Brett.

"Are you drunk?" I asked.

"Yes, and that's your fault too. Every fucked up thing that has happened since I met you is your fault. You think you have some hold on me, don't you? Like you're some fucking femme fatale. You're subtle, I'll give you that."

The breath stalled in my chest as I realized what he was saying. He thought that I had set him up. That I was a gold digger. He was basically calling me a whore. "You have a terrible memory, Brett," I managed to say. I wasn't sure if my voice quavered, but the rest of me was definitely shaking.

He shook his head. "Oh, no, I see quite clearly now. You knew I'd go to that paper shop before Christmas and knew my reputation with women."

"Plastic women, Brett. Not women like me."

He sneered as his gaze scraped over me again. "You're right. You're not my type. But you worked that wide-eyed, innocent schoolgirl charm on me. When did you know that Lindsay wasn't going to come to the cabin? I bet it was before you left Boston. But you came so you could be alone with me."

"What do you want, Brett?" There was no use arguing. I knew there was no changing his mind, especially when he was in one of his moods.

"I want you out of my fucking head."

"If that's true, why are you on my porch? I did what you asked. I've stayed away from you. You're the one stalking me."

He jerked. "I'm not stalking you. I don't need to stalk women to get them in my bed."

I closed my eyes, hating that sex was all he saw in me. In all women, really. "Then why are you here?"

"I don't like to be played or lied to. I want you out of my life."

"Well, then, let me give you some advice. It's the same advice you gave me on New Year's. Stay the fuck away from me." I slammed the door, flipping all the bolts and locks, then sagged against it, sliding to the floor as the endorphins crashed through me. I shook from the pain of his words, from the things that he thought of me, and the things he could still do to me if he found out the truth.

I wasn't sure how long I sat there, but I crawled over to the window, peeking through the curtain, and saw that he was no longer on the doorstep. I stood on shaky legs and went through the house, making sure all the doors and windows were locked. He never made any move to suggest he could be violent, and Lindsay never mentioned he'd ever been violent, but I wasn't going to take any chances.

I made my way back to my room, cleaning up my books, notepads, and laptop off my bed, setting them on my desk. There wouldn't be any more studying tonight.

I took a shower because Brett's words clung to me, making me feel dirty. I put on another pair of leggings and a T-shirt and climbed under the covers, hoping that when I slept, everything about Brett would disappear.

I was so tired and emotionally wrought that sleep came quickly. But with it came the nightmare. I was back at the front door, and every rotten thing Brett had ever said to me he was repeating. Each awful comment or accusation was like a punch in the gut until all I could feel was my stomach cramping and burning.

"You think you pulled one on me, don't you? But I'm going to teach you a lesson, Miranda. Because when that baby is born, it will be mine. I will use all my resources, every power I have within me to keep you from seeing your baby."

I woke up with a start, sitting up, panting, and crying. My stomach cramped hard again, and I realized that it hadn't just been a dream. This time, the terror that filled me had to do with the baby.

I flung the covers off and padded my way to the bathroom. When I saw blood on my leggings, I cried out, "Dad! Dad, help me."

I wasn't even sure that he was home. I didn't know what time it was. But I heard him running down the hall, sliding into the doorway. "What's wrong, baby?"

I looked up at him, feeling sadder than I could ever remember feeling. It was as sad as I felt when my mother died. "I think there's something wrong with the baby."

"I'll call an ambulance."

"Maybe you should drive me. We can't afford an ambulance."

"Now is not the time to be worrying about that, Miranda." He rushed away from the door, and with him gone, loneliness and emptiness filled me. Somehow, I managed to pull myself back together, getting up and slipping on shoes and a coat as I waited for an ambulance.

I looked at my father, and his expression was as stricken as I felt. I could only imagine that he was reliving losing my mother.

He reached out and pulled me in for a hug. "I'm not going to let anything happen to you or your baby. You hear me, Miranda? You and the baby are going to be fine." It was as if he was trying to will that into the world. It was a promise I knew he had no control over. But being afraid, I latched onto it, wanting to believe that my father could make everything right.

When the ambulance came, it was a whirlwind of activity. I was poked and prodded and asked what I was feeling and what happened. Soon, I was in the back of an ambulance. My father rode with me, grilling the paramedics on my status.

We finally arrived at the hospital, and they started to wheel me down the hall.

"I'm going to call your friend Lindsay," my dad called after me.

"No, Dad, don't do that." God. That was the last thing I needed.

"You should have a female friend with you since you don't have your mom."

It was such a sweet thought, but I didn't want her here. Unfortunately, my father disappeared from my view as they rolled me into a room.

Again, hospital staff busied themselves with tests and questions.

"Your blood pressure is a little bit high," the nurse said as she removed the cuff that I hadn't even realized was on my arm. But of course, my blood pressure was high. Brett was ballistic on my porch, wondering if he was the father of my baby. In my dream, he threatened to take my child. What was going to happen when he learned something was wrong? In what sort of crazy, twisted way would he decide that I had ruined his life if I lost the baby?

19

Brett

An incessant buzzing pulled me from an unconscious stupor. As I began to wake, I realized I was face down in my bed, with a jackhammer rumbling in my brain and sandpaper in my mouth. I moaned as I groped around in the dark for my phone, realizing that was the source of the buzzing.

I wrapped my fingers around it, pulling it toward me, opening my eyes just enough to note that it was three thirty in the morning and the caller was Lindsay. In an instant, I was alert, nearly sober.

I poked the answer button. "Lindsay. What's wrong?"

"I'm sorry to call you so early, Dad, but it's important. An emergency."

I didn't know what the hell was going on, but I shot to my feet looking for my clothes until I realized I was still fully dressed in my tux.

"What's wrong?" I staggered out of my bedroom, noting that while I was mentally understanding what was going on, I wasn't yet ready to drive. I'd have to order a car to get to wherever Lindsay needed me.

"It's Mira. She's in the hospital."

My bumbling up the hallway abruptly stopped as I leaned against the wall. "What do you mean?"

"I don't have the details. Her father called me when he brought her in because she was bleeding. I'm so afraid she's losing the baby."

For a moment, everything inside me went still as the words I said to Miranda on her porch came back to me, haunting, menacing. Miranda had stood up to me, but I hadn't missed the stricken look in her eyes, the paleness in her face. Jesus fuck. Was this my fault?

"Mr. Hathaway, that's Mira's father, he's worried sick. Not just about her, but he's also concerned about the level of care she's going to get."

With each word the lingering fog in my brain started to dissipate. "Why wouldn't she be getting the best care possible? What the hell hospital are you in?"

"It's not about the hospital, Dad, but about how much insurance they have. Or more about what it might not cover. I hate to ask you, but could you use your influence to make sure she gets the best care possible? And maybe . . . maybe you could help pay for it. I know it's a lot to ask—"

"I'm on my way. You tell whoever's over there that whatever Miranda needs, she'll get. It'll be paid for. I promise."

"Thank you, Dad. Thank you so much."

When Lindsay hung up, my fingers fumbled to dial a ride share. I had to look like hell as I stumbled out of my home in a rumpled tuxedo. My hair was probably sticking up all over the place, but none of that mattered. All that mattered was getting to the hospital and ensuring that Miranda and her baby were fine.

I gave the driver the address to the hospital, and fortunately, traffic wasn't too bad at three thirty in the morning. When he dropped me off, I rushed into the emergency room, sliding up to the reception desk.

"Miranda Hathaway."

"Dad."

I looked over my shoulder to see Lindsay hurrying up to me. I turned to her. "Is there any news?"

She shook her head as she threaded her arm through mine and tugged me to the waiting area, where I saw an older gentleman with despair etched all over his face.

"Right now, we're just waiting. Mr. Hathaway? This is my dad, Brett McKinnon. Dad, this is Mira's father, Mr. Hathaway."

Mira's father looked up at me, weakly extending his hand. "You can call me Peter."

I shook his hand. "I'm Brett. What's going on?"

Peter looked down, shaking his head. "I don't know. I heard her cry out, and when I got to her, she was in the bathroom, bleeding. I got her here as fast as I could and they took her back, but I haven't heard anything. I was hoping Lindsay would be able to be with her. I can only imagine what Miranda is feeling. The last time we were at a hospital, her mother was dying."

As if the guilt I was feeling wasn't enough, the memory of learning how Miranda's mother had died, and Miranda having to take on adult responsibilities, heaped on more guilt.

Her father hiccupped, clearly trying to keep back tears. "Miranda would be the first to tell you that losing her mother broke me. If not for her, I don't know that I would still be here. If I lose her and my grandchild, I don't know—"

I reached my hand out, putting it on his shoulder. "That's not going to happen. Whatever Miranda and her baby need, they're going to get it. I promise."

The man looked at me with such anguish in his face. "I should be able to take care of my girl, but I'm not too proud to refuse your help."

"Good." Guilt urged me to confess the truth. Miranda was mine. The baby was mine. It was my job to take care of them. I told myself that this wasn't the right time or place to tell them, ignoring the truth that the reason for my silence was because I was a coward.

"Let me make sure that they have my information and affirm that she needs to get the best care possible, okay?"

He nodded. Lindsay sat down next to him, taking his hand. She also looked terrified that something was wrong with her friend, but she'd been able to manage it so that she could be there for

Miranda's father. Another wave of guilt filled me as I realized that I was so hard on Lindsay in terms of her scholastic achievement and getting a job, I hadn't recognized what a good person she was. I had no clue where she had gotten that from because there was no doubt that I was a fucking asshole. Her mother wasn't any better.

Lindsay looked up at me and mouthed, *thank you.* I nodded and then headed to the nurse's station to give them information about Miranda's care. It made no sense to me how difficult it was to convince hospital administrators that whatever intervention Miranda and the baby required, I would pay for, but finally, they seem to have gotten the message, and I signed a few papers and then went back and joined Lindsay and Peter in their vigil.

The sun was rising when a doctor appeared in front of us. The three of us shot up from our chairs. My breath stalled in my lungs as I waited to find out about Miranda and the baby and whether or not I'd be able to ever look at myself in the mirror again.

The doctor held her hands up in a calming manner. "Miranda is fine."

The three of us took a breath, but the relief wasn't completely here yet. Not until we knew about the baby as well.

"The baby is fine too."

"Thank God." Peter sank down into his chair as if his legs had given out on him. Then he wept, surely tears of relief.

"What happened?" I had to know for sure if the vile things I'd said to Miranda were the reason she was here. The reason she and her baby were at risk.

"We found two issues. While we need to watch them, we do believe that her and the baby's health should be fine."

For the first time since I got a call from Lindsay, I felt my heart beat again. She would be fine.

"She has a subchorionic hematoma, which is when blood collects between the wall of the uterus and the chorion membrane. We also found a cervical polyp. In most cases, each of these resolve themselves, but we will monitor them."

“What if they don’t resolve?” I asked, not sure I was happy with the wait-and-see approach.

“They don’t have to fully resolve. The only issue if whether they cause problems—”

“She’s here now. That’s a problem,” I growled.

The doctor wasn’t fazed by my outburst. “Right now, neither of these issues are impacting the baby’s health. We’ll monitor to see if they reduce in size or fully resolve. If they don’t, if they get worse, then we’ll discuss treatment options such as medications or surgery to remove the polyp.”

"Would that be safe for the baby?" I asked.

The doctor nodded, cocking her head at me, probably wondering who I was. She looked at Peter.

"Whatever you do, Doc, just make sure they're both safe,” he said.

She nodded. "Of course."

“What about the bleeding?” Lindsay asked. “That can’t be good.”

“Both of these issues can lead to bleeding, but we were able to see that the baby was fine through the ultrasound. The heartbeat was exactly as it should be."

Whatever Peter had in his knees swept through me, and I sank down onto the chair. The idea of hearing the baby’s heartbeat brought the reality of the situation crashing in around me.

"You can hear the heartbeat this early?" Lindsay asked.

"Yes. We can usually detect the heartbeat anywhere from six weeks with a vaginal ultrasound, but in this case, since she’s eight to ten weeks, we picked it up through fetal doppler.”

A knot formed in the back of my throat. Either Miranda didn't know how far along she was or she lied about being six weeks pregnant. I had a flash of anger about that, but it was quickly doused by the fact that I couldn't blame her for wanting to lie. When I wasn’t fucking Miranda, I was a cruel and dismissive bastard. All because of the way she made me feel, the loss of control because of the hold she had on me. That wasn't her fault.

Peter managed to stand. "Can I see her?"

"Yes, but just for a few minutes. We're still doing some monitoring and she needs to rest."

"Can we all go?" Lindsay asked. She looked at Peter. "I mean, if that's okay with you."

He nodded. "I'm not so good in hospitals, myself. It would be good to have you there with me." He looked over at me. "And you too, Mr. McKinnon. Her guardian angel."

Bile threatened to come up at the way Peter looked at me like I was some sort of savior. I was fully the opposite of that. An angel would've declined to go with them, knowing I had no right to see her, but I was no angel, so I followed them toward Miranda's room.

"We'll be moving her to a private room shortly. We'll make sure she'll get the best care possible," the doctor said as we followed her up the hall.

"Yeah, only because my dad is here to pay for it," Lindsay murmured.

"Linds."

She came in step next to me, leaning closer, and in a harsh whisper said, "It's not right, Dad. She should get the top care no matter what."

I nodded. "But that debate is best left for another day. Let's not antagonize hospital staff."

"Right."

As we reached the door, Peter stepped in, rushing over to his daughter's bedside. "Miranda, you're going to be okay. Dad's here. And so are your friends."

Lindsay moved in, going to stand next to Peter. "You gave us quite a scare there."

Taking a deep breath, I stepped into the doorway. Miranda's tired and glassy eyes slowly moved, tracking me in the doorway. For a moment, her face was expressionless, but a second later, she tensed, everything about her moving as if she were in distress.

She lifted her palm out to me in a stay away gesture, her head shaking. "No. I don't want him here. He can't have my baby."

Lindsay and Peter's heads swiveled toward me, probably

expecting to see somebody else standing in the doorway. They both frowned and turned back to Lindsay.

"It's okay, Mira. It's just my dad. You remember my dad, don't you?"

But Miranda's distress continued.

"I'll just leave." I wanted to tell Miranda I was sorry. I wanted to get on my knees and grovel for her forgiveness. But I understood that the best thing I could do for her at this moment was to leave her alone.

I left the doorway, heading back up the hall, trying to decide whether I would sit and wait for Lindsay to finish her visit or just go home. I'd only made it about ten steps up the hall when Lindsay called after me.

I stopped, gathering my wits about me before turning to look at her.

"I don't know what that was about," she said as she reached me. "She's just scared. Please don't read anything into it and stop help—"

"It's okay, Linds." I hated that Lindsay thought I would withdraw financial support simply because Miranda couldn't stand the sight of me. Miranda's words came back to me.

He can't have my baby.

I realized now that no matter what, the secret would be revealed. I suspected that Miranda didn't want me involved in the baby's life and would possibly ask me to continue our agreement, to keep her secret and with that, the paternity of her baby. If I were truly an angel, I'd honor that. I'd give her everything she needed to raise the child in a stable, healthy, happy home and stay away. But as I'd already admitted, I was no angel.

There were only two things in this world that I was any good at. One of them was building a successful business, and the other was being a father. Lindsay was proof of that. There was no doubt that if I had to choose between Lindsay and anything else in this world, including my businesses, it would be her. From the moment I first held her, she had become the center.

And now, I had another child growing in Miranda's womb, and the only thing I could think about wanting was to be a father. I wanted to be there on the doctor's visits, listening to the heartbeat, and watching the child grow as Miranda's belly swelled. I wanted to be there for the birth, seeing my child open their eyes and cry for the first time. And that unexplainable pull toward Miranda had me wanting to be by her side through it all. Through late-night feedings and diaper changes. From the first day of kindergarten through graduation.

I ran my fingers through my hair as clarity came. I knew what I wanted, and that was Miranda and the baby. I had no right to either of them. And at this point, Miranda would likely keep me as far away from her and the baby as possible. But I finally recognized that my heart wanted what my heart wanted, and I was an idiot and an asshole to continue to fight against it.

But in order to have it, I needed to come clean to Lindsay.

"How about we go to the cafeteria and get some coffee? I need to talk to you."

"Now?" She checked her watch. "I'm not late for class. But surely, you're not going to give me a lecture for not going to school when my best friend is in the hospital."

"It's not about that. It's important. It's about Miranda."

Her brow furrowed, but she nodded, and we went to the elevator, riding up silently to the floor with the cafeteria. I got us both coffee and we sat at a table.

"So, what about Miranda?" Lindsay asked when I remained silent.

From the time I told Lindsay that I needed to talk to her, I found it impossible to make eye contact with her. But now, it was time to face the truth. What was that saying? The truth will set you free.

I turned my attention to Lindsay. "I'm the father of Miranda's baby."

20

Miranda

I awoke completely disoriented. Opening my eyes and looking around, I saw Lindsay sitting in a chair reading a magazine. Where was I?

Then it all came flooding back. The blood, the fear. Not just the fear of losing the baby to a health crisis, but to Brett as well. What had he been doing here? He had to know or at least suspect the truth.

"Hey," Lindsay said, standing up and putting her magazine aside. She walked over to the side of my bed. "How are you feeling?" She was being sweet like she normally was, and at the same time, there was something in her expression that told me something was up.

"Am I going to be alright?" I had a vague recollection of being told that me and the baby were okay, but maybe that was a dream.

"Yes. You and the baby are fine. There's a couple of things that the doctors will monitor, but they seem to think they aren't that big a deal."

I nodded.

She studied me, her expression turning more serious. “Were you ever going to tell me, Mira?"

I could try to pretend that I didn't know what she was talking about, but it was bad enough that I had kept something important from her. Why insult her by continuing to pretend? "Did your dad talk to you?"

"He seems to think he's the father of your baby. On the one hand, I'm completely shocked that you would have slept with my father. But I also know that my father wouldn't lie about that. And since I can't imagine your sleeping around, I suspect that maybe he's right. Then again, I didn't think you'd sleep with my father, so maybe you are sleeping around."

Studying her, my impression was that she was more hurt than anything that I had betrayed her. She didn't seem particularly angry.

"I didn't know who he was—"

She held up a hand to stop me. "He gave me all the disturbing details. And I'll be honest, Mira, you two hooking up without knowing who each other was, that I can deal with. But after that? At the cabin? That feels really weird to me."

I nodded. "I know. I'm sorry."

Her eyes narrowed. "I still don't see how it could have happened. You've always seemed so focused on school. You hardly ever went out, and when you did, you never spent time with men. I don't understand how you'd hook up with a total stranger and then continue to do it even knowing he was my father."

I looked down, not sure how to explain it to her. To be honest, I didn't completely understand it, especially since it turned out Brett could be so cruel. "I don't know. We ran into each other, and initially, I didn't like him and yet he invited me for a drink. We talked, and I don't know, I just felt something and decided for once, I would go with it. It was the same at the cabin. Initially, we were butting heads and I was trying to avoid him, and then all of a sudden, we weren't. It was almost like I was outside myself. I was away from school and all the stress and everything, and I just wanted to be different. And to answer your question, although I'm ashamed to admit it, I hadn't planned to tell you. We agreed that we wouldn't. We figured once we got home, we were back to our old lives, and what happened was gone in the past."

"But then, you found that you are pregnant. That's why you left, right?"

I nodded.

Anger flashed in her eyes, an unusual sight from Lindsay. "You were going to keep the baby from my father."

Her accusation made me think that Brett hadn't told her everything. "The last time I saw your father, he told me to stay away from him."

She sighed. "He told me all about that. The guy is beating himself up with guilt over the way he treated you, but even so, he doesn't deserve to miss out on his child, or his child to miss out on having him as a father. I know my father can be a jerk, but he's a good father. And considering your dad is worried about paying an ambulance bill, my father can provide financial support that you and your child need."

My own anger flared, but I tried to tamp down on it, knowing that she was right. "I did try to see him," I said, feeling I needed to defend myself. "I went to his office, but his secretary looked at me and treated me like I was lower than pond scum. She said he was out, and after I left, I saw you go into the building and you stayed there, so he had to have been there."

"So you just gave up?"

"I suppose I did, but then he showed up on my doorstep saying things." I wanted to tell her just how awful her father could be. At the same time, I wanted to protect her from it. She loved her father.

"He hates himself for that." She shook her head, letting out a humorless laugh. "My father has been immune to women ever since he and my mother divorced. But there's something about you, apparently."

I had no idea what she meant, so I didn't respond.

"I think my father's half in love with you, but because he can't deal with it, because it makes him feel out of control, he takes it out on you. I'm not saying that it's right that he did that. I'm just trying to explain."

Even without explanation, I knew there was no future for me and Brett. Even with the secret out and Lindsay dealing with it as well as she was, there was no way I could put me and my child in a position to have Brett's vitriol spewed on us whenever he felt he couldn't manage his feelings. There were a lot of things Brett and I needed to figure out if he was going to be in my baby's life, and the idea of having to co-parent increased my stress. He had money and power and influence, all things he could use to take the child from me. But I didn't feel that this was a fear I could share with Lindsay.

"Maybe we shouldn't talk about this now. You need to rest. The doctor says that you will be able to go home if the next check-in goes well. Your dad has gone home to get the car so that when you're discharged, he can take you home. In the meantime, my father has arranged for whatever healthcare that you need while you're here, and any aftercare."

My agitation increased. "I don't need—"

"This isn't just about you, Mira. I get it. You're angry at my father for being a jerk, but he is the baby's father. He has a right and a responsibility to make sure you two have the best care."

A few hours later, my doctor gave me the okay to go home. My only discharge instructions were to rest for the next week and not have intercourse, like that was going to be an issue. I'd have to call my student-teacher placement to let them know, but I hoped that rest just meant being in bed. I could take my courses and do my homework from there.

I was beyond relieved that the baby was fine and there didn't seem to be a serious concern about the pregnancy. At the same time, I was agitated at Brett's appearance earlier and Lindsay's seeming lack of concern about the fact that I slept with her father. In fact, her biggest concern seemed to be that I didn't want anything to do with him.

Then there was the fact that while Lindsay knew my secret, I still hadn't told my father. But for right now, I just wanted to get home and into my own bed to rest.

When it was time for my discharge, I was wheeled out in a wheelchair to my father's car. Lindsay had left earlier to go to class. She said she was willing to stay and help me, but because this whole situation was so odd, I encouraged her to go. I needed a respite from the drama.

As my father drove us back home, he was quiet, making me wonder if he was worried, reliving the past with my mother, or maybe he knew the secret as well.

"That Brett McKinnon is sure being generous," he finally said with a tone that sounded as if he suspected something was up.

I closed my eyes, wishing I didn't have to have this conversation now. I wished I didn't have to have it at all.

"Your friend Lindsay told me that she didn't make it to the cabin over Christmas, which means you were alone with her father. I know I'm a simple man, Miranda, but . . ."

I let out a sigh. "It's what you think."

My father glanced at me, his expression one of shock and maybe disappointment. He turned his eyes back to the road. "I'm not sure what to think about that. I guess I've always seen you as my little girl. I mean, I figured you dated, but Mr. McKinnon is so much older than you."

"I don't know how to explain it." I'd made an attempt with Lindsay, but hearing it come from my mouth, it hadn't made sense.

"Sexual desire is a powerful thing."

I closed my eyes, turning my head toward the window, not wanting to talk about my sex life with my father.

He was quiet for a moment. "If you can't be talking about the deed, Miranda, you shouldn't be doing it. There's a child involved now, and trying to avoid it isn't going to make it go away. If Mr. McKinnon is the father of your baby—"

"He is."

"Then he has responsibility to you and the baby."

I shook my head. "He has no responsibility to me. I might've been stupid to sleep with him, but I wasn't ignorant. I knew the potential ramifications. He might have responsibilities to the baby, but I don't want him involved."

My father glanced at me with a frown on his face. "Why not? Did he hurt you? Is he abusive? Lindsay doesn't give off the vibe of an abused child."

"He's not a physically abusive dad, but he is powerful and has money. Did Lindsay tell you about her mother? Brett got full custody. I don't want him taking my child from me."

"Do you think that's a possibility?"

In my mind, Brett was capable of anything. After all, he'd shown up on my doorstep drunk and called me a gold digging whore. "I don't know."

We drove on, my father's fingers flexing and then re-gripping the wheel as if he was deep in thought. Finally, he said, "I guess that means that you and he aren't in love. This was just a sexual relationship."

I nodded.

"Are you sure there is no possibility of you two being together? I only ask because he's quite intent on taking over your care, making sure that you have everything and anything you and the baby might need. He seemed genuine in his concern about you in the hospital. I just wonder if maybe he feels something for you."

I remembered Lindsay mentioning that she thought her father was half in love with me, but that was laughable. People don't call the people they love gold digging whores.

"Taking over could be part of him wanting to be in control and eventually get custody. I don't want him around, Dad."

My father's expression was pained. "If he's the father, Miranda, I don't know how we can keep him away."

We turned onto my street and pulled up to the house. A fancy SUV was parked in front.

I shot a look at my father as he pulled into the driveway. "Is he here?"

"Yes. He insisted on making sure everything in the house was prepared for you. He's giving you everything I wish I could give you. I didn't know how to say no."

I desperately wished my father were a stronger, more assertive man, but at the same time, I understood the difficult situation he was in. I reached over and took his hand. "We'll figure it out."

Just then, the door of my car opened and Brett was there. He reached into the car as if he were going to pick me up.

I batted his hands away. "What are you doing?"

"I'm going to carry you inside to your room."

"I can walk."

"You're supposed to rest. Did they let you walk out of the hospital?" His voice was gruff and irritated.

"The wheelchair is hospital policy. I can walk."

"I'm going to carry you into this house, Miranda. Are you really going to let your anger and pride keep you from doing what's best for this baby?"

"Let him take you inside, Miranda," my father said, making me feel betrayed.

Brett reached in, picking me up.

I put my arms around his shoulders only to steady myself. "I really hate you," I said into his ear so only he could hear.

His jaw tightened. His eyes remained forward as he carried me up the walk. "I know." He carried me into the house and to my room.

As soon as he set me on my bed, I pushed him away, scrambling to the middle of the bed and away from him. "You can go now."

He stood beside my bed. For a moment, he just watched me. "Look, Miranda, I know you're pissed off at me, and I don't blame you. My behavior toward you has been beyond vile. It's knowing that that keeps me from being angry that you were going to let me live my life never knowing that I had a child."

I glared up at him. "You can't have it both ways, Brett. You can't tell me to, and I quote, *stay the fuck away*, unquote, and know about the baby."

His hands settled on his hips and he gave a curt nod. "I know. Like

I said, I understand. But now I do know about the baby, and that means you and I are connected from now on."

Tears stung my eyes as I rested my hands over my belly. "I won't let you take my baby from me."

He frowned. "I don't want to take the baby from you. Why would you think that?"

"That's what you did to Lindsay's mom."

He gave me an exasperated eye roll. "Janine didn't give a fuck about Lindsay. The only reason she fought for custody was to get at me. To get more money from me."

"You called me a gold digger."

His expression turned pained. "I don't believe that. I don't want to take the baby from you, but neither will I let you keep this baby from me." He let out a long sigh. "We don't have to figure this all out now. You get some rest. Do you need anything? Water? Something to eat?"

The only thing I needed was for Brett to be gone. I scooted down on my bed, lying on it and turning away from him. "I just want to rest."

He didn't say anything, but the silence told me he hadn't left yet. What was he doing? What was he thinking? Finally, the floorboards creaked, signaling his exit from my room.

His words came back to me. *You and I are connected from now on.* How was I going to raise my child to respect their father when I hated Brett's guts?

21

Brett

Janine used to look at me with the same loathing that Miranda did, but it hadn't bothered me. But Miranda's hatred of me was difficult to swallow because I knew it was my fault. I was angry that she hadn't told me about the baby, that she hadn't planned to, but I understood the reasons and couldn't blame her for them.

As I exited the room and headed up the hallway to the kitchen where I heard Peter, I realized I hadn't apologized for my behavior. I had admitted it, but mostly, I had focused on my intent to be in her and the baby's lives. I stopped in the middle of the hallway, cursing myself for being so self-centered and selfish. I wanted to turn around and go back, to let her know how profusely sorry I was and how I wanted to make it up to her. But I couldn't face her looking at me with such revulsion. Especially since she was pale and tired. Once again, the best thing I could do for her would be to leave her alone. That didn't mean I wouldn't look out for her and the baby. Like it or not, I was in her life. The good news about that was perhaps over time, I'd be able to make it up to her for the terrible way I treated her. Maybe she'd even come around to stop hating me.

I continued up the hall and to the small kitchen.

"I'm making grilled cheese and tomato soup, an old staple for Miranda and me. It's probably not frou-frou enough for you." Peter stood at the stove, not bothering to look at me. I wondered how much of my heinous deeds Miranda had shared with her father.

"I didn't grow up rich. I ate a lot of grilled cheese growing up, and it's still one of my favorites." I understood that if I had any chance of changing Miranda's mind about me, I would likely need her father's help. Yes, I'd have to rebuild the relationship, build her trust, but if her father was on my side, that could be a help. She clearly loved her father.

"I'm going to take these to Miranda. I'll be right back." He picked up a tray with a sandwich and a cup of soup on it. I was about to tell him that she was sleeping, but it was possible she said she wanted to rest just to make me leave.

I waited in the kitchen, looking out the window toward the backyard. Like the rest of the house, it was tired, needing a little bit of cleanup and maintenance. My initial instinct was to pour money into this place, sprucing it up, fixing all the needed repairs. But I knew it wouldn't matter to Miranda or Peter. Spending money on them wasn't going to earn the trust and respect that I wanted.

When Peter returned, he put the other two sandwiches on plates and poured the remaining soup into mugs. He picked up his plate and mug and headed to the small table in the eat-in area of the kitchen.

I picked up the others and joined him. Peter wasn't much older than me, but as I sat there, I felt like a teenage boy talking to the father of the girl he was interested in.

"I don't have to ask you about your intentions with my daughter. I understand that you used her and abused her."

My sandwich stuck in the back of my throat. Had she told him the things I had said to her?

"I'll be honest, I'm a little surprised by Miranda's behavior. She's smart, and she's focused on her future. And while she is a woman, the idea that she would be with someone like you, her friend's father, is a little bit difficult to take. I want to blame you for that. But while Miranda might've been innocent, she's not so naïve. She gave you something, but I don't believe you respected it."

I was finally able to get the sandwich down and gave him a nod, letting him know that he was right.

"I'm not like you, Mr. McKinnon."

I wanted to ask him to call me Brett but understood that this was not a friendly conversation.

"I'm not aggressive or assertive. I'm a simple man, a weak man, really. I don't have your money or influence, but if you hurt my daughter, if you try to hurt that child of hers, I will go to my grave making you pay."

"I don't want to hurt Miranda. I know that doesn't mean much considering I already have. Your daughter is a special woman. And you're right, I took something I wanted without appreciating it. And in fact, I resented it."

His eyes shot up to mine. "What the hell does that mean?"

"When I'm around Miranda, she makes me feel things that I don't understand and don't want to feel. I was powerless against them, powerless against her, and I took it out on her. The truth is, Mr. Hathaway, I'm the one who is weak. And I don't mean weak in not being able to avoid the temptation, the lure of your daughter."

He scowled, and I realized that the words *lure* and *temptation* weren't the best words to use at this moment.

"I was weak, and I couldn't face up to or admit what was going on with me, my feelings. I lashed out at her for that, and it was wrong." I realized these were the things I needed to say to Miranda, not to her father. I hoped I would have a chance.

"I don't . . . I don't really care about you. I care about my daughter and the baby she's carrying."

"As you should."

"Miranda doesn't want you in her life. She doesn't want anything from you."

I opened my mouth to let him know that wouldn't be a possibility, but he continued.

"You seem to be a terrible man in terms of how you treat the women you sleep with, but having met your daughter, I can see that you are a good father. It appears that you want to be a father to this child. That is your right. And of course, you have a responsibility. If Miranda had her way, she would release you of all of that, but I recognize that you can provide for my daughter and her child in a way that she and I can't. And as I've already told you, I'm not so proud that I'm going to turn away what you can offer."

I nodded. "Whatever they need, I will provide it."

"But what I said earlier still stands. I don't know what your intentions are now. Maybe you just want to be in the child's life and you're doing your duty by Miranda, but if you hurt her, I will do whatever I can, and likely fail at it, but I will still try to make you pay."

"If I hurt them again, I'll deserve it." I thought for a moment whether I wanted to say more. I really should be talking to Miranda about all this, but who knew if she would ever listen? "I am not acting only out of duty or responsibility here." I wanted more. I realized that now. But I also understood that it was too late.

He studied me as if he was trying to see the truth of my words. I hoped to hell that I looked sincere. Finally, he said, "Just so long as we're clear."

"We're clear."

After eating with Peter, I didn't want to leave and at the same time knew that if I was ever going to earn Miranda's trust and respect, I was going to need to be patient. Peter would take good care of Miranda, and I knew that Lindsay would be stopping by after her classes. Although I wasn't happy that Miranda and the baby had a scare, the silver lining was that Lindsay was focused more on Miranda and less on Liam. I didn't like how Lindsay appeared to be giving up everything in her life for that young man.

When I left the Hathaway home, I drove to my office to check in on work. I also made arrangements to see Duncan later for drinks.

Not wanting to go out into the bar scene now, I invited him over to my place.

When he arrived, he studied me as if he was trying to gauge my mood. "I understand from Lindsay that everything's okay with Miranda and the baby."

"It appears so. She'll go back next week for a follow-up, but so far, no one seems overly concerned."

He patted me on the shoulder. "I'm glad to hear it. Now where's my beer?"

I got us each a beer and we went into the living room. I thought about turning on the TV, but I knew I needed to talk with Dunk to let him know how I needed to focus on Miranda and the baby for a while.

"Thank God you are so good at managing the gems because I need to dedicate time to making sure Miranda and the baby have everything they need."

"Of course." His brow furrowed as he took a sip of his beer. "What is the deal with you and Miranda?"

"She hates my guts. And with good reason."

"Is she going to try and keep you from the baby?"

I shook my head, knowing that she would prefer for me to be out of her and the baby's life, but she wasn't spiteful like Janine. She would put the child before her own needs, something Janine never did. "She'd prefer if I stayed out of the picture, but that's not going to happen."

"For all your faults, Brett, you are a good father. As Lindsay's friend, she must know that."

"Her father said something similar to me today."

Dunk let out a loud bark of a laugh. "Oh, my God, man, you got a talking to by her father like a teenage boy on a first date."

My cheeks heated with embarrassment. "I did. But I deserved it. I was really shitty to her, Dunk."

"I see that you feel guilty about that. Is the fact that she hates you a problem?"

"Yes, it's a big problem." I shook my head as all those crazy feelings in my chest swirled again. I didn't completely understand what they were, only that they represented my need to be with Miranda. "You know that saying about how little boys who like a girl pull on their pigtails?"

He nodded.

"I was like that. Only much worse. I couldn't deal with the things I was feeling, and I said the worst things possible. I'm ashamed of it, and because of it, I've ruined everything."

Dunk studied me again. "Are you saying you're in love with her?"

I shrugged. "I don't know if it's love. All I know is that I can't stop thinking about her. I can't stop wanting her. Is that love?"

Dunk shrugged. "How the hell do I know? But it sounds like something close to it. And if that's the case, I know you'll do what needs to be done to make things up to her, and maybe she'll forgive you."

"I don't know. I can't imagine her ever forgiving me." I couldn't get the image of her pale and stricken face from my mind. I was sure on my deathbed, that was the vision I'd leave this world with on my trip to hell.

"What did you say?"

"It was bad." So bad that I didn't want to repeat it, even to Dunk. Neither had I told Lindsay the heinous details. I'd only said that I had behaved badly, and it made sense that Miranda would hate me. I hated myself for it and hoped that over time, Miranda's hate for me would lessen.

"So, what's next?" Dunk took a swig of his beer.

"Next, I will do what I can to take care of Miranda and the baby."

"Maybe you should send her flowers and candy or something."

It was a thought except for the fact that there was no amount of flowers or chocolate in the world that could make up for what I had done. Still, maybe there were some small gestures that I could do that would help soften her to me.

I pulled my phone out, searching my list for the art gallery owner.

"What are you doing?"

"Instead of flowers and candy, I think I'm going to buy her a piece of art."

"Does she like art?"

"She likes anything that speaks to or creates history." It was a dumb idea, but since I had no good ones, this would have to do. I'd lusted for Miranda practically from the moment I bumped into her. But I'd fallen for her over long discussions of history, art, and life. I couldn't possibly know if she'd felt anything beyond lust for me, but if she had, the best way to rebuild her trust and respect was by connecting to her through her passions.

22

Miranda

I awoke the next morning ready to start my life as usual but then remembered my life wasn't usual anymore. I was supposed to be resting, which meant I wouldn't be doing student teaching.

It was probably just as well. My life was in turmoil. I wanted Brett out of my life, but I knew that wasn't a possibility. Not now that he knew about the baby. I needed to use this rest time to figure out what I was going to do to protect my rights.

Looking at my phone at the side of my bed, I saw it was nearly eight in the morning. Dad would have already left for work, which meant I had the house to myself. I got out of bed, stopping by the bathroom to wash my face and brush my teeth, and then made my way to the kitchen to fix myself tea and maybe some toast.

I nearly came out of my skin when I saw someone sitting at the kitchen table. Brett. What was he doing here?

He looked up at me, his eyes taking inventory of my body. It wasn't a sexual look. More like he was checking to make sure everything was all right.

I crossed my arms. "What are you doing here?"

"You know why I'm here."

I huffed out a breath. "I'm not an invalid. I don't need a babysitter."

He watched me for a moment and then let out a breath as he stood. "Can I make you some tea?"

"I don't want anything from you."

"I was about to make myself some eggs and toast. I can make some extra for you as well."

I gaped as I stared at him. "So now you're going to disrespect me by ignoring me?"

His jaw ticked, his eyes flashing with pain. "I'm not trying to disrespect you. You and I both know that I'm not going anywhere. I want to help you recover, and I want to make it up to you for how badly I treated you."

"You know that's not possible, right?" I couldn't see any scenario in which Brett was able to redeem himself in my eyes.

"I know, but that's not going to stop me from trying." His expression morphed into one of guilt and shame, and I wouldn't deny feeling happy to see it. To know that he understood just how vile he'd been. "I'm so sorry for all the things I said and did going all the way back to the cabin, and New Year's, and the other night. I've never met a woman like you. Someone who makes me feel things I don't understand."

His words tried to worm their way into my heart and soften it, but I locked it down tight. "Do you always verbally abuse things that you don't understand?"

He shrugged, looking helpless. "This is all new territory for me. And I get that you will never be able to forgive me—"

"It's not about forgiveness, Brett. I would never be able to trust you. How could I? By your own admission, you don't understand why you do what you do."

He gave a single curt nod. "I understand, but you and I are going to have to find a way to work together for the baby." He gave me another sad stare. "If it weren't for the baby, I would absolutely do as you want, and I would be out of your life. I don't want to hurt you. It guts me to see the way you look at me."

I scoffed. "You're trying to make me feel bad for you, for the man who called me a gold digging whore?"

He winced. "No. I deserve your anger and mistrust. I deserve the disgust and revulsion, the hate that you feel for me. I'm sorry for what I did to cause it. And I'm sorry that I can't give you what you really want, to disappear off the face of the earth. I'm going to be here, in your life, if only peripherally, to help raise the baby. And before that, I want to be at all the doctor's appointments. I want to be there for the birth. And I will do my best to stay out of your way as much as I can, but for right now, at least until your next doctor's appointment, I'm here. Especially when nobody else is with you."

I realized I wasn't going to be able to get rid of him, so I turned on my heel and went back to my room.

For the next two days, I woke and started my regular routine, only to discover Brett sitting in my kitchen working on his laptop. Each time, he offered to make me breakfast, and each time, I got mad and left him there.

I spent my days studying and researching my parental rights in my room, coming out only to make my own meals. In the evening, my father would come home and make dinner, which I would spend complaining to him about Brett babysitting me. My father told me he wasn't sure about Brett and at the same time, he supported Brett coming over and taking care of me during the day. Traitor.

Twice, Lindsay stopped by. I wanted to complain about her father to her but didn't and was relieved when she didn't bring it up either. Instead, I listened as she chatted about Liam and her concerns about the crowd he'd started hanging out with.

On the fourth morning, I was prepared to enter the kitchen and see Brett, so it was a surprise when he wasn't there. Finally, he got the message.

"Would you like me to make you some tea?"

I jumped as Brett's deep voice spoke from behind me. "God, you scared me to death." His hands reached out to my arms to steady me.

For a moment, I felt the warmth of his hands, but then remembering that I hated him, I pulled away. "I thought you got the hint and were gone."

He gave me a smirk. "You're the one who needs to get the hint that I'm sticking."

"Where were you?" All the other mornings, I had found him working in the kitchen.

"I was in the living room. I got you something."

My eyes narrowed at him in suspicion. "I don't want anything from you."

"I know. Come and look anyway."

He started to take my hand, but I tugged it away. Even so, I followed him to the living room. Resting against the back of the couch was an art piece that looked to have pages from a book and toys attached to it.

I wanted to ignore it, but as I got closer, I found myself intrigued by it. I walked over to study it more closely. "What is this?"

"It's a piece of art. What do you think?"

I examined the work, forming my impressions. I crossed my arms as I turned to look at Brett. "I think it speaks to how throughout history, society kept women in a certain lane, a box, but despite progress, those attitudes still exist."

He flashed a grin. "I knew you'd say that. I could totally hear you saying it when I first saw it."

My eyes narrowed. Was this a game? "You know, you and my father both continue this archaic attitude when you try to keep the weak little pregnant lady barefoot and at home."

That effectively removed the smirk from his face. "Nobody thinks you're weak or incapable. Even independent women like you, Miranda, need support and help sometimes."

I tried to shrug his comment away, hating that he was right. "Maybe so, but I don't need it from you. I don't want it from you." I headed back toward my room, looking back over my shoulder as I reached the hallway.

Brett stood facing the painting, running both hands through his hair as he blew out his breath. "You deserve this, McKinnon," he murmured to himself.

I almost felt sorry for him. But then I remembered that he was right that he deserved my anger. He had destroyed my faith in him. There was nothing that he could do to get it back.

EVEN KNOWING that I was never going to trust him again, Brett continued his routine of coming over and spending the day with me. In a few weak moments, I wondered if it meant that he felt something for me. But then I remembered that his visits had to do with the baby. After all, he'd said that if not for the baby, he'd be out of my life.

A week and a day from when I was discharged from the hospital, I had a doctor's appointment and there was no way that I could go to it without Brett. He'd been sticking to his word to stay out of my way and not trying to make conversation, so the ride over was quiet.

I felt good physically over the course of the week. There had been little to no cramping or spotting. Even so, as we approached the clinic, my nerves ratcheted up. Just because everything seemed okay didn't mean everything was okay.

We walked into the clinic. I checked in and then sat in the waiting room.

"Are you alright?" Brett asked, sitting next to me.

I turned to look at him, his steel gray eyes watching me with concern. At that moment, I desperately wanted to give in to the need for him. For his strength. But I couldn't. I wouldn't.

I turned my attention away from him. "Yes, I'm fine."

Several moments later, we were called back to the examining room. My doctor questioned me about how things had gone over the week, and to his credit, Brett didn't intervene to complain about how I wouldn't let him wait on me hand and foot.

"We'll do another ultrasound and see how things look today. Before we get started, do you have any questions?"

She looked from me and then to Brett.

"If everything looks good today, what will that mean for the pregnancy down the road?" Brett asked. I frowned at him, feeling like he had no right to ask questions about my pregnancy.

"Let's see what we have going on before we discuss that, shall we?"

I laid back on the table, lifting my shirt and pushing down my yoga pants as she squeezed a warm gel over my belly. She put the wand on my belly, moving it around. "Hmm."

Panic shot through me. What did "hmm" mean? My hand shot out toward Brett, grabbing his and squeezing. I looked at him, and as if he understood, he rose, folding my hand in both of his hands. He brought it up to his lips and kissed it. I hated that I needed him at this moment but couldn't deny that I appreciated that he understood.

"There's no change from last week—"

I let out a little gasp. I wasn't getting better.

The doctor looked at me. "That's not a bad thing. The good news is it's not getting any worse, and if it's going to resolve itself, it will take a few weeks. Everything about the baby looks fine. Would you like to hear the heartbeat?"

Brett's hand squeezed mine, causing me to look up at him. Emotion swam in his eyes as he looked at me hopefully. I will admit that for a moment, my pettiness wanted to refuse his being able to hear the heartbeat. But while I wanted to protect myself from him, I didn't want to become mean like him.

I turned my attention back to the doctor. "Yes. I'd like to hear the heartbeat."

She flipped a switch, moving the wand a little bit on my belly again until a fast-paced flickering sound echoed through the room. My breath stalled in my lungs and tears sprang to my eyes.

I was listening to my baby.

"It's amazing." Brett leaned over, giving me a kiss on my temple. "You're fucking amazing."

For a moment, and only for a moment, I basked in the perfectness of this moment. My baby was alive and well. And Brett, the man I had fallen for at the cabin, was here. While I would let myself savor this moment, I was never going to forget the other side of Brett.

23

Brett

I'd missed doctors' appointments when Janine was pregnant with Lindsay. I was a hotshot twenty-year-old kid who had taken his senior project in business and turned it into a half-million-dollar online nutritional company. But to do that, I had to work night and day as well as keep up on my studies. Janine supported my work, urging me on, telling me not to worry about her and the pregnancy. At the time, I thought it was love talking. I learned later that it was her desire for money.

Intellectually, I understood what I had missed by not being on those visits, but until this moment, until I saw the gray image on the screen and heard the heartbeat, I hadn't truly understood it. Here was my child, growing, thriving, and the emotion of it threatened to bring me to my knees. The only reason they hadn't given way was that I was holding Miranda's hand, doing my best to support and reassure her. I couldn't stop this well of emotion from bursting forth, from leaning over and kissing her temple in awe of her.

As the appointment finished up, hope bloomed that Miranda's attitude toward me was changed. Not that she had forgiven me or now trusted me, but perhaps she was open to the possibility. Open to the idea that I could earn her trust, earn her love.

But the minute we left the doctor's office, she put distance between us physically as well as emotionally.

"Now that we see that everything is okay, you don't have to babysit me anymore." She sat in the passenger seat, as close to the passenger side door as she could.

I gnashed my teeth in frustration. "I don't have cooties, Miranda." I snapped and then chastised myself for my temper. This was what got me in trouble in the first place.

My outburst earned me a slanted glare from her that told me I had just reminded her why she wanted me out of her life.

I should've kept my mouth shut and yet I still couldn't. "Are you punishing me? You want to get back at me?"

She pursed her lips at me. "I'm not punishing you, Brett. But what is it they say? Once bitten, twice shy? In your case, I'm what? Three or four times bitten?"

I turned my head, glancing out the driver's side window, hating that she was right. Hating that I continued to do the very thing I didn't want to do. Hating that I would never be able to make it right.

"What do you want from me, anyway?"

Respect. Trust. Love. Jesus fuck. I wanted her to look at me like she did in front of the fire at the cabin. Like the sun rose and set by me. Of course, I couldn't tell her that.

"I just want us to be able to get along for the baby's sake."

"I'm doing the best I can, Brett. It can take awhile for gold digging whores—"

"Fucking hell, Miranda. I know what I said. You don't have to keep reminding me. I don't believe that. I never did. I was just . . ." God, I couldn't tell her I was jealous. She'd never believe it.

"Just what?"

"Drunk."

She shook her head. I'd never felt so small, so insignificant in my life.

When I got us back to her place, she retreated to her room as usual and I went to my spot in the kitchen to check in at work. When her father arrived home, I gave him a quick update, knowing that Miranda would give him the details, and then headed home.

I thought about going to the gym but instead changed into running clothes and decided to run in the neighborhood. I wanted to pound away the anger and frustration and self-loathing that were threatening to consume me whole. But no matter how hard, fast, or long I ran, my demons kept pace.

Physically and emotionally exhausted, I returned home to find Lindsay and Dunk in my kitchen dancing to eighties tunes as they got out plates and opened a box of pizza.

"We were going to start without you," Dunk said, grabbing a third plate.

"What are you doing here?"

Lindsay looked up at me, her eyes shining with sympathy. "We knew today was the doctor's appointment and we wanted to find out how it went."

"It was fine." I made a beeline to my bedroom, stripping my clothes, climbing into the shower, and dunking my head under the spray. But just like the run hadn't warded off my demons, neither did the water wash them away.

When I returned to the kitchen, I'd hoped they'd given up and left, but of course they hadn't.

Dunk opened the oven and pulled out the box of pizza. "This time, we really will eat without you if you don't sit down now."

Two minutes later, we were all at the table with pizza and beer.

"Was everything really all right?" Lindsay asked again, sincerity shining in her eyes.

I took a long swig of my beer. "The doctor said there hadn't been much change in the last week but that it wasn't bad. It's not getting worse, and if the issues are going to resolve themselves, it will take a couple of weeks."

"Whew," Lindsay's expression brightened. "Did you get to see the baby or hear the heartbeat?"

The memory of it filled me with emotion. I reached out and took

Lindsay's hand. "I did, and it was amazing. As if I needed more guilt, it made me regret that I hadn't been a part of all that when your mother was pregnant with you."

"Luckily for you, I had no idea what was going on inside the womb." She gave my hand a squeeze, telling me that I was forgiven.

I thought back to the time at the cabin with Miranda and how we both marveled at the way Lindsay went through life. Living moment by moment often seemed directionless and flighty to me, but at the same time, she wasn't letting past bitterness or grievances hold her back. Here I was, her father, having slept with and knocked up her best friend, and she didn't hate or resent me for it. I needed more of whatever it was about her that could stay calm and accept life. God, how I wished Miranda would have more of that as well. Maybe then I'd have a chance to put things right.

"Is Miranda still giving you the cold shoulder? She didn't like the gift?" Dunk asked, shoving his pizza in his mouth.

"I think she liked the gift, but she still has no interest in me. There was a moment when she took my hand during the doctor's appointment, but it didn't mean anything. I think it was nerves or emotional overwhelm."

"You were there for her, right, Dad?" Lindsay asked.

"Yes." *And then in the car, I blew it by snapping at her*. "I think I'm just going to have to accept that whatever my future holds with Miranda, it's going to be a distant civil arrangement."

Dunk shrugged. "It's only been a week. In time, you'll be able to make her fall for you again."

"To be honest, I'm not sure if she ever actually fell for me."

"Oh, I'm certain of it," Lindsay said.

It was odd talking about my love life with my daughter in general. But when it involved her friend, it seemed even weirder. Probably inappropriate.

"How do you know so much?" Dunk asked. "Did Miranda say something?"

For a moment, I hoped Miranda had revealed something to Lindsay. Maybe I would learn that she was softening toward me, and I just needed to be patient and persistent.

She shook her head. "No. That's a topic we stay away from. I know because Miranda isn't the type of person to sleep with somebody if she doesn't like them."

I arched a brow at her. "It's not exactly true." But again, feeling weird, I didn't want to tell my daughter that I slept with Miranda the night we met.

"Okay, so maybe it was quick before you two hit the sack."

I winced. Really. This was not a discussion to have with my daughter.

"But you had drinks, right? You talked, right? And the same at the cabin. Face it, Dad, she saw something beyond all that surliness of yours."

If that were true, my situation was even more tragic. It meant that if I had behaved better in all areas, not just in how I treated Miranda but also by being open with my feelings and not trying to hide our situation from others, perhaps there could've been something between us.

"Well, unfortunately for me, I am full of surly." And cruelty too.

"So go to counseling." Lindsay said matter-of-factly. As if the solution was right there for the taking.

"I am what I am, Linds. I don't need counseling."

She gave a pointed stare, pursing her lips. "No, you don't need counseling. All you did was sleep with your daughter's friend and knock her up. And then because you still yearned for her, you told her to stay away. And then when you learned she was pregnant, you were so jealous that she was with another man that you got drunk and showed up at her house and called her a gold digger and a liar. No, you don't need counseling."

Every single word out of her mouth punched me in the chest. "How do you know about my being drunk at her house?" While I had shared a great deal with Lindsay, I hadn't gone into detail, particularly the part about being drunk and calling Miranda a gold-digging liar.

"It's all the talk of the neighborhood, Dad. People heard you. They were getting ready to call the cops."

Dunk tried to stifle a laugh by covering his mouth with a napkin. "I should've called that PR fixer after all."

I glared at him.

He shrugged. "She's not wrong. I mean, can you say for sure that you won't ever say anything you regret to her again because you have feelings that you don't like or don't understand?"

Considering I'd been trying so hard to not do that and yet still, just minutes after hearing our child's heartbeat, I had done just that, clearly, I couldn't say that for sure.

"I'm sure that's what she's thinking. She doesn't trust that you won't do it again." Lindsay dunked her pizza crust in ranch dressing.

I looked over at Lindsay. "How did you get so smart?"

"I took a psych class, but mostly, it's common sense. I mean, it doesn't take a rocket scientist to know that your revolving door of hookups is because you're afraid you'll meet someone like Mom again who will trample on your heart and try to take your money." Lindsay took a bite of her ranch covered pizza crust.

"She didn't trample my heart," I grumbled.

"She kicked at it a time or two, though," Dunk said.

"My temper is a part of me. My personality. My temperament."

Lindsay shrugged. "Well, if you're going to think like that, like it's not something you can change, then you should probably stop bothering trying to win her trust." Her gaze held mine. "Or maybe you could go to counseling and figure out how you can knock it off. It's just a matter of what you want and what you're willing to do."

Dunk looked over at her. "You are wise beyond your years, young grasshopper. But don't you find it weird about your dad and your friend?"

"It's hella weird. But this isn't about me. I can see that Miranda means something to Dad and Dad had meant something to Mira. Plus, they're having a baby. We're a family now, no matter what. Personally, I'd prefer to be a happy family, but whatever."

Dunk looked at me. "I have to say it again, Brett. I think Lindsay was switched at birth. There's no way you and Janine made a child as smart and insightful and forgiving and loving as Lindsay."

I might've agreed with him if I didn't know for sure she was my daughter because of the paternity test I took during her custody battle. That was another doozy Janine tried to lay on me. She tried to tell me she'd fucked someone else. She probably did, but Lindsay was my child.

That night after they left, I lay in bed wondering if Lindsay was right. Maybe what was wrong with me could be fixed. Then again, what if it couldn't? I was a forty-two-year-old man set in my ways.

It's just a matter of what you want and what you're willing to do. Lindsay's words came back to me.

The truth was, I was willing to do anything for Miranda and the baby. And because of that, tomorrow, I would be calling a therapist.

24

Miranda

I was supposed to be doing homework, but I found myself continually looking up at the wall with the art piece Brett had given me. I'd hung over my desk, and a part of me wondered why I still had it, much less hung in a place where I could easily see it. I told myself it was because the artwork was lovely and compelling, too much so to get rid of it simply because I didn't like the man who gave it to me.

But I couldn't look at it and not think about Brett. He'd said he'd known exactly how I would've responded to it and that was part of the reason he bought it for me. What did that mean?

I shook my head and returned my gaze to my computer sitting in my lap as I studied on my bed. It didn't matter what the gift meant. It didn't change anything. The way Brett snapped at me in the car ride back from the doctor's office was a reminder that he was too easily triggered into lashing out. Did he really think buying me art and holding my hand at the doctor's office yesterday would make up for the terrible things he'd said?

My gaze lifted again to the picture.

You're fucking amazing.

Brett's words and the kiss on my forehead came back to me. Somewhere deep inside, I wondered if it did mean something.

But why the hell did I still care? How could there be a piece of me that still cared for him? It made no sense. The only explanation was that all the time he was spending with me recently, especially his understanding how nervous I was at the doctor's office, had somehow softened me. I would have to do better to guard against it because I couldn't allow myself to be in a position where he could shatter me again.

For the umpteenth time, I pulled my attention back to my homework. I'd been able to keep up on my studies during my medical rest period, and next week, I'd be able to resume my student teaching. I was back on track to get my degree, and hopefully, a job that would allow me to be financially secure without Brett.

I was just finishing up a video when there was a knock on the front door. I closed my eyes and hoped to God that it wasn't Brett. When would the guy get a hint and stop showing up? I didn't need help anymore.

I slid off my bed and headed to the front door, yanking it open, ready to tell Brett to go home. The words stalled in the back of my throat as I took in who was standing on the doorstep.

"Loretta?"

My former stepmother worked her face into concern. "I just heard, Miranda. My goodness, you're the last person I ever thought would accidentally get pregnant. You were always so responsible. But no worries. I'm here to help you."

My eyes narrowed. Loretta didn't have an empathetic bone in her body. She had to be here for some other reason. "How did you know?"

"It's all the buzz of the neighborhood, including how that beast of a baby daddy treated you." She still had friends in the neighborhood? That was news to me.

She stepped forward, and I moved out of the way, knowing that she would've walked into me if I didn't.

She stood at the entryway, taking in the house. "I see not much has changed. Your father was never one for housekeeping, was he?" She smiled, and like her concern, it was fake.

"Dad's not here."

"I figured as much. But I'm here for you. A baby." She clapped her hands together and smiled. "This is exciting. I mean, I know it wasn't planned, but still. Now that I'm here to help, everything's going to be okay."

"Does Dad know you're here?" I was still standing with the door open, hoping she would turn around and leave. She made her way through the living room toward the kitchen. With a sigh, I shut the door and followed her.

"As I said, I'm here for you."

"For how long? I mean, won't your husband miss you?" The rumor was that she had been through two husbands in the years since she had left my father.

She was opening the cabinet doors and the refrigerator. What was she looking for?

"Oh, no. I'm free as a bird now. Why do husbands become such a disappointment when you marry them? You're lucky that you know the type of man you're dealing with. It's just unfortunate that you can't fully get rid of him now that you're having his baby."

I pressed my hand over my belly, not liking her talking about my baby. Or knowing my business.

She stopped her rummaging and turned her attention to me. "I have to say that I am shocked, simply shocked, at who your baby's father is. I have to admit, Miranda, I didn't think you had it in you to attract a man like Brett McKinnon." She said it like it was a compliment, but it was actually an insult.

I had an epiphany. She wasn't here to help me. She was here to get access to Brett. She might talk about him like he was a jerk, but I knew Loretta. She saw dollar signs in my situation.

"It's very sweet of you, Loretta, to stop your life to come help me, but I assure you, I'm fine." I don't know why I thought that would make her leave, but I had to try something.

"You definitely need my help. First of all, someone needs to grocery shop. You have a baby growing inside you. The heir to the McKinnon fortune."

And there it was. She was after money.

"Lindsay is the heir."

"And so is that little baby growing inside you. And imagine if it's a boy. Men love to give everything to their little boys."

It was clear she was focused on Brett's money, but if all his money went to my baby, what was in it for her?

"And of course, I can help you make sure that he pays you his fair share. In fact, I don't know why you're still in this hovel. You would think a man like Brett McKinnon would put you in a nice home, have servants taking care of you night and day."

"This is my home." I couldn't hide the offense I felt at her calling this house a hovel. It wasn't fancy, and in fact it needed work, but it wasn't a hovel.

She gave me a sympathetic stare. "I don't mean to insult your home, Miranda. I know you love this place, but that's because it's all you've known. Of course, you're going to love it. But now you have the opportunity for nicer things. And I'm going to help you get that."

She walked over to me, setting her hands on my shoulders. I wanted to shirk them away, but I also didn't trust her to not do something terrible if I offended her.

"He might try to say that the baby isn't his, so we're going to have to have a DNA test. Are you sure the baby is his?"

There was no doubt in my mind that her question had nothing to do with wanting to help me and everything to do with gathering as much information as she could to figure out how she could use it to her benefit.

"I'm sorry, Loretta, but this is really between me and Brett."

Her eyes flashed with heat. In a nanosecond, it was gone, but not before I had seen it.

"Well, if it's between you and him, then I guess that answers that question. Now, I'm going to order some groceries and have them delivered. And I'll have somebody come by to clean the house." She started back toward the front door.

"That's not necessary," I said as I followed her.

She waved her hand as if she were flicking away my comment. "You have a baby to think about now, Miranda. I'll be in touch." She opened the door, and I wanted to tell her again not to bother, but then I didn't want to do anything that would stop her momentum of leaving. When she finally stepped outside and shut the door behind her, I sank down onto the couch, blowing out a breath. This wasn't good.

I should do something but was at a loss for what that something should be, except to hope that she would never come back. Thank goodness my father wasn't here. Thinking of my father had me checking my watch. Noting the time, I decided I would go make dinner since he'd be home soon.

As I cooked spaghetti, I tried to ignore the fact that I was hoping it was as good as Brett's and instead focused on what to tell my dad about Loretta's visit. Losing her hadn't been like losing my mom for him. But that didn't mean she hadn't broken a part of him. She made him feel duped and stupid, and it continued to affect his confidence.

By the time he got home and we sat down to eat, I was still at a loss for what to say and ultimately didn't say anything. After dinner, we hung out watching TV, and then I went back to finish my studies.

At nearly nine o'clock, I was thinking of getting ready for bed when my phone pinged with a message. I checked my phone. Brett.

I started to set my phone down to ignore it but found myself unable to do so. I was one of those people who had to respond to everything whether it was a text, a voicemail, or a phone ringing. I remembered Loretta and her saying she was going to make sure he paid his fair share. God. Had she gone to visit him?

I poked the button to open the text.

How are you today?

That little part of me that hoped he really cared tried to rise up, but I pushed it down. What he was really asking about was the baby.

Fine. Hopefully, my one-word answer would give him a clue that I didn't want to converse with him.

I'm glad to hear it. I'm fine too.

I couldn't help it. My lips twitched upward at his text. He was ignoring my terseness, just like he had when he was babysitting me. But I wouldn't let it sway my feelings. I set my phone down and turned off my computer.

A few moments later, my phone pinged again. With an exasperated groan, I picked it up to read the text.

Do you still hate me?

Hate was a strong word. I couldn't say for sure that I hated him. But I definitely hated things he did.

Yes.

I waited for a moment, and when I decided he was done texting and started to put my phone down, it pinged again.

Goodnight, Miranda.

I studied the text, wondering what he was up to? Maybe he wasn't up to anything. It was probably that stupid part of me still longing for the sweet Brett I had met at the cabin.

I tossed the phone on my bed and went to do my nightly routine. I told my dad goodnight and climbed into bed.

It wasn't unusual for Brett to appear in my dreams. After Christmas, those dreams were usually erotic. But after New Year's, and especially after the night he'd been drunk on my doorstep, he'd showed up in nightmares. Tonight should have been no different, considering the way he'd been upset with me in the car. So it was a surprise when he took my hand and brought it to his lips.

That's not going to stop me from trying, he'd said when I told him he couldn't do anything that would make up for his behavior. He repeated it in my dream as he guided me to the fire at the cabin.

"No. I won't do this again." I tried to tug away. Tried to get out of the dream. Back to reality.

"Are you trying to punish me?"

I wasn't, was I? No. He said terrible things to me. Even if I was punishing him, he'd deserve it.

"No, but I don't trust you."

"I know. But you and I are connected from now on." He tugged me close again, and all the warmth and caring and desire from the cabin swarmed through me. I was helpless against it, melting into him. His lips covered mine and I groaned at his taste. Oh, how I'd missed that. Why did he have to be such a jerk?

But this wasn't the real world. This was my dream, and there, he could be the man I wanted. Sweet. Sexy. Mine.

So I gave into it. I didn't resist as our clothes disappeared and he laid me in front of the fireplace. I pulled him to me, opened for him, taking him in.

You and I are connected from now on.

Tears came to my eyes as I realized that the baby wasn't our only source of connection. Despite it all, he was a part of me. No matter what, a part of him would always be with me.

25

Brett

Trying to wear Miranda's defenses down probably wasn't the best game plan, but it was the only one I had. Her answer to the question of whether she still hated me didn't help my confidence in the scheme.

The truth of the matter was that I didn't know what the hell I was doing. I'd always had good luck with women. I'd had good luck with Miranda the night I ran into her just before Christmas. But whereas other women I'd been with were happy with just sex, or in the case of Janine, hoping for fortune, Miranda didn't care about either of those.

I'd like to put all the blame for the demise of our marriage on Janine, but I had said some pretty heinous things to her too. The difference was she didn't give a shit as long as I was forking over the money. The marriage ended because I wanted it to, not because I was an asshole.

During our marriage, I grew to despair that for the rest of my life, I was going to be miserable. The only time I saw glimpses of contentment was in business, and I had happiness with Lindsay. Still, there had to be more to life than being married to a woman who didn't give a shit about me. If I went broke, she'd have left in a second.

When I finally ended the marriage, for a short time, I wondered if I could find love. Not the transactional kind I had with Janine, but the real thing. The type of love poets wrote about. It didn't take long for me to come to the realization that true love didn't exist in reality. Every woman I met saw dollar signs when they looked at me, and so I decided that love wasn't going to be in my future.

It wasn't just ironic that I had given up on the idea of love and then Miranda literally fell into my life. It was ironic that I would accuse her of being a gold digger when in fact, she had never looked at me as anything but me. She didn't see my money. She didn't see my connections. She saw me, the man. Maybe that was why I was so mean to her. Perhaps it wasn't just that I struggled to deal with the power she had over me, but also that she saw through me. Saw to the man I tried to keep hidden.

I recognized now that I was looking at a lifetime of regret and despair if I didn't get my shit together and earn Miranda's trust, and maybe her love. In some ways, I was grateful she was pregnant because if she wasn't, I would have no reason to be around her. Or more accurately, she'd have no reason to be around me. With the baby, I had an excuse to see her. This child was my chance to get everything right this time. The only question was whether Miranda would ever come to believe in my sincerity, come to trust me.

When I got up this morning, I researched and found a therapist and made an appointment to meet with them. To prove to Dunk that I wasn't shirking my responsibilities to him, I headed to the gym where we reviewed reports and our game plan for the next quarter. Then I headed downtown to my office, where I took care of my other business.

When I noted that sales of prenatal supplements and nutritional products were on the rise, I realized I could be supplying those to Miranda. Of course, we'd want to check with her doctor first, but I went ahead and ordered a few cases to give to her. She wouldn't like it. She'd tell me to leave her alone. But Miranda was smart. She'd put the baby first, so if the doctor okayed it, she would take them.

Later in the afternoon, Connie's voice rose outside my office. She appeared to be trying to keep someone away from my office. This particular person wasn't taking no for an answer.

There was a time I was curious about these people who tried to get past Connie. Sometimes, I would poke my head out to watch. The problem was, once they saw me, it was hard to make them leave. Connie, in particular, got pissed when I did that. So, instead of indulging my curiosity, I stayed focused on my work. Ten minutes later, the commotion ended.

Another five minutes after that, Connie entered my office.

I smirked. "Did the intruder leave all in one piece?"

She looked at me like I was a petulant child. "I don't much like hearing things about you from gossip. It's one thing if it's not true but something totally different if it is."

I arched a brow. "I don't know what you're talking about." Even as I said it, though, I imagined she'd heard about the pregnancy. All of a sudden, I wondered if it was Miranda whom she had ousted.

I stood up. "Who was that?"

"It was a woman claiming to be the stepmother of the woman she claims you, and I quote, *knocked up*."

I frowned as I sank back down into my chair. Why would Miranda's stepmom be visiting me?

Connie pulled out her phone, scrolling through it and then handing it to me. "Is this the woman you've knocked up?"

I stared down at Lindsay's social media profile that had her and Miranda grinning like two best friends. It occurred to me that if I were on social media, I would have known Miranda's name and what she looked like. That would have saved me a great deal of angst. Granted, I couldn't resist her when I did know who she was, but I felt chances were good that I wouldn't have seduced her that first night outside the paper shop if I'd known who she was. And yet, I couldn't help but be grateful that I didn't know her. As fucked up as everything was, the hope she gave me for something fuller in life was worth it.

I handed the phone back to her. "Yes." It really wasn't her business, except for the fact that she couldn't do her job if I kept important things from her.

She sniffed, glaring at me in annoyance. "That woman, not the one today but the one in the picture, was here."

"Just now?" Fucking hell.

"No. It was several weeks ago."

"And you didn't send her in?" My head was reeling. Miranda had been here? Why?

"She didn't have an appointment."

"Did she say who she was?"

"If you mean did she tell me that you knocked her up? No. She told me she needed to see you and I told her that was impossible. Besides, you weren't here. She left without giving me a name."

My gut burned until I thought I might be sick. Had she come here to tell me about the baby? This news made what I did at her house the other night all the worse. I felt justified in my anger if she'd planned to never tell me about the baby. It was the way I'd gone about it that was wrong. But now, it was possible that she had planned to tell me but hadn't been able to see me.

I rose from my desk and grabbed my coat. "And what about the stepmother? What did she want?"

Connie had an expression on her face that suggested she thought the stepmother was no good. I had a sinking feeling she'd given Miranda a similar expression. "We didn't get that far. She did say something about making you pay, but it's not like you haven't heard that before."

She wasn't wrong. Janine had said it plenty of times. And before I figured out how to read women when looking for a no-strings-attached hookup, a few had hunted me down, angry at my dumping them and threatening to make me pay.

I wasn't worried about the stepmom. My concern was that Miranda had come to visit me. I left my office and sped like a demon over to Miranda's house. When I banged on the door, I realized I needed to take a calming breath. I didn't need her thinking that I was showing up as Mr. Hyde again.

She opened the door, and her expression reminded me of Lindsay in the height of her teenage years, her hand on her hip and a large eye roll. "Why are you here?"

"Did you try to see me at my office?"

She blinked, her expression immediately changing to suspicion. "Why?"

Annoyance took root, but I did my best to rein it in. "Why do you have to fight me on every little thing? It's just a question."

She blew out a breath. "Yes."

"Was it to tell me about the baby?"

She glanced out the door, and I turned to where she was looking. A neighbor who was walking from their car to the house was looking over in our direction.

She stood back, opening the door. "I don't need any more gossip about me from the neighborhood."

Inwardly thanking the neighbor, I entered the house. It appeared that she intended for us to stay in the entryway, but I made my way to the living room, taking a seat on the couch.

With weary eyes, she followed me but remained standing with her arms crossed.

"Were you there to tell me about the baby? I asked again.

"Yes. But your secretary wouldn't let me see you. She told me you weren't there, but I know you were."

I frowned because Connie told me I hadn't been there either. "Didn't you leave your name or a message?"

"She threatened to call security if I didn't leave. She told me if I wanted to join the gym, I should do that, but not to bother an important person like Brett McKinnon. She looked at me like I was a fat slob, and how dare me to try to see you?"

I closed my eyes, rethinking the benefit of having Connie as my admin.

I stood and walked toward Miranda, but as I got close, she put her arms out in front of her and stepped back to block me.

"I'm sorry, Miranda. I had no idea that you came by."

"I guess you should give your secretary a raise since she's able to keep people away, even when you're there."

I shrugged, not sure how to explain the situation. "It's quite possible I wasn't there. I divide my time between two businesses."

She crossed her arms again. "I saw Lindsay go up and waited. After fifteen minutes, she didn't leave. That tells me you were there."

I shook my head. "Not necessarily. I often arrive at my office to find Lindsay waiting for me. But that's not really the point. My admin might've been rude—"

She arched a brow. "Might've?"

I huffed out a breath to keep from snapping. "Let's say that she was. But I wasn't. If I'd known that you were there, I would've seen you."

She shook her head, her expression telling me she didn't believe me. "You wouldn't. The last time I saw you before then, you told me to stay the fuck away from you."

For a moment, I didn't say anything because what could I say? "I immediately regretted that not just because it was hurtful, but because it wasn't true." I looked down in shame and disgust with myself. I finally met her gaze again. "But you had no way of knowing that, so I understand that you don't believe me." I took a chance, reaching my hand out, wanting to run my finger down her cheek.

She tilted her head away, wrapping her fingers around my wrist to keep me from touching her. I tugged my hand enough that I could slide it out from her fingers and instead clasped them just like I had at the doctor's appointment.

She stared up at me with wary eyes. "What are you doing?"

I watched her, willing her to see that I wasn't a monster even though I knew it still resided in me. "Do you still hate me?"

Tears swam in her eyes, and while I didn't want to see her cry, it gave me hope that maybe she was changing her mind even though she didn't want to. "Yes." Her lips quivered when she spoke.

"Someday, I hope you won't." I brought her hand to my lips, giving it a kiss, all the while wishing I could hold her and kiss her more thoroughly. But I still didn't have the right. Then I left.

As I drove home, I realized I had forgotten to ask about her stepmom. I decided it wasn't important. If the woman tried to approach me again, then I would figure out what to do about it. Instead, I focused on the news that Miranda had tried to see me. I replayed my visit with her, wondering if I was being a fool to think that while her words and wariness told me to stay away, there were glimpses that she would be able to forgive me. Maybe I needed to lay it all out on the line. Maybe I needed to tell her that what I wanted was her in my life. Her and the baby.

But all I could imagine that she would do would be to laugh at me or tell me in no uncertain terms that she would never, ever stop hating me. I wasn't ready to hear that. I couldn't give up on having something that I had long ago given up thinking I could ever have.

26

Miranda

When Brett left, I cursed myself and how precariously close I came to giving in to his touch. When I looked into his eyes and really studied them, they appeared sincere. It was almost as if he wanted more from me. What else could I read into the kiss he gave my hand? But for all I knew, my silly schoolgirl dreams were clouding the situation. And whether he wanted something more from me or not, there was the fact that he had the potential to be cruel. One minute, he would desperately want me, and then the next, he would be pushing me away, calling me names, acting as if I'd done something wrong simply by existing. I didn't want to go through that anymore. When I went to bed that night, I vowed I wouldn't get caught up again.

But my willpower continued to be tested each time Brett visited me. Sometimes, he'd come in the evenings, and sometimes, during the day when he knew I'd be home doing my online classes. I finally gave up asking him why he was there, but when he would leave, he'd ask if I still hated him and I croaked out the word "Yes" to protect myself. Each time I said it, his eyes flashed with pain, but he would say that someday, he hoped that my feelings would change.

I wanted to come right out and ask his intentions but didn't want to be humiliated to discover all his effort was simply so that we could get along when the baby came. That he didn't actually feel anything for me.

A few weeks later was the beginning of April, and while spring had officially started, it wasn't until now that it felt like winter had broken. My dad was out at the bar with his friends when Brett showed up carrying a bag from a toy store.

I opened the door to him, knowing it would be fruitless to try and keep him away. "Are you buying presents for the baby already?" I hadn't begun to think about creating a nursery for the baby. Luckily, there was an extra bedroom in the house, although I needed to clean it from its use as a storage room.

He shook his head. "Nope. This is for you." He handed me the bag as he shrugged off his coat and hung it on one of the pegs in the hall.

I used the handles to pull the bag open wider and looked in. "*Trivial Pursuit*?"

"I thought maybe for once you can beat me up in a game instead of with your words."

Inwardly, I winced because I was frequently snarky and curt with him, but that was only to help keep my distance, or more accurately, hoping that by behaving that way, he'd stay away.

Resolved that he was going to spend the evening with me, I carried the game into the living room. As he set it up, I went to the kitchen and got him a beer and myself a glass of milk.

"You really are a glutton for punishment. You know that?" I set his beer in front of him on the coffee table.

He flashed me a grin that I felt all the way to the bottom of my heart. "I know, but at least tonight, it will be related to your kicking my ass with trivia."

He was right. I did kick his ass. But that wasn't what made me enjoy it. It wasn't what brought up the concern that I was losing the battle to keep him at a distance. What affected me were his responses to my answers. I not only got the questions right, but I was often able to elaborate on them, explain the greater context of the topic. When I did, he looked at me in awe.

I finally beat him six pies to four. He laughed as he shook his head. "Well, at least I'm improving. I got four pies this time."

I started to put the game away, wishing that he would leave while at the same time hoping he didn't. That was how I knew I was in trouble.

"What did you ever do with the piece of art that I got you?" He took the final drink of his beer.

"It's hanging in my room."

He had a look of relief.

"Did you think that I threw it out?"

He gave me a shrug. "It crossed my mind. I hoped that maybe you sold it, though."

It never occurred to me that the artwork was worth something.

"Can I see it?"

"You don't believe me?"

"I believe you. I just want to see it again. I want to see it with you when you're not pissed off at me."

I wasn't pissed, and for a moment, I thought about what my answer was going to be tonight when he asked me if I still hated him. Being with him like this was making it harder and harder to hold onto my anger.

I led him to my room, thinking it was no big deal since he had been there before when I came home from the hospital. But as we entered my room and he stood next to me looking at the art piece on the wall, my room felt very small. He felt very close.

He backed up a bit, hitting the edge of my bed and sitting down. His hand clasped around mine and tugged, bringing me down to sit next to him. My heart ached with yearning while at the same time, warning bells clanged in my head.

"Do you like it?" he asked.

"You know I do. I wouldn't have kept it if I didn't like it so much."

He looked at me for a moment. "Meaning you liked it more than you hated me?"

I turned my attention back to the painting, not wanting to confirm his statement. He let out a sigh and turned his gaze back to the painting as well. For a moment, he just stared at it. "Have you shown it to Lindsay?"

"Yes. Sometimes, when she comes over to study, we work in here. She likes it too."

He gave a short nod. "She didn't go with me to the gallery the night I saw this. In fact, we haven't been to a gallery together in a long time."

I wondered what he was getting at. "Did something happen between you and Lindsay?"

"I don't think so. But she's back to being totally consumed by Liam." He looked at me again. "It feels almost obsessive. Do you think I'm overreacting?"

I see-sawed my head, not quite sure how to answer. As a parent, he was probably overly worried, but he wasn't wrong that Lindsay was spending more and more of her time around Liam.

"I think that's what happens when people are in love. Everything becomes about the other."

His head swiveled toward me again. "It does, doesn't it?" Something in his eyes told me that his words held more meaning. But I was too afraid to believe them. He couldn't possibly be saying that all this time that he spent with me was because he was in love with me. If that was the case, why not just say so? So perhaps he was talking about the baby. There was definitely an all-consuming love where the baby was concerned.

"I'm just worried about her. There's something about Liam that strikes me as off," he said.

I hadn't seen Liam since New Year's Eve. He had always struck me as somebody who was trying to move and shake in the right circles. Someone who was striving for money and power. But I remembered a few times Lindsay saying things that suggested that Liam was getting involved with the wrong crowd. When I asked her to elaborate, she'd always wave the concern away. She told me she was reading too much into the situation and everything was fine. I started to tell Brett that but then considered that maybe he and I shouldn't be talking about Lindsay in the same way that Lindsay and I never talked about him.

"Lindsay is smart. If there's something off about him, she'll deal with it. But my guess is she won't appreciate our talking about her."

His brows rose, conceding my point. "Do you and Lindsay talk about me?"

"No."

He let out a long sigh. "It's probably because you don't want to tell her that you hate me. And because she doesn't want to hear it."

I didn't answer because that was the truth. Or at least it had been.

He continued to look up at the picture. "I didn't know what the hell I was doing when I became a father to Lindsay. I just knew I wanted to be good at it."

My heart clenched in my chest at the worry in his voice. "You are a good father."

"I don't know. You'd think by now, I'd have the hang of it, but I'm still not sure what to do." His gaze turned downward to my belly. "I don't want to fuck it up again."

I pressed my hand against his back, gently rubbing. "You haven't fucked anything up. Not with Lindsay, anyway."

He looked at me, his eyes filled with regret and pain. "I wonder how that can be true. I mean, I've never treated her like I've treated you. And yet, that part of me is inside me."

"I think it's normal. We all present differently to different people depending on the situation."

His gaze looked up at me. "I hate that sometimes, I present to you as a beast. Your Mr. Hyde."

I brought my hand back to my lap, looking down at it. "I don't much like it either."

He was silent for a moment. "I'm going to counseling."

I jerked my gaze back to him.

"I don't want to be Mr. Hyde. I want to be better."

Emotion welled inside me, although I couldn't quite determine why. He wasn't saying he wanted to be better for me, that he wanted a future with me beyond coparenting. And yet there it was, emotion blooming, so full that I couldn't stop myself from wrapping my arms around him in a hug.

His arms came around me, and he buried his face in my shoulder, at the base of my neck. For a moment, we just held each other, and then he peppered soft kisses along my neck and up along my jaw, and then his mouth was on mine. I nearly gave into it but finally caught myself pulling away.

"I've missed you, Miranda. I've missed how we were at the cabin."

Oh, how my heart ached to have that again as well. "But we're not at the cabin, Brett. And if you remember, at the time, we only allowed that to happen because it was a moment away from reality. But we're not there anymore."

"Fuck reality," he barked, and I flinched. "Fuck. I'm sorry. That wasn't toward you. It was just general frustration."

I understood what he was saying because I could feel the difference. He hadn't told me fuck off. He'd lashed out at the situation.

My lips twitched upward slightly. "Those pesky cravings for things you shouldn't have are getting to you again."

He settled his forehead against mine. "Why can't I have what I want?"

His words caught me off guard. He lifted his head, his gaze inventorying my face as his fingers traced my cheek. His thumb brushed across my lips. Desire along with yearning filled my chest.

"Why can't I have what I want?" His lips were on mine again, and I found myself helpless to answer his question. Why couldn't he have what he wanted? Why couldn't I?

He pulled me back on the bed with him. "Let me touch you. Let me make you feel good." His hand slid under my shirt, rubbing over my nipple, making it impossible for me to deny him. He tugged my shirt and bra up. "Miranda," he murmured as he wrapped his lips around my nipple.

I let out a sigh, giving myself over to him. It was wrong. I'd likely regret it, but right now, I wanted this. I wanted him.

He kissed and caressed me as my clothes came off. Soon, I was naked on the bed next to Brett, who'd taken his shirt off but nothing else. "Let me make you feel good," he said again. "Just feel."

I did as he asked, letting him do whatever he wanted as I lay on my bed enjoying it. "Brett," I sighed as he suckled my breast again.

"I'm here, baby." He trailed his lips down my body, stopping at my belly, kissing me there. His fingers slid between my thighs, rubbing over my clit.

My hips shot up as I gasped.

"You're so needy. I'm going to take care of you." He moved up my body, kissing me again as his fingers stroked through my folds. The combination of his licking and sucking my breasts as he teased my clit had me writhing with need.

"Come for me," he murmured against my nipple. He gently tugged on it with his teeth as his fingers swirled around my clit. Pleasure burst through, white-hot and so good.

I cried out, moving my hips with his fingers, seeking to prolong the pleasure as much as I could. *Why can't I have what I want?* The question swirled through my mind, seeking a solution that wouldn't put my heart at risk.

27

Brett

I hadn't come tonight expecting to kiss Miranda, much less touch her. I'd come to believe that it could never happen. And yet here I was, listening to her moans echoing in the bedroom, filling my heart with such hope.

As she came down from the high, I wanted to sink into her, not simply for the sexual release I was craving but to finally be a part of her. Like joining with her body would fill the emptiness I'd been feeling. But I knew I couldn't. Not tonight, anyway. I didn't want intercourse to impact her or the baby, even though the doctor had said everything was fine.

I leaned over to kiss her, trying not to read anything into the fact that her kiss felt stilted. I lifted my head to look at her, seeing regret in her eyes. My heart sank.

She gave me a wan smile. "I know that you're not finished yet, so maybe—"

"I wasn't planning to have sex with you. I don't want to do anything to hurt you or the baby."

She looked down toward my groin. It was impossible for her not to see my dick straining to be free.

"I guess I could help you out."

I had a moment of wanting to lash out at her for making it seem like getting me off would be such a chore. But I'd been practicing the suggestions my therapist had given me in noticing my feeling, taking a breath, and counting to five before speaking.

I rolled on my back, taking my breaths and counting.

"Are you mad? I could—"

"I'm not mad." Ultimately, I undid my pants, shoving them down until my dick sprang free. I wrapped my hand around it and stroked it. "It's all right. I can take care of it." For the life of me, I don't know why I did that. Maybe I was hoping that if she saw me, she'd want to touch me, not out of duty but out of desire.

Her eyes drifted down to where my hand still wrapped around my dick. Her eyes flared with heat, and for the first time, I thought one of my cockamamie plans was going to work. I stroked him again, letting out a groan as I did.

Miranda's gaze stayed on me, entranced at watching me stroke myself. Would I have rather had her mouth on me? Absolutely. I'd rather have any part of her on me. But I couldn't deny how sexy it was to have her watch me pleasure myself. So I gave in to it. I wanted to ask her what it did to her to watch me. Did it turn her on? I wondered if I could get her to talk dirty to me. But I was worried I would break the spell, and so I kept my mouth shut except for the heavy panting as I continued to stroke my cock and fondle my balls, turned on by her watching me.

I watched her watching me, and it wasn't long before my hand was pumping quickly and my cum shot out, landing on my stomach and chest. It felt good, and yet empty, too.

I excused myself, going to the bathroom naked to grab tissue to clean up. Only when I was heading back to her room did I consider the possibility that her father was home. Oh, well. He had to know I slept with his daughter considering she was having my baby.

When I reentered the room, Miranda was sitting on the edge of the bed wearing a robe. Disappointment filled me. I sat down next to her, pulling her to me.

"I'm sorry, Brett. I can't do this." She stood, walking away from me. Her room wasn't very big, but it seemed to me she was trying to get to the farthest space from me as she could. Was this two steps forward and one step back? Or had it been one step forward and two steps back?

I rose, grabbing my jeans, slipping them and my shirt on before I stood across the room looking at her. The time it took to get dressed gave me a moment to gather my thoughts so that when I spoke, my frustration didn't hurl out at her. "If you can't do this, then why did we just do it?"

"The things that attract us are still there, Brett. But I don't trust you. You scare me."

She could've stuck a knife in my chest and gutted my heart and it wouldn't have hurt as much as those words. "I scare you? I assure you, Miranda. I'm not a violent man."

"You don't need to be violent to hurt someone. I've been there, I've done that, and I don't want to do it again."

Goddammit. Why couldn't I do the thing or say the thing that would make her change her mind? Couldn't she see that I was trying? Couldn't she see that she meant something to me?

The words of my therapist came back. She was talking to me about communication and how nobody was a mind reader. "You need to tell her how you feel. It's the only way you can get what you want."

But standing here vulnerable in front of Miranda, who just told me that she was never going to trust me, I didn't have the courage to tell her what was in my heart. I felt certain it wouldn't matter if I did. It wouldn't change the past, and the past was why she was determined to keep me away. I couldn't ever remember feeling as dejected as I was at that moment.

I gave her a nod to let her know that I understood. "I'll go now." I headed out her bedroom door and down the hallway. I put my coat on and reached for the front door.

"Aren't you going to ask?"

I turned to see her standing at the entryway, her arms wrapped around her.

"I already know the answer and I can't bear to hear it again tonight."

Her eyes softened as she approached me. "I'm sorry, Brett."

"I am too."

I opened the door, stepping out.

"I don't hate you, Brett."

I stood on the porch feeling more pain than I ever had before. How was it that the words I'd been waiting to hear over all these weeks only filled me with more sadness?

"I'm glad." I headed to my car, and as I drove home, I replayed the night in my mind, wondering if I had done something different, had said something different, things would change. The pessimistic part of me said no.

I tried to think about how Lindsay might view it. She had a glass half full type of attitude. Lindsay would have seen the kiss as positive. Miranda's telling me she didn't hate me was positive. Did this mean there was hope? Maybe I needed to do more. Maybe not more kissing and touching, but more proving that I was devoted to her. Committed to her and the baby.

When I arrived home, I headed upstairs and down the hall to a bedroom right off my room. It was currently empty because I had no use for it, but the original purpose of the room was as a nursery. Maybe if I created space for her and the baby, coupled with the counseling, she would see the depth of my commitment.

The next day, I made calls to several contractors to get estimates on turning the bedroom into a nursery and then creating another space in the house just for Miranda. It could be an office or whatever she wanted.

I'd just finished making an appointment with the third contractor when my phone rang. The caller ID said the police, and as normal for any human being, my heart rate skyrocketed. Why were the police calling me?

"Hello?"

"*Is this Mr. Brett McKinnon?*" a gruff male voice came over the phone.

"It is."

"*Mr. McKinnon, I'm calling because we have your daughter, Lindsay McKinnon, down here at the station.*"

What the fuck? "What, why? Was she a victim of something?" God. If I lost her, I didn't know what I'd do. Immediately, all the wrong moves I'd made in raising her came to the surface.

"*Not exactly.*"

"What does that mean?" I wanted to reach through the phone and throttle this guy.

"*Your daughter was picked up with a group of young men we have arrested. We have determined that she is not liable for any criminal activity. But we need somebody to come get her to bring her home.*"

"Why? Is she incapacitated?"

"*Yes. We think she's taken something. She insists that she hasn't, and it's possible she was unaware she was consuming something, but we cannot be sure of that.*"

Holy hell. "I'm on my way."

I made it to the police station in record time, and the police were right that Lindsay wasn't quite right. I immediately took her to the hospital where I was told that she had been drinking and had ingested some sort of street drug I knew nothing about. Fortunately, they said she wasn't in any immediate danger and the effect would wear off in a few hours.

Three hours later, I had her in the car heading back to my place.

"Lindsay, what the hell—"

Her hand came up in a stop position next to me, even as she was still slumped against the passenger door. "I don't need a lecture, Dad."

"I just had to pick my daughter up at the police station. I think that automatically comes with a lecture. What the fuck are you doing?" She was so close to graduation. She had a job lined up. Was she really going to throw it away? "If this has anything to do with Liam, I will stop you from seeing him. That kid is bad news."

"It wasn't Liam's fault. He's as much a victim as I am. We were drugged. I promise, Dad, I didn't take it on purpose."

In my mind, this situation was bullshit, but I was so filled with rage that I couldn't trust myself not to say things that would hurt her in the same way I'd hurt Miranda.

I took her to my place and put her in her childhood room to let her sleep. Once the drugs and alcohol wore off, I would talk to her.

I headed downstairs to my office, sitting in my desk chair as I downed a couple of fingers of scotch. I wondered if this was the universe punishing me. I'd had it so good for so long. Maybe I had been a little too cavalier with women and my money. Maybe my daughter getting involved with people who could derail her future, and Miranda, the one woman I've ever loved, who couldn't look at me without disdain were my punishment for being a dick.

How could I keep on like this?

I had to keep on. Lindsay was my daughter. Miranda was my love carrying my child. I couldn't waste my time on pity. I had to suck it up and be a man.

28

Miranda

I didn't hear from him or Lindsay for a few days, and I thought that perhaps he'd finally gotten the message. When he'd left the night I'd let him touch me, he looked so defeated that I felt sure he had given up. I told myself that it was a good thing. But deep down, my heart ached. His giving up was not what I really wanted. What I really wanted was the sweet, kind, gentle man he was showing himself to be. And yet, I still couldn't fully trust him to control his darker side.

A few days later, I learned that Lindsay had been picked up by the police high on drugs and alcohol. I remembered Brett was so concerned that he wasn't a good father. I could only imagine this made it worse.

Lindsay minimized the situation. She chalked it up to not paying attention like she should to her surroundings.

"Someone put drugs in your drink, Linds. Maybe it's your friends, not your surroundings."

"It will be fine, Mira." While Lindsay made the whole thing to be no big deal, she did refocus on finishing school and ended things with Liam. I took that as a good sign. Brett must have too as he started showing up again. I had to hand it to Brett. The guy was persistent and patient.

He showed up wanting to play *Trivial Pursuit*. Another time, he came by during the day with a picnic basket, taking me to lunch in the park. Every other day, sometimes everyday, he showed up. While there were a few more stolen kisses, there was no more sex, and to be honest, that was frustrating because all of a sudden, my libido had cranked up two hundred percent.

Tonight, he took me to an art gallery. It was after hours, but he had been able to get us in, and we took our time as we checked out the exhibits. We reached an artist that I recognized had done the piece hanging in my bedroom.

When we stopped at a piece of art, we talked about it. Well, mostly, he'd ask a question and then I'd prattle on like a know-it-all. But he seemed to like that.

Afterward, he took me to dinner in a quiet, secluded restaurant where it felt like we were the only two people in the world. As the dinner ended, I realized that I was precariously close to losing my ability to keep from loving him.

He reached across the table, taking my hand. "Over the weekend, I need to go up to the cabin to check things out and get it ready for summer."

I sat across the table feeling warm and safe as I stared into his eyes.

"I was hoping you'd come with me."

I blinked, not expecting his invitation.

As if he expected me to retreat, he held my hand tighter. "We don't have to do anything, except perhaps you could beat me at *Trivial Pursuit*. And of course, there won't be peppermint liquor in the hot chocolate. But it could be nice. We haven't done a lot of talking about the baby."

I frowned. "This is about the baby?" Disappointment filled me. I thought he was making a move to tell me he loved me, but it was all about the baby.

"Is that wrong?" he asked.

This time, I did tug my hand back, telling myself I was such an idiot. "No, but we don't have to go out of town to do that. We could do it here."

He rose, moving his chair closer to me as he sat down facing me. One of his hands pushed the hair away from my face as his other hand rested on my forearm. "I know we could do it anywhere. But I want to do it there. I want to spend some time with you. Away from everything."

"What about Lindsay?"

"I told her I would take her up there after graduation. With things between her and Liam being over, finally, thank fuck, she's back to studying and recommitting to her future. That's her effort, not me making her do it."

I nodded, knowing it was true. She had been in touch with me a lot more. I'd hoped that she'd realize Liam wasn't good for her. At the same time, I knew the breakup was hard on her.

"So. Will you come?

I wanted to tell him no, but as I looked into his gray eyes, I couldn't form the word. "Okay."

His fingers brushed my cheek. "Are you doing this only for the baby?"

I was confused about why he was repeating my thoughts back to me.

I hesitated to answer, and he reached out, pressing a finger over my lips. "No, don't tell me. It's enough that you said yes. "

And that's how on Friday afternoon, a few days later, I was beside him in his SUV as we drove back out to the cabin. As we approached it, bittersweet feelings filled me. This place was where I had fallen in love for the first time. I mean really fallen in love. Not a little crush or infatuation. But it had gone so horribly wrong.

We entered the cabin, and I wondered why he needed to come. It felt fresh and ready for summer fun.

"I had the guy who keeps up on the place come earlier in the week to make sure we had food, and everything was aired out. But I do need to check on a few things before we settle in."

I nodded. "I can make dinner if you'd like."

He shook his head. "I'm making dinner. This is a respite for you."

"Well, I won't argue with that."

I don't know if it was being at the cabin or maybe the fact that over the last few weeks, I was softening to him, but as the evening wore on, the animosity and the desire to keep Brett away were practically nonexistent. Only the fear still remained. But even that was dissipating.

After dinner, he made hot chocolate, and he sat on the couch while I lay in front of the fire enjoying the warmth. My hands rested on my belly, where I noted that it was finally starting to protrude. Movement under my hand caught my attention. Was that my stomach growling? It happened again, and I realized that it was the baby.

"Oh, my God."

Brett was off the couch and by my side in an instant. "Is something wrong? Jesus fuck, where's my phone? I'll call 9-1-1."

I let out a giddy laugh as I grabbed his hand. "No, everything's fine. It's the baby. I think I can feel the baby." I pressed his hand over my belly, and for long moments, we waited. I began to wonder if I'd imagined it. But then it was there again.

Brett's eyes shot to mine, filling with tears. "Holy shit." He leaned over, his lips pressing to mine in a kiss that was so intense, so emotional that I had no other choice but to respond.

My hormones fired up hot and needy. I tugged him over me, wanting to immerse myself in him. "I want you."

He groaned as his hands roamed. "I'll take care of you."

"No. I want you in me."

He stopped touching, forcing a whimper from me. "What about the baby? About your condition?"

"It's fine. The doctor said sex was okay."

His fingers brushed my cheeks. "Are you sure, Miranda? I don't want to hurt you."

I pushed him back, straddling him. "You're the one who will be hurt if I don't feel you in me."

He laughed. "Well, alright, then."

With love and laughter, we undressed. Once naked, the mood turned slow and seductive. Brett's lips kissed me everywhere, followed by the caress of his fingers until all my nerves were humming with need.

"Brett." I reached for him.

"I'm here." He maneuvered me over him again. "Take what you need, Miranda. Whatever you want, take it from me."

I ran my hand down his chest, desperately wanting to tell him I wanted his love. I was certain he cared for me, but love? I couldn't be sure. This could just be friends with benefits. Or maybe coparents with benefits.

Deep down, I had a niggling fear that I would be hurt again, but at this moment, rising over him to take him inside me, there was only him, only me, only us.

"God, Miranda." He levered up as I sank over him. His lips wrapped around my nipple and sucked. I felt it all the way to my center.

I rocked over him, holding his shoulders as I slowly, then with more speed, more need, moved.

"Ah. So fucking good." He lay back, his hands rubbing my thighs as he moved underneath me.

I rested my hands on his chest as my body ached, reaching for the pinnacle.

"That's right, baby. Ride me. Come on my cock."

Pleasure hit me hard, rocketing through me. "Brett." I never wanted to stop. Never wanted this moment to end.

"Yes." He bucked up, filling me with his essence. Together, we moved, drawing out the pleasure as long as we could.

I collapsed over him, catching my breath. His arms wrapped around me, holding me. I rested my head on his chest, feeling the steady beat of his heart. I fell asleep wishing it beat only for me.

29

Brett

I was on the verge of having everything I could ever want. For so long, I thought that had been money and raising Lindsay, and while it added to the quality of my life, having love, having a child conceived of love and raised in love, that was the pinnacle.

Holding Miranda, having her say she wanted me, it felt like I had finally broken through her walls. She had opened to me. Not just physically, but fully. Not that she had said the words, but I swore I could feel it in her touch and the way she looked at me.

For the first time in a long time, I could see my life laid out in front of me. With graduation only five weeks away, I planned to ask Miranda to move in with me once she had her college degree. The work on the rooms in my house would be done by then.

Once she was in my home and saw that I was a changed man, maybe not perfect, but definitely better, then I would ask her to marry me. I hoped that would happen before the baby came in September, but if not, that would be okay as long as she was with me. Along with learning to understand and deal with my anger, I'd learned patience.

Feeling secure that Miranda was open to the possibility of us, I was able to refocus on business. Luckily for me, Dunk was a whiz in business and the gyms were doing fine. The summer and the kids' programs were going to be a big hit.

In my other company, things were also moving along well. The continued growing trend toward health and wellness, particularly with natural and organic foods, was a real boon to my business.

Yes, life was good.

Tonight, Lindsay and Miranda were going to be studying together and I was grateful that Lindsay was spending more time with Miranda. I had to hand it to her for how well she accepted the fact that her father loved her best friend. But more than that, I was grateful that Miranda was her friend because Lindsay was struggling over the breakup with Liam. She swore to me that it was over, but I worried that if he showed up on our doorstep groveling, she would forgive him.

I knew she was in contact with his brother, Oliver. I didn't love that idea, but my sense was that he was suffering from his brother's behavior too, and I couldn't find a good reason to try and forbid Lindsay from seeing him.

Since Lindsay and Miranda were busy, I made arrangements to meet Dunk at a pub we both enjoyed. I arrived a little early, and as I sat down with my drink, I got a text from Dunk saying he was running a few minutes late.

I pulled out my phone to see if I had any messages from Miranda. Not that I was expecting one, but I found myself always wanting to hear from her.

"Brett McKinnon, as I live and breathe."

I looked up to find a woman in her mid-forties with a shit-ton of effort to try and look thirty taking a seat at my table.

I managed to smile because I didn't want to be rude, but at the same time, my hookup days were gone. "Do I know you?" That question was always guaranteed to upset women. They didn't like to be forgotten. With that said, I hadn't forgotten her as I was certain I'd never met her.

"You do now. I'm Loretta, and I have to tell you, Mr. McKinnon, after seeing you and this brief exchange, I'm shocked by all that I've learned."

I had that feeling in the pit of my stomach that I was about to be played. "Well, you wouldn't be the first person who was shocked by anything I did."

She let out a hearty laugh. It made my teeth grind as I could see it wasn't genuine.

"Well, maybe I'm not surprised. But I am surprised by Miranda. I mean, she's smart and lovely. Clearly, you could do so much better."

Anger boiled deep in my gut, and I could hear my therapist reminding me to take a breath and count to five. I'd only made it to two. "Don't talk to me about Miranda." Who the hell was this woman and how did she know me?

"I don't mean any disrespect toward you or Miranda. It's just unfortunate that your good time with her has resulted in a lifetime commitment. She's so young, and inexperienced, if you know what I mean."

The bastard in me wanted to tell her that Miranda got my rocks off better than any woman I'd ever had. But of course, that would be gauche.

Then it came to me. This had to be Miranda's stepmother.

"Miranda is such an independent woman. She doesn't know how to be there for an important and powerful man like you. And I'm not just talking about in bed, although that too. I know how to make you look good out in the world. I'm trim and toned, working out all the time—at one of your gyms, in fact. I know how appearances mean everything. Miranda is a nice girl, but she can't represent your brand."

"What are you after, Loretta?"

"Like I told you. You need a woman who understands your needs and your business needs. I can do that so much better than Miranda."

Wow. I'd met a lot of women who wanted to be my woman, but none had laid it out quite like Loretta. What the hell had Peter seen in this woman? Or what had Loretta seen in Peter? The only thing I could think of was his wife's inheritance.

"I think you overestimate your appeal, Loretta, if I may call you that. The truth is, Miranda is the most beautiful woman I've ever met. I have to admit I find it a little bit disturbing that you would try to seduce me, knowing my relationship with Miranda."

The agreeable, seductive exterior vanished. Her eyes narrowed. "It's no more disturbing than your sleeping with your college-age daughter's friend."

I suppose she wasn't wrong, but I wasn't going to take the bait. "The point is I'm not interested in what you're offering."

She leaned forward, practically sneering at me. "That's fine. It's clear that you're a bit of a pervert, anyway."

I felt that dig in my psyche, wondering if that was true. Was my love of a woman half my age a perversion? How could it be? She made me a better man. A happier man.

"My goal was to be able to help you manage Miranda and not ruin your reputation," she said.

"I don't know where you get off thinking that I need that. Because I don't."

She sat back, giving me a satisfied smirk. "You might want to rethink that, Mr. McKinnon. Once I go to the press and tell them about how the hotshot businessman has slept with his daughter's friend and gotten her pregnant . . ."

I ground my teeth, wanting to haul this woman out of the bar and out of my life.

"I wonder if people will continue to do business with you when they learn that your coed lover is pregnant with your child, but she still lives in a hovel."

"What do you want?"

"A hundred and fifty thousand would be nice."

"What's going on here?" Dunk said, looking from me to Loretta. His expression suggested that he thought I was picking up this woman.

"This is Miranda's stepmother. She's trying to bribe me or extort me. I don't know which it is, but I know when I talk to my lawyer, he'll be able to sort it out."

She looked at me, incensed. "It's all true. I haven't said anything that isn't true."

"I'm not suing you for defamation. I'm suing you for trying to get money out of me to keep you quiet."

"I'm shocked that you're out with the boys, drinking it up while Miranda is stuck at home with her drunk father. You really are a piece of work. Wait until I tell her."

My eyes narrowed. "Is Miranda part of this?" Even as I asked, I felt guilty about it.

"You don't think you owe her anything after what you've done to her?" Her response wasn't a yes, but it wasn't a no, either. It didn't make any sense that Miranda would try to get money from me when I spent all my time trying to show her how much I wanted to give her. But maybe that was the answer. Maybe in showing her the kind of life I could give her, she fell in love with the money and not me.

Loretta stood. "I'll be in touch for your answer." She turned and strutted toward the bar door.

"It's a no," I called after her.

Dunk sat down, but I stood up. He looked at me in confusion. "Where are you going?"

"I need to go talk to Miranda."

Dunk stood up, stepping into my path. "Maybe that's not a good idea when you're pissed off. Isn't that the kind of behavior that got you in trouble in the first place?"

It was, but there was no way I was going to be able to calm down until I knew for sure whether Miranda had duped me.

"I'm all right. I need to do this."

Dunk shook his head, but he moved out of my way. I drove to Miranda's house, trotting up the front walk to the door. I wouldn't call my knock a bang, but neither was it soft.

It occurred to me that Lindsay was supposed to be here, which was all the more reason for me to contain my anger.

She opened the door, and her smile was sweet. As if she was happy to see me. Was it real?

"You just missed Lindsay."

Thank God. "What's going on with your stepmother?" I tried not to be angry, but my voice was definitely terse.

Her smile faltered. "What are you talking about?"

"I just had a visit from your stepmother, and she's trying to get $150,000 out of me. Are you a part of that?"

For a moment, she just looked at me, studying me like she didn't know who I was. And then I could see it in her face, the moment everything inside her shut down, and with it came the panic that once again, I was letting my anger get the best of me.

I took a breath and counted to five. "I just need to know what's going on."

She shook her head and started to shut the door. My hand came out, holding it open. "Listen, if I am wrong, if I'm out of hand, tell me. Tell me what's going on. This thing can't work if you just shut me out."

She shook her head. "We can't work at all, Brett."

"Don't say that. I've been working my ass off so that I can be better. The only reason I'm doing that is for you."

"You're just doing it for the baby."

I brought both hands up to my head, grabbing my hair, feeling like I was going to yank it out by its roots.

"Of course, I love the baby, but all these weeks, it's been an excuse for me to see you. Jesus fuck, Miranda, can't you tell that I'm in love with you?"

Her eyes rounded in surprise, and I thought, hoped, that I was reaching her.

But then she closed down again. "If that were true, you wouldn't be here asking me if I was working with my ex-stepmother to take money from you."

I'd done it. I had told her what I wanted and how I felt, and it didn't make a difference. My brain buzzed with all sorts of things I wanted to say, most of which would probably make my situation worse. Then again, how much worse could it get? I'd gone as far as I could go, but there was no having the dream that I'd been trying so hard to put in place. The only thing to do was to let it go.

I turned away, heading to my car. When I reached the street and opened the driver's side door, I looked up toward the house, I suppose, hoping that she would stop me. But the door was closed and the porch light was off. It was a metaphor for my life.

30

Miranda

What was the saying about always doing the same things and expecting something different? How had I thought that Brett wouldn't lash out at me again? Granted, this time, he didn't call me names, but the idea that he thought I would be in cahoots with my stepmother to get money from him was ludicrous. Hadn't I spent the last few months telling them I didn't want anything from him?

He asked me to explain to him what was going on, but what was the point? This was a pattern, one I didn't want to be a part of anymore.

After I shut the door and moved back into the house, my father appeared, clearly having heard it all.

"Why didn't you tell him you had nothing to do with Loretta? Or tell him the type of woman Loretta was?" he asked.

"What would be the point?"

"Because the man was desperate to know that you weren't part of it."

How was it that my father was siding with Brett? "If he truly loved me, he would know that." Had he really said that? That he loved me?

My father cocked his head, giving me a look like I was naïve. "From what I heard, he didn't say anything as awful as you indicated he'd said before. His only crime was having doubt, questioning you. But you remember Loretta. Do you have any doubt that she said something to him that might make him think she was working with you?"

I hated that he was right. In fact, thinking about the entire encounter, it was true that Brett's only crime was in doubting me. He hadn't said mean things. He hadn't even come right out and accused me. He'd only asked about her and then begged me to explain.

Miranda, can't you tell that I'm in love with you?

He was asking me to confirm what he wanted to believe, which was that I wasn't involved. And while he told me he loved me in frustration, he'd said it. And I'd shut the door on him.

"I guess I overreacted."

My father nodded. "It's understandable considering your history, but he's right. If you're going to overcome it and be together, you're going to need to work through it. But is that what you want? Do you love him too?"

"I do." I headed back toward the door, pulling my jacket from the hook and slipping it on.

"It's a little late to be going out, isn't it?"

"I need to go see him. I need to tell him about Loretta."

I HAD NEVER BEEN to Brett's house, but I knew where it was because Lindsay had talked about it enough times. I found a place to park and then made my way up the sidewalk toward his brownstone. Just before I reached it, Loretta came out of nowhere.

"What are you doing?" she hissed.

"What are you doing?"

She looked up toward Brett's door and then back at me, putting her hands on my arms as if she were pushing me back out of his view.

"I'm about to make a great deal of money and I don't want you ruining it."

"By threatening to ruin his reputation? Why don't you just seduce him?" I always thought that was her M.O. anyway.

"I tried, but the man is clearly in love with you." Her face pinched with disgust.

Meanwhile, I wondered how she'd been able to notice that and I hadn't.

"So instead, I'll ruin him unless he pays. I was planning on giving you $10,000, Miranda. I mean look at how he lives and look at where you live. You're having his child and he treats you like this."

I shook my head. "It doesn't matter."

I turned and started toward the door, but Loretta stopped me. "Don't you ruin this for me, Miranda. Your baby daddy isn't the only person I could ruin here. Do you think anybody's going to want a teacher who has been sleeping around and getting pregnant?"

"What is wrong with you?"

"Or how about your father? I can ruin him as well."

I couldn't imagine how. My father didn't have money, and he wasn't well-known so nobody would care if he ended up in the news.

I made another attempt to go up to the door when it opened and Brett stood on the threshold. At first glance, I worried that seeing me with Loretta would confirm his suspicions about me.

"The cops are on their way and I'm planning to press charges, starting with trespassing, but then extortion or whatever my lawyer decides you're doing."

Loretta sent him a smug smile. "It won't work. You have responsibilities to Miranda. There's nothing wrong with asking the father of her child for help."

I shook my head. "I don't—"

He glanced briefly at me. "Miranda knows I'll give her anything that she wants." There was something in the words and the way he looked at me that gave me hope that he understood what was going on.

He turned his attention to Loretta. "It's time for you to go. And if I ever see you around here again, or around Miranda or Peter, for that manner, you will pay."

For a moment, Loretta looked like she was going to argue.

Brett looked at his watch. "You have about two minutes before the police arrive."

"You ruined everything, Miranda." She stormed off.

I looked up at Brett, a small smile on my face. "I always like to watch her leave."

He didn't respond, so I hesitantly climbed the stairs to him. Brett stepped back, letting me into the foyer of his home. That was a good sign, right?

As I looked up at him, he appeared tired and wary.

"I came to tell you three things, although I'm not quite sure which to start with." I looked at him with hope that he would forgive me. Would he be stubborn like I was and make me work for it?

"It's usually best to just start from the beginning."

"Loretta is a greedy, conniving bitch. And I absolutely am not doing anything with her. She learned about our connection and tried to take advantage, but it's all her."

His response was just a curt nod, so I wasn't sure if he believed me.

"The second thing is that I'm sorry. I realized after you left that I was having a sense of déjà vu seeing you angry on my front step. I overreacted. You weren't mean to me. You doubted me, and that hurt, but it wasn't like before. I'm sorry that I didn't recognize how hard you've been working on your anger issues."

"Thank you." And still, my words didn't seem to sway him. He looked at me like he'd given up on me. "You said there were three things."

I nodded and stepped closer to him, glad that he didn't back away. "Perhaps I should've led with this. I love you too."

He studied me, and I hoped he saw what he was looking for.

"Do you still love me?" I asked. "Did I mess that up?"

He closed his eyes and his head tilted upward, as if someone were pouring a balm over him. When he finally returned his gaze to me, the tender, sweet man I knew was back.

His hand cupped my cheek. "I should be asking you that. Ah, Miranda, how much of all this craziness would I have saved us if I'd told you this earlier?"

"I don't know that you would've saved any time. I'm not sure I would've heard it."

"But you hear it now, don't you? You trust me now, don't you? I mean, I know I fucked up tonight, and I can't guarantee that I won't ever fuck up again. I know that's why you're wary of me. I love you, Miranda. What I said earlier is true. Anything you want from me is yours. But God, how I need you to love me back."

I cocked my head and gave him a sassy smile. "Didn't you just hear me tell you that I did?"

He smiled, one of the rare wide, wondrous ones. "I have a surprise for you."

"Okay, but first . . ." I reached up, gripping the collar of his shirt and tugging him down, plastering my lips over his. He groaned and pressed me up against the wall, taking the kiss deeper, not just with the heat, but with the love.

When he finally tore his lips away, he said, "I'm really tempted to get to the makeup sex part, but I really want to show you my surprise." He took my hand and led me up the stairs and down a long hallway. "I made this for the baby." He opened the door to a room that was clearly a nursery.

"Since we don't know if it's a boy or girl, I tried to do it with non-gendered colors."

I looked around at the pretty yellow walls and the jungle animal decor. If I hadn't already loved Brett, I would have fallen for him right then and there.

"I love it." But then I realized that I was thinking I would be in this house with him and the baby, but he hadn't asked me to move in too.

"There's more. Follow me." He tugged me to another part of the house, opening a door to a room done in soft, muted grays with accents of white.

"This is your room."

I looked up at him, wondering what he meant. While the room was painted and had a desk, there was no bed. "Where do I sleep?"

His brow furrowed and then he laughed, taking both of my hands in his. "I was going to wait until after graduation, but I find that I can't. I want you to move in with me. And not because of the baby. I want you to move in with me because I can't stand to be away from you."

"And this is my bedroom?"

"Hell no. Your bedroom is my bedroom." Then he stopped. "Unless you're not comfortable with that. If the only way to get you to live in my house with me is separate bedrooms, I'll do that. But this room, I was thinking, could be an office or whatever you want it to be. It's Miranda's Room."

I smiled, giddiness filling me that he wanted me to have a place of my own in his house.

"So, will you move in with me?"

I launched my arms around him. "I want to see your room."

"Ah, the best for last." He carried me back toward the nursery and to the room next door. To be honest, except for the large, comfortable bed, I didn't see much of the space because my attention was all on Brett.

We undressed, but this time, everything was different. There weren't worries or questions. There was just love. Out in the open.

"Do you think I'm a pervert?" he asked as he trailed kisses down my body.

"What?"

He looked up at me from where he'd been swirling his tongue in my belly button. "Loretta says I'm a pervert for being with someone so young."

"Don't ever think about anything that woman says." I frowned. "Does the age thing bother you?"

"Bother? No. I mean, I'm a cliché, right? But my life is yours, Miranda. Whether you're twenty or thirty, that doesn't change. But when you're my age, I'll be in my sixties. A senior citizen."

"And I'll still love you then."

His expression filled with tenderness and awe. "Thank you for giving me another chance."

"You can thank me by giving me a screaming orgasm."

"Whatever you want, Miranda, I'll give it to you."

EPILOGUE I

Brett – Christmas, One Year Later

I did it. I fucking did it. I found a woman who loved me for me. I raised a daughter who was strong and independent, but kind and generous, and she graduated college and started a job in her dream industry. A year ago, I'd never thought about love and I worried that Lindsay wasn't going to make it through school.

What a difference a year makes.

A year after thinking I'd made the biggest mistake in my life by sleeping with my daughter's friend, I was back at the cabin, living a life I couldn't imagine I'd ever have, and certainly, one I didn't deserve.

Miranda and I, along with three-month-old Grayson, were celebrating the holidays at the cabin, now as a family. Once Miranda moved in with me, my plan worked like a charm. The day after she graduated from college, I proposed to her and she said yes. I told her I'd give her the biggest wedding ever, but she said all she wanted were family and a minister. And of course, I gave it to her in mid-July.

And then in early September, I watched with utter awe as

Miranda delivered our son, Grayson McKinnon, into the world. How the fuck did I get so lucky?

We arrived at the cabin two days early, partly to get ready for Christmas but also because it was an anniversary of sorts. While Miranda and I couldn't pinpoint when Grayson was conceived, we both agreed that our time at the cabin had been magic and we wanted to celebrate it.

Lindsay would be driving up tomorrow on Christmas Eve. Once she arrived, I knew this was going to be the best Christmas I'd ever had. The only difficult part was Lindsay was still reeling over the loss of Liam. My worry about Lindsay and Liam back in April was justified. He came groveling back, and Lindsay forgave him. Maybe he tried to change, but it never stuck. In fact, it got worse. Liam was attracted by the lure of money and power, which put him in the path of dangerous people, and four weeks ago, it got him killed.

Despite Miranda's being Lindsay's stepmother, they've maintained their friendship dynamic. I was grateful that Lindsay had someone to talk to through the last eight turbulent months. I hoped that Christmas with us all together would help Lindsay begin to heal from her loss.

When we arrived at the cabin, we settled in. I brought our bags up to our room and checked the nursery to make sure everything was okay for Grayson. Once settled in, I pulled out the decorations. We went through them but didn't put them up, instead waiting for when Lindsay arrived.

Later in the evening, after Grayson was in bed, I put a fire in the fireplace and made hot chocolate, without the liquor since Miranda was nursing.

"Did you see how he almost rolled over tonight?" I asked Miranda as we sat on the floor by the fire. "He's brilliant like you."

Miranda grinned up at me. "I wonder how long before he can beat you in *Trivial Pursuit*."

I gave her a look but smiled because her knowledge and the way she put it all together, like an intricate puzzle, always amazed me.

"Maybe he gets it from you. You are smart. Plus, rolling over is a physical thing. That's your area of expertise."

I knew she was talking about the gyms, but I much preferred the innuendo. "You think I'm an expert in physical things, eh?" I pushed her back and lay over her.

"Oh, I know it." She looped her arms around my neck.

"You're not bad yourself." I slid my hands under her sweater, tugging it off her.

"Everything I know, I've learned from you." Her hands tugged at my shirt until I pulled it off.

"I must be a good teacher, then."

"The best. Or at least I think you are."

I frowned. "You think?"

"Well, I was a virgin. You're all I know."

I ground my dick against her. "I'm all you'll ever know."

She smiled. "What more could I want?"

God, I hoped that I'd continue to make her happy. That I wouldn't fuck up, because I didn't want her to want anyone but me for as long as we lived.

"You know, Miranda, whatever you want, I will give you. You have my heart." I kissed her neck. "My body." I kissed the other side of her neck. "My soul." I looked down at her. "You have all of me."

"Then I have all I could ever want or need. Except maybe an orgasm. I do love it when you give me those."

I laughed. "You're insatiable."

"Do you mind?"

"Hell no."

I took her in my arms, and with my body, I showered her with love and affection, and of course, all the orgasms she wanted. And in return, she gave me life and love, and yes, orgasms.

EPILOGUE II

Lindsay

I was often asked if it was weird that my father and my friend were now married and had a baby. I'd be lying if I said it wasn't. But most of the time, I didn't think about it. When I was with Miranda, she was my friend. And when I was with my dad, he was my dad.

Now that they were married, it was sometimes a little weirder because it was hard to keep their roles separate. As long as I didn't think about them having sex, I was usually okay. Mostly, I was happy for them. And of course, I loved my new little brother, Grayson.

I tried to focus on this as I sat with all of them in the living room, listening to Christmas music and making Christmas ornaments, Miranda's idea of a new family tradition. This was our first Christmas as a family, and I wanted it to be perfect for them. So I plastered on a smile, even though my problems weighed heavily on me.

A month ago, my on-again, off-again boyfriend was killed in my house. It still sent chills down my spine to wonder what would happen if I had been there. Or if Oliver, Liam's brother, had been there. I couldn't figure out why Liam was there as I'd kicked him out yet again.

I still grappled with wondering why he couldn't change. What hold had the people he worked with held over him that he was willing to risk his life and break the law just for money? I finally decided it was the money and power.

So many nights, Oliver and I would stay up together, worried sick about Liam, and he'd saunter in, cocky and high on something, acting like we were a bunch of whiny pansies. I wanted to help him, but he wouldn't listen. Even when I ended up caught up in one of his schemes and was nearly arrested, he didn't care. He thought I was overreacting to be upset.

From that time until just before Thanksgiving, he was in and out of my home like a revolving door because I kept hoping that this time, he would change. The last three times, Oliver, who still rented a room in my place, told me not to take Liam back. But I couldn't say no, and so Liam would move back in with me until everything went horribly wrong. Thank God Oliver wasn't one to say, "I told you so." Instead, he'd listen when I'd scream in anger. Or hold me when I cried. Oliver was the only reason I had been able to stand up to Liam that final time.

Why he was in my house when he was killed, I don't know because I had finally resolved that I was done with him. Did he think he could just show up and all would be well? Had he left something there that he was looking for?

"How's this?" My father held up a paper chain of multicolored paper.

"Very Christmassy," I said.

He winked.

"It looks like someone here needs to go to bed," Miranda said, looking down at Grayson sleeping in her arms.

My father stood up and took the baby from Miranda. "Let me get him down. I'll give you two girls a chance to talk."

Normally, I might've corrected my father and told him we were women, but I was still off my game.

"Come sit with me." Miranda moved closer to the fire and patted the floor next to her.

Finding my inner snark, I arched a brow. "Is there any possibility that Grayson was conceived there?"

Her cheeks blushed. "There is. But come sit with me anyway."

I did as she asked. She put her arm around me, and I rested my head on her shoulder.

"I know that you are still grieving the loss of Liam."

"I was so done with him." Maybe if I said it enough, it would be true.

"I know, but that doesn't mean you didn't care for him. But it seems like something else is going on. Your father's worried sick, and I agreed that I would talk to you about it because as you know, he's not always really good at this stuff."

I smiled. "He's better, but . . ." I sat up and turned my body to face her, knowing there was no more putting off this discussion. "There is something else going on."

She took both my hands in hers and looked me in the eyes. This was what had made Miranda such a great friend. She was here one hundred percent. That didn't mean I wasn't scared to tell her what was going on. Or maybe I was just more nervous about what my father was going to do.

"In October, I went to a Halloween party and Liam was there."

Her expression told me she knew where this conversation was going. In a weak moment, I'd given in to Liam's charm again, wanting to believe all his promises even though by then, I knew he couldn't keep them.

"You can't beat yourself up for loving somebody who couldn't get their act together. For a time, I did the same."

She had, but my father was strong enough and willing to get help to deal with his issues. Liam couldn't or wouldn't.

I realized I was trying to draw out the inevitable. I needed to treat it like a Band-Aid and rip it off. "The thing is, Mira, I'm pregnant."

In an instant, her brows shot up to her hairline. But a second later, she schooled her expression back to concern. She squeezed my hands. "How long have you known?"

"Long enough to know that I want to keep it. I mean, I know I'm not going to have what you and Dad have, but I think I could be a good mom."

She nodded. "I can't blame you for that. For all his troubles, you cared for Liam and now you have a part of him. No matter what, I will be here for you. And he might rage and say crazy things, but your dad will be here for you and the baby as well."

I let her pull me into a hug, and I did feel better, except for the fact that I was still lying.

The truth was, I hadn't been with Liam, as I'd suggested to Miranda. I'd been with his brother. The baby I carried was actually Oliver's.

Lindsay and Oliver's story is available here. Get it NOW!

And you can binge read the entire series here.

SEAL DADDIES NEXT DOOR (PREVIEW)

DESCRIPTION

Becoming rich overnight led to a series of nightmares.
But the three *much* older Navy SEALs that entered my life as a result were more like a fantasy come true.

The electricity I feel with them makes me forget that the man who surprisingly left me an inheritance has been murdered... *and I'm the prime suspect.*

Reed, a protective single dad, has a rugged charm that could steal any woman's heart.
Asher could cut glass with his razor-sharp features. Yes, he's exceptionally strong but what draws me to him is his heart of gold.
Miguel has Spanish blood in him. His temper is unmatched, but you'd never guess that when he cracks dad jokes.

These men fill my heart with joy... and my bed with heat.
My soul belongs to them, but do I even know who they really are?

Their traumatic past won't let them get too close to me, even though the two pink lines on the stick bind us together.

I may not know who the dad is, but I'm taking a leap of faith.

They say I'm too innocent for my own good.

Am I naïve to think that I can trust them with my life, and with my baby?

***Our* baby?**

1

Juniper

2021

Item one: go on a date before Mama chews my ears off.

Item two: don't say anything stupid on the date.

Item three: don't run away if he calls you sugar.

Item four: okay, maybe run away, but tell Mama you ran because you got a case of the collywobbles. Do not, I repeat, do not tell her the date went to pot.

I'd had it up to here with my mama telling me I was gonna die a "lil' ole spinster." It used to be cute about five years ago.

But now, at the tail-end of twenty-nine, it was like I had this massive time-bomb strapped to my chest, and it'd explode any second.

I could almost hear her southern drawl in the back of my ears. For context, most of our conversations flowed along the same pattern these days.

"Well, sugar, I was just wondering if you'd met any nice fellas lately."

"Oh, Lord. Here we go again."

"Now, don't you go getting all huffy on me, Juniper. I just want you to be happy."

"I'm perfectly happy, Mama. I don't need no man to make me happy."

"Now, that's just plain silly. Everybody needs somebody."

"I've got plenty of somebodies in my life, Mama. I've got my friends, my books, and that dratted cat who visits me now and then. I think he likes me more than he does his folks."

"I don't know about that. That cat's not gonna take you out to dinner or dance with you under the stars."

"I can take myself out to dinner, Mama. And as for dancing under the stars, well, I'll ask the cat. Who knows, maybe I could bribe him into it."

"Hey, Ms. Davis?"

I looked up, pen in my mouth, at the little kid standing in front of me.

"What is it, Janie?" I smiled at her. Cute kid.

"Well, ma'am, I was just wonderin' if it'd be alright if I kept holdin' onto that *Faraway Tree* book for a spell longer."

"I know I missed the due date and all, but it's just so dang good, and I got a heap of homework that's been eating up my time somethin' fierce.

"Could I maybe bring it back in four days or so, pretty please?"

Janie's tongue grew sweeter than the tea in front of me with each word she uttered.

Her eyes enlarged in a dual attempt to convince me she was an adorable little Dachshund and that I had to excuse the late return.

It never failed.

I covered my lips with my hand in a poor attempt to conceal my grin.

"Okay, Janie, but this is the last time. Do you promise to read to the younger kids next week in return?"

She bobbed her head of golden hair enthusiastically. "I do!"

"Good girl. Off you go."

It was an unseasonably warm day here in the heart of Oakmont, Georgia, but I wasn't complaining.

I sat behind the circulation desk of The Quill and Hearth Library, a place as whimsical as its name. We actually allowed patrons to sip on sweet tea while they read their books.

I enjoyed the slow heat and the bird-like chattering of children. I loved the lower level for this very reason. It was a wonderland for the little 'uns.

We had a storytime event later that day. I could count on the little regulars to show up and demand a new fairytale. I'd been studying up for it too.

Maybe I could just talk about how Rapunzel should have gone renegade and used her hair to whip the shit outta that evil woman who'd caged her.

Or maybe I was just mad because I'd had a pretty sour conversation with Mama not ten minutes ago.

Funny thing about people who adored you—they knew your cues.

They didn't need to say much, but oh, when they were positioning to attack you, and I mean verbally decimate your soul, all they needed was one word.

Or a line. Or a few of them. You get what I mean.

"You're about to hit the big three-o and still ain't got yourself a man. What the hell are you waiting for?"

"When you gonna find a beau who's worth his weight in grits?"

Ugh. She didn't need to tell me I was old and single. In fact, no one did. I could feel the life force between my legs drying up.

I tried to focus on the pretty little place that gave me so much joy.

Big windows let in buttery-yellow sunshine, and every nook and corner had a cozy reading space.

There were rows and rows of books, neatly arranged by subject and author and utterly orgasmic for my OCD-fueled mind. Hey, I was a girl who loved her lists and her shelves.

You wanted fun? You had to have a method to it.

I let out a satisfied sigh as a ray of light fell most becomingly over the dark wooden shelves. They looked lush as a lover's embrace, a comfortable in-between of secrets and safety.

My job was to make sure this place remained as calm as it looked.

Easier said than done when I was always around kids.

I couldn't help chuckling as I heard a "'squee'" from their section. Some newbies had to have found a new adventure. That's why we turn to books anyway, right?

We couldn't physically be everywhere all at once. But in the library, you could train your mind to take you wherever you wanted to go.

You could even get married to the fanciest Prince Charming. Not that it would ease my mama's heart.

Life was good in Oakmont, though, all things considered. As they said around here, "If you don't like the weather, just wait five minutes."

And I didn't mind sticking around longer. Better than going home to nothing. I could call Sadie or one of the girls.

I just didn't want another pity party today. Hell, I'd get enough of it in a week when I actually hit the big three-o.

Bam!

I jumped up from my desk to investigate the source of the loud crash. On crossing two rows, I found a group of kids who'd built a fort out of picture books.

They were all hooting and hollering, running around as if they were facing down an army of monsters.

I could hear one of them, a scrappy little boy with a missing tooth, shouting, "Y'all ain't gonna beat us! We got the strongest fort in all of Oakmont!"

Another little girl, a bandana wrapped around her head like a pirate, squealed in her tiny voice, "We'll see about that! We're gonna knock that fort down and take all your treasure!"

The boy with the missing tooth turned to me with a big smile and said, "Hey, Junie. Wanna join our army and help us beat the bad guys?"

I bit back a laugh and replied, "Well, I don't know if I have what it takes to be a soldier, but I sure can cheer you on!"

The kids all laughed and kept on battling, and I stood there a little while, basking in the warmth of their innocence.

They'd gone and made a whole little world inside the library. Anything was possible, and the only limit was their imagination.

Suddenly, my eye fell on a dark-haired boy standing some rows away and eyeing the tyrant group with sad, dog-like adoration.

I walked over to him and knelt down. "Hey there, what's your name? Are you new here?"

He shot me a furtive look before nodding. "Yep. I'm Billy. I came to get an action book."

I looked him up and down, and my gut instinct kicked in.

"How'd you like something with more adventure and magic? We're doing a reading of *The Hobbit* soon. Wanna stick around for that?"

He blushed. "Ah . . . I don't think I can."

"Why not?"

He shuffled his feet and looked down at the floor. "I . . . my dad says magic is for little sissy girls, and I need to be a man."

Ah. Of course his dad said that.

I pursed my lips together and thought for a second before replying.

"Well, little Billy, what do you want to read?"

His face was immediately lit by hope. He looked like a sunny day. You know, the kind where trees sway gently in the breeze and leaves rustle softly in the wind. You look overhead and see a brilliant shade of blue, with just a few straggly clouds drifting lazily. It's everything you hope for, especially if it's hurricane season and you don't know what the next moment holds.

"I'd love to read magic books," Billy mumbled, "but I know my dad won't be happy about that."

"Where's your dad right now?"

"He's at work. He said my nanny will come pick me up after one."

"What if we make ourselves a little secret? You stick around for *The Hobbit* readin', and I'll treat you to a good ol' fashioned fairy tale 'bout a Wishing Chair that can take you anywhere you want to go.

Why don't you give it a try and see how it makes you feel? Don't let your dad be the one callin' the shots all the time, now."

The hope that burst across that little face made my heart churn. Man, I was sure his dad loved him, but fathers could be assholes sometimes.

But then again, at least his one stuck around. Mine wasn't even there to see me get born.

"You won't tell on me?"

I made a three-finger salute. "Scout's honor."

After Billy pottered away to join the other kids, I made my way to the history section. I was doing a bit of reading about the Ku Klux Klan, and it caught my interest.

This fascination had begun the very night I finished my tenth re-read of *Gone With The Wind.* Say what you would, but I'd never get enough of O'Hara and her damned gumption.

I was neck-deep in the Civil War era when I felt a gentle tap on my shoulder. Turning, I smiled. "Hey, Harold. Here for some history?"

"No, I just came to meet you. And I saw you getting that young'un into trouble!"

Harold Montgomery, sixty-something, missing two teeth (one he'd retouched in gold), and as eccentric as a pink-haired lady driving a blue Cadillac.

He'd become my friend over the last six months. I'd met him when he was scouring through the Civil War section, looking for titles on ancestry.

We got on like a house on fire, so to speak. It was actually funny, the things we had in common.

I squared my shoulders defensively. "Ain't no one telling a kid that they can't have their fairy tales. The world will mess 'em up soon enough. Let 'em be young while they can."

Harold chuckled. "Young lady, I have no complaints. In fact, I think you did the right thing. The father deserves a sentence for trying to deprive his son!"

I relaxed. "Maybe I could go all Avenger on him."

He walked with me to the counter. "What are you doing tonight?"

Nothing. I was just gonna go home and sit on the back patio in a pair of pajamas with my mama's quilted throw over me. I'd probably bury my face in a tub of bourbon pecan ice cream straight from the tub with extra bourbon and maybe a drizzle of dark chocolate.

A perfect dinner for a single lady on the verge of discovering her first gray hairs.

In all fairness, this dinner would pass muster with my mama.

She approved of a lot about me, even some parts that could make others run the instant I opened my mouth.

Harold probably surmised the extent of my evening adventures from the dreamy look on my face.

"I can see you're getting distracted, so I'll be quick. I'm hosting a dinner at my mansion. I want you there."

My eyes bulged. No way.

Nestled amid old oaks and magnolias in the very heart of Oakmont's historic district, the Montgomery mansion had become the stuff of local legend.

The house itself was a masterpiece of Antebellum architecture with its grand columns and sweeping porches, but it was the rumors that made me uneasy.

It was common hearsay that Harold's ancestors were all members of the Klan, and they'd even used the house as a meeting place during the Civil War.

Some even whispered that the hidden rooms and secret tunnels beneath the mansion housed the Klan's loot.

But despite what I'd heard, I believed my heart more.

Harold was a gentle soul, always ready with a smile and a kind word for his neighbors.

Sadie used to tell me it'd take him a lifetime to undo the reputation of his ancestors, but you had to give a man props for trying.

He continued surveying my face like I was some fascinating archaeological artifact. Or a gecko.

"So, what's it gonna be?"

I smiled. "Will you have bourbon pecan ice cream for dessert?"

Why did he look so relieved, like he *needed* me to be there?

His Southern drawl came through immediately, although he'd spent almost his entire life out of the country and in London.

Harold wasn't one for convention—it seemed to hurt his soul.

But in moments like these, he was as Southern as the rest of us.

"Bless your heart for sayin' yes. I reckon this shindig is gonna open doors for you. It's gonna be like a lit matchstick, sparkin' up a whole new flame in your life."

Well, bless his heart too. What in tarnation did that mean?

2

Juniper

I unlocked the door to my lonely, single life.

Okay, I totally did not mean to sound that bitter. At least I had my own little space in Oakmont's central precinct.

Magnolia Street was home to my quaint apartment, filled with charming brick buildings and old-world trees.

I stepped in through the front door and immediately found myself surrounded by the warm glow of the setting sun. It cast a soft halo of light across my living room.

The neighborhood cat, Bumbles, was already snoozing out on the balcony, his furry body stretched out on the cushion I'd left for him.

This was the fourth night he'd stayed with me. I knew the neighbors were gonna say I'd kept him high on catnip.

From my window, I could see a pair of graceful egrets flying toward a nearby marsh.

A group of chatty cardinals hopped along the branches of my old friend, the oak I'd named, well, Mr. Oakwood Hardy.

Yes, not all was bitter about this place. It was small, and there were days I wished I could open the door and shout, "What's for dinner?" but . . . it was okay.

I was okay.

Sighing, I made myself more sweet tea and settled down on the sofa with a new list. The sound of a distant train whistle floated through the open window.

My phone drawled out a lazy tune. I looked at the name on the screen and groaned.

"Hey, Mama."

"June bug! How about you come on back to the nest and let Mama feed ya? I'm fixin' to fry up some chicken."

My mouth watered at the words. No one could make fried chicken like my mama. Juicy and tender, it exemplified Sunday meals with her.

She did mashed potatoes and gravy, collard greens and cornbread . . . the whole nine yards.

I loved to soak up the gravy and potatoes in the bread and do a perfect bite with a bit of everything.

But again, after I moved out, my mama's invitations to dinner became more and more of a call to an unavoidable war.

She'd feed me and bombard me with questions I had no clear answers to.

Some of them weren't all that bad—like what kids I'd met at the library or what Sadie's husband was doing.

The moment she moved to Sadie's husband, she'd redirect to ask me when I'd catch my own.

Like this was an unavoidable bout of a new strain of COVID that I just had to have.

I sighed and shook my head, almost picturing her crestfallen face.

"Mama, I'd love to, but I can't tonight."

"Oh?"

It was plain as day that her curiosity had been piqued by my words, as I could hear the telltale lilt in her voice.

Lord have mercy. I reckoned I could've phrased that a mite bit better.

No doubt she'd be fixing to inquire about my plans and whether there were any fine gentlemen involved in them.

"You headed out with a good-lookin' fella tonight?"

Talk about hitting the nail straight on my own fuckin' head.

"No, Mama. No date. I just got an invite to this fancy dinner."

"Where?"

I hesitated for a second. My mama, like all the old-timers in this city, did not trust men with a tarnished reputation—even if this reputation had nothing to do with them, per se.

They could be golden, but if there was one black sheep in the family, it meant they had a little devil in them.

Plus, my mama hated Harold Montgomery.

I honestly had no idea why. It began the day he met me in the library and insisted on dropping me home. In his Aston Martin DB11.

At the time, I was still living with Mama. I'd only moved to this place about twenty days ago, mostly because I wanted to be able to walk to work. And I felt like I was getting too old to share space with someone I loved but who also drove me nuts.

Mama took one look at him and told me never to see him again.

I didn't push it then, and I didn't want to push it now. But I was never good at one thing when it came to her. I didn't lie to her. I couldn't.

Not when that's what she'd known the entirety of her life before I came along. That's all she had from the one other person she loved—the one who got away.

"Harold Montgomery's party, Mama."

She sounded like she'd choked on a peach.

"Hell no, Junie! You're not going to that man's house! You know what they say about that place and the secrets? You know his ancestors used to torture others to get money and loot their jewels, right? Why do you want to associate yourself with that?"

Why did I, actually? Apart from the obvious curiosity I had about the house, there was just something so affable about Harold.

He was old and weathered and sweet. He talked to me like he really cared and wanted to be part of my life, even if it was just a sliver.

That meant something.

"Mama." I spoke sotto voce. "Harold's tried to undo all that his entire life. Maybe we could just give him a chance."

"Child, I ain't givin' no man like that the time of day, and neither should you. Don't you remember what I done told you about your daddy? You gotta be strong, just like your Mama. You hear me?"

Okay. Not the way I'd hoped this would go. Against my better judgment, a swell of bitterness rose inside me.

"Mama, I don't want to have this conversation. Not when I've asked you about Dad so many times and got nothing back."

"Honey, you know good and well he was nothin' but pure evil. The second he found out I was carryin' you, he up and left without a second thought."

And you've never let me forget it.

"I'm sorry I'm such an inconvenience." I spoke sharply. "But I'm old enough to make my own decisions. I understand you may not agree with them, but I hope you'll care enough to respect them, anyway."

"Junie, now you listen to me—"

I hung up.

Oh, I'd never hear the end of this. But I'd deal with her temper and tears tomorrow. I knew she meant well.

But even I got tired of being made to feel like I was responsible for her never getting married.

All I ever knew about my dad was that he was super rich, and his folks told him he could either be livin' in the boonies with my mom or he'd have to leave her and return to his roots.

No points for guessing what he chose.

I wanted to make peace with it. But that was damn hard when the topic kept cropping up like an unrelenting tide of heat poking like nails on my skin.

My phone rang again. I just flipped that switch to silent and high-tailed it outta there.

I reckoned I needed to blow off some steam, so I went to dump a bucket of ice-cold water over my head.

By the time I got out, it was already sundown. The buttery glow of the last rays of amber sunlight had melted into soft pinks and purples against a deep blue sky.

My invite said I needed to be at the party by nine, so I took some time to gussy up.

Hell, I'd be a Southern belle ready to stir up some trouble at that party.

I slipped into a ruby red cocktail dress, feeling like a hot tamale in a sea of ice cubes.

The entire next hour saw me hurling a tirade of cuss words as I tried my best to coax my curls into shape. I managed to tease my hair up high and let it fall in loose, beachy waves around my shoulders.

I could have sworn Dolly Parton would be proud of that hairdo.

The figure smiling back from the mirror was all curves, gentle, swaying, and redolent of summer scents. And I loved it.

I loved every stretch mark woven like lightning on my skin, each freckle and meander and wrinkle.

It had taken me years to come to this place where I was learning to fall in love with myself. I'd spent two decades on the other side.

Then, two heartbreaks and a side of controversy later, I realized I could spend all my life at war with myself, but it would never make living any easier.

And I didn't want to remember myself that way. When I turned gray and crocheted my way into retirement, I wanted good memories.

This was me making those happen.

I finished by adding just the right amount of sparkle to make my eyes pop and my lips pout. With that, I strode into the living room and immediately regretted my decision.

You ever been around an introvert?

You know, that special breed of people who get excited to make plans and then immediately run out of social battery the second the plans are about to begin?

Yup, that was me.

Too late to back out. My Uber had already arrived.

I stepped out of my apartment, suddenly feeling like a toad in a dress. Thankfully, my Uber driver, Hank, was an angel.

"Howdy, Ms. Davis. I'll be your Uber driver for the evening. You look pretty as a peach in that red dress!"

I chuckled. "Thank you kindly, Hank. You sure do have a way with words."

As the ride began, I lost myself in the easy ramblings of Hank's thick drawl and the sights I saw on the way.

Old oak trees blurred into a bouquet of brown, green, and yellow draped in a soft evening wind and Spanish moss.

Every brick building here had something that tied it to the remnants of life from the Civil War era.

I leaned back and sighed. "I don't think I'll ever be able to live anywhere else but the South."

Hank cleared his throat. "Well, speakin' of living here. A few years ago, I was driving this very car when all of a sudden, I hit a pothole so deep it swallowed my tire. I was stuck there on the side of the road, wondering what to do. That's when a bunch of good ol' boys in a pickup truck pulled up beside me and asked if I needed help. And you know what they did? They pulled out a rope, tied it around the car, and yanked me outta that pothole like it was nothin'!"

"Only in the South, right?"

Hank grinned. "You got that right, Miss Juniper. We may have our share of potholes, but we sure do know how to help each other out."

Before I knew it, the easy ride brought me to the drop-off leading up to the main door of the Montgomery mansion.

The pathway was lined with lights and an abundance of heady flowers. I followed a trail of guests to the door.

A tall, silver-haired figure stood at the threshold.

He looked like a direct import from England. Like he'd been flown in after a long-standing decade of serving the Queen herself.

"Name, please?"

"Ha!"

Why did I say that? Why was I so awkward? I wished the marble floors would just swallow me whole.

"I mean . . ." I fumbled, trying not to let his hawk-like eyes pierce through me. "I'm Juniper. Juniper Davis."

He took a minute to go over the names on the list he held in his hands. A very agonizing minute.

Maybe this was some joke Harold had played on me?

I nearly turned and pulled a Cinderella before he spoke again, his tone cold as day-old turkey right outta the freezer.

"Welcome to the Riviera party, Ms. Davis. You may go through to the salon."

"Thanks, you too."

Before I could give him the chance to throw me out for the stupidest comeback ever, I ran into the salon.

I was immediately bombarded by an onslaught of people in clothes worth more than my year's salary.

On any other day, I'd curse myself for being a social anomaly, but right now, I was absolutely blown away by the opulence of the interior.

The entire salon could have swallowed my apartment, with ceilings so high they could go on forever. Tall windows, rich, warm walls, and ornate moldings were everywhere.

I meandered through the room, but not before I overheard a conversation between two guests.

"My dear, it comes as no surprise that Mr. Montgomery has spared no expense for this evening's affair."

"I hear he's preparing to make a rather momentous announcement. No doubt, an attempt to conceal the origins of his vast wealth."

"Truly, the Montgomery family has a dubious reputation in certain circles. There are whispers of thievery and deceit."

"I have heard tales of a scandalous affair involving Mr. Montgomery and a woman of questionable reputation in his younger days."

"It is quite clear that he is a man with many secrets."

They turned around and saw me, and one of them—a big ol' fella in a fancy vest, his eye accentuated by a ridiculous monocle, scowled.

I took off running quicker than a spooked hen.

Trying to shake off the heaviness of the air, I approached a group of people near the bar.

"Hey there," I said, raising my voice and giving in to the sudden burst of social energy. "What's everyone drinking?"

One of the men in the group turned to me and grinned. "Whiskey, of course. We're in the south, honey. What else would we be drinking?"

I chuckled and shook my head. "I shoulda known better. Make mine a double."

A few drinks later, my bladder had a mind of its own. I rushed out of the salon and found myself in a maze of a corridor. Where the hell was the washroom?

I was about to give up when one of the doors burst open and Harold stormed out, his face red, angry, and unlike anything I'd ever seen before.

Something made me hide behind the wall opposite the room.

A young man followed him his hands bunched into fists.

"You're gonna regret this. You hear me?"

I realized I knew his face. And it was one of the few things I wanted to forget most in the world.

End of preview. ***Get the entire story here.***

ABOUT THE AUTHOR

Ajme Williams writes emotional, angsty contemporary romance. All her books can be enjoyed as full length, standalone romances and are FREE to read in Kindle Unlimited .

Books do not have to be read in order.

Heart of Hope Series

Our Last Chance | An Irish Affair | So Wrong | Imperfect Love | Eight Long Years | Friends to Lovers | The One and Only | Best Friend's Brother | Maybe It's Fate | Gone Too Far | Christmas with Brother's Best Friend | Fighting for US | Against All Odds | Hoping to Score | Thankful for Us | The Vegas Bluff | 365 Days | Meant to Be | Mile High Baby | Silver Fox's Secret Baby | Snowed In with Best Friend's Dad

The Why Choose Haremland (Reverse Harem Series)

Protecting Their Princess | Protecting Her Secret | Unwrapping their Christmas Present | Cupid Strikes... 3 Times | Their Easter Bunny | SEAL Daddies Next Door | Naughty Lessons

High Stakes

Bet On It | A Friendly Wager | Triple or Nothing | Press Your Luck

Billionaire Secrets
Twin Secrets | Just A Sham | Let's Start Over | The Baby Contract | Too Complicated

Dominant Bosses
His Rules | His Desires | His Needs | His Punishments | His Secret

Strong Brothers
Say Yes to Love | Giving In to Love | Wrong to Love You | Hate to Love You

Fake Marriage Series
Accidental Love | Accidental Baby | Accidental Affair | Accidental Meeting

Irresistible Billionaires
Admit You Miss Me | Admit You Love Me | Admit You Want Me | Admit You Need Me

Check out Ajme's full Amazon catalogue here.

Join her VIP NL here.